MY FAVOURITE HALF-NIGHT STAND

CHRISTINA LAUREN

piatkus

PIATKUS

First published in the US in 2018 by Gallery Books,
an imprint of Simon & Schuster, Inc.
First published in Great Britain in 2018 by Piatkus
This paperback edition published in 2019 by Piatkus

1 3 5 7 9 10 8 6 4 2

Copyright © 2018 by Christina Hobbs and Lauren Billings

The moral right of the author has been asserted.

A CIP catalogue record for this book
is available from the British Library.

ISBN 978-0-349-42273-2

Printed and bound in Great Britain by
Clays Ltd, Elcograf S.p.A.

Papers used by Piatkus are from well-managed forests
and other responsible sources.

Piatkus
An imprint of
Little, Brown Book Group
Carmelite House
50 Victoria Embankment
London EC4Y 0DZ

An Hachette UK Company
www.hachette.co.uk

www.littlebrown.co.uk

Christina Lauren is the combined pen name of longtime writing partners/besties/soulmates/brain-twins Christina Hobbs and Lauren Billings, the *New York Times*, *USA Today* and #1 international bestselling authors of the Beautiful and Wild Seasons series and various standalone romances.

You can find them online at:

ChristinaLaurenBooks.com

Facebook.com/ChristinaLaurenBooks

@ChristinaLauren

For all of the CLo friends who helped us swim
through the shark-infested waters of internet dating

chapter one

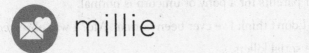 millie

When I was in grade school, my best friend, Alison Kim, was obsessed with horses. She was *the horse girl*—you know the one. She took lessons, came to school in cowboy boots, and always smelled faintly of barn. Not *necessarily* a bad thing, but certainly unique among the student body at Middleton Elementary. Her room was covered in pictures of horses; her clothes were all horse-themed. She had trading cards and figurines. This girl was *invested* and could be called upon at any given moment to answer a horsey question or rattle off an equestrian fact.

Did you know horses can run a mere six hours after birth? Nope.

What about their teeth—were you aware a horse's teeth take up more space in their head than their brain does? Didn't know that, either.

Most little girls are obsessed with *something* at one point, and for the most part it never gets a second thought. Puppies: standard. Princesses are also frequently idolized. An obsession with boy bands is to be expected. Begging your parents for a pony or unicorn is normal.

I don't think I've ever been normal. Me? I was obsessed with serial killers.

More specifically, I was obsessed with the idea of female serial killers. Hear the phrase *serial killer*, and most of us probably picture a man. It's not surprising—let's be real, men are responsible for at least ninety-two percent of the evil in the world. For centuries, women have been socially programmed to be the nurturers, after all—the protectors, the emotional bridges—so when we hear of a woman who takes life instead of creating it, it's instinctively shocking.

My particular fascination started around the time I played Lizzie Borden in my seventh-grade theater class. It was an original musical—the brainchild of our eccentric-would-be-an-understatement teacher—and I landed the lead role. Before then, the concept of murder was still loose and shapeless in my head. But, ever studious as a child, I gobbled up everything I could about Lizzie Borden, the gruesome hatchet murders, the dramatic trial, the *acquittal*. The fact that, to this day, the murders remain unsolved was enough to get the wheels in my mind spinning: What is it about the male brain that makes it not just more aggressive in general but more prone to serial violence—and what trips that same switch in a woman? It's why I read every book on the subject I could find as a teen, watched every crime drama and mystery, and why I now teach criminology at UC Santa Barbara, and am working on my own book about the very women who so fascinated me as a child.

It's probably also why I'm drinking it up with four of my strictly platonic best guy friends, instead of out enjoying myself on an actual date.

No man wants to hear "I wrote my thesis on gender differences in serial murderers" during the *Tell me about yourself* portion of an initial rendezvous.

"Millie."

"Mills?"

My attention first snags on Ed's voice, and then focuses on Reid's. "Yeah?"

Reid Campbell—one of the aforementioned strictly platonic best guy friends, the reason we're here celebrating tonight, and a man whose genetics never got the memo that it's unfair to be both brilliant and beautiful—grins at me from across the table.

3

"Are you going to pick your game piece or stare slack-jawed at the wall all night?" He's still waiting, still smiling. It's only now that I notice the game board on the table, and the pastel money he begins distributing.

Apparently while zoning out, I inadvertently agreed to play Monopoly. "Ugh. Guys. Again?"

Reid, who for some reason is always the banker, looks back up at me with faux-wounded blue eyes. "Come on. Don't even pretend you don't love it. Getting a monopoly on Park Place and Boardwalk gives you an *obscene* amount of joy."

"I loved it when I was ten. I still mostly liked it two years ago," I say. "But why do we keep playing it when it always ends the same?"

"What do you mean it always ends the same?" Ed—or *Stephen Edward D'Onofrio!* if you're his mother—pulls out the chair to my left. Ed's hair is this wild mop of reddish-brown curls that always looks like he either just got up or should really go to bed.

"For starters," I begin, "Reid is always the top hat, you're the car, Alex is the ship, Chris is the shoe, and I'm the dog. You'll go to the bathroom twelve times right before it's your turn so we all have to wait. Chris will hoard his money and then get mad when he keeps landing on Alex's hotels. Reid will only buy the utilities and somehow still

4

manage to clean the floor with all of us, and I'll get bored and quit six hours into a never-ending game."

"That's not true," Ed says. "*I* quit last time, and Chris bought up all the orange properties to get back at Alex for the rooster-shaped birthday cake."

"Man, that was a great cake," Alex says, dark eyes downcast as he laughs into his drink. "Still worth Chris putting salt in my beer for two weeks."

"What's greater," Chris replies, "is how you never once expected the salt, even after the fourth time."

In typical fashion, Reid won't be distracted from his goal, and pipes up from where he's organizing the property cards. "The rules were very clear tonight: my party, my choice."

We groan in unison because he has a point. Reid and Ed are both in neuroscience—also at UCSB—but while Ed works as a postdoc researcher in Reid's lab, Reid is a newly minted associate professor, just awarded tenure. Said tenure is why I'm wearing both a dress and a party hat, and why there are somewhat droopy crepe-paper streamers hung throughout Chris's living room.

Chris is always Team Reid; he's gathering up the game pieces, but not to put them away, to compromise. "We'll switch things up. I'll be the dog, Mills."

"I think you're missing my point, Christopher."

Four sets of eyes stare blankly back at me, urging me to give up the battle.

"Okay then," I say, resigned as I stand and walk into the kitchen for another bottle of wine.

An hour later, I've lost track of how much pretend money I've paid Reid, and how many times Alex has refilled my glass. Alex is a professor of biochemistry, which explains how he can always be counted on to get me drunk. And oh, I am drunk. I don't know what I was complaining about: Monopoly is awesome!

Chris reshuffles the Community Chest cards and places them facedown on the board. "Ed, are you still seeing that redhead?"

I have no idea how Chris remembers this. Between Alex and Ed it seems there's never a shortage of odd dating stories to go around. Alex, I get. He's tall, dark, and wicked, and even though he's originally from Huntington Beach, he spent every childhood summer with his extended family in Ecuador, giving him an accent that stops women in their tracks. He's also never serious about anyone, and rarely sees someone again after getting a cab home in the morning.

Ed is . . . none of these things. Don't get me wrong, he's not unattractive and he has the aforementioned full head of hair, but he's more like a grown frat boy than a manly man. If we went to his place right now we'd find ketchup and a case of Mountain Dew in his refrigerator, and a living room full of pinball machines instead of furniture. Still, he goes out more than me, Reid, and Chris combined.

Not that that's saying much.

Reid is a workaholic. Chris is gorgeous and accomplished, mentoring fellow African American chemists right here at the university. But he's also picky and serious, and works the same insane hours as Reid does. And me? Honestly, maybe I'm just lazy.

Alex counts out his spaces and sets the dice in the center of the board. "You're talking about the one with the eye patch?"

Okay, *that* jogs my memory.

Ed isn't amused. "She did not have an *eye patch*."

"Actually, I remember her, too," I say. "I distinctly recall seeing a patch covering an eye." I motion to the board and the neat row of hotels lined up there. "PS, it's your turn and if you roll anything other than a two—which will land you in jail—you are fu-*ucked*."

"Slumlords," Ed mutters, but rolls the dice anyway. I have no idea how, but he does—miraculously—roll a two, and does a celebratory fist pump before scooting his little car into the space marked *Jail*. A momentary reprieve from the rows and rows of Alex's hotels. "And it wasn't an eye patch, it was a small bandage. We were being . . . amorous and things got a little crazy."

"A little crazy as in . . ." I trail off, deciding I might not really want the answer.

Reid laughs over the top of his glass. When Ed doesn't immediately clarify, though, his smile slowly straightens, and a hush falls over the room as we're all left to mentally unravel this, logistically. "Wait. Seriously?"

I tidy up the meager remains of my money. "He did say it was a *small* bandage."

Reid falls forward onto the table laughing, and maybe it's the fact that half my blood has to be wine at this point, but I'm reminded all over again that the first thing I noticed about him was his smile.

Just over two years ago, Reid and I were introduced by my then-boyfriend Dustin, the department chair for criminology. (Yes, this means that my ex-boyfriend is now my boss—the reason I will never date someone I work with again.) Reid was new to UCSB, and at the dedication of a new computer science building, Dustin made some crack about it being the first time anyone had seen Reid outside his lab. Apparently Reid and his fiancée had just broken up; her first complaint was that Reid spent too much time at work. I didn't know that at the time, but I found out later that Dustin had. Reid laughed at the little dig and continued to smile warmly as we shook hands. I had a tiny, immediate crush on that sparkling, crinkly-eyed smile that survived the sting of Dustin's underhanded jabs.

For un-Reid-related reasons, I broke up with Dustin a few months later, but because it turns out no one liked Dustin anyway, I got to keep Reid, and all his friends, too: Chris and Reid went to graduate school together, Ed joined Reid's lab as a postdoc shortly after he was hired, and Alex shared lab space with Chris when they were both new faculty at UCSB. I'm the only non-sciencey person in the group, but at work and at home, these guys have become my sweet little chosen family of sorts.

"So," Chris says, "I'm going to take that as a no, on the still dating question."

Ed rolls again, happy when he doesn't manage a double and gets to remain safely in jail. "Correct."

"Then who are you inviting to the commencement banquet?" Chris asks.

Reid pulls his attention from the board and over to Chris. "Do we have to think about that yet? The banquet is in June. It's only March."

Chris smiles and looks smugly around the table. "I take it none of you heard the rumor about this year's speaker."

Reid searches his expression. "The speaker will make me want to bring a date?"

Chris stands and walks into the kitchen to grab another beer. "I heard a rumor that Obama is giving the commencement address, and a keynote at the Deans' Banquet. Black tie, plus-one, the whole nine."

We all gasp, deeply, in unison.

"I got word that the chancellor is going to announce it this week," he adds.

"No way." Ed stares at him, eyes wide behind his thick glasses. "Oh. I am definitely going this year."

Reid laughs, picking up the dice. "You're supposed to go *every* year."

"Last year the commencement speaker was Gilbert Gottfried. I don't think I missed anything."

"I actually wanted to talk to you guys about this," Chris says. "None of us is dating anyone—" He stops, glancing to where Ed is balancing a cork on his nose and counting to see how long he's able to do it.

"Look at this, Millie." Ed stretches his arms out. "Ten seconds, no hands."

Chris turns back to the rest of us. "—or has any serious prospects," he continues slowly. "Who *are* we taking?"

Ed straightens, catching the cork in his palm. "Why can't we all go together?"

"Because it's not junior prom," Chris says.

"We can't just go solo?"

"I mean, you could," Chris says, "but this is gonna be a big deal with dancing and coupley stuff. Go solo and be the loner, go in a group and we're the table of dudes—and Mills—sitting there awkwardly. We should get dates."

Reid rolls his dice and begins counting out his turn. "I call Millie."

"You *call* me?"

"Whoa, whoa." Derailed from his initial argument, Chris turns to Reid with a frown. "If we're just going to pair up, why'd you pick her?"

Reid shrugs and gives a vague nod in my direction. "She looks better in a ball gown."

Ed seems genuinely insulted. "You have obviously never seen me in one."

"I took you to the Deans' Banquet last year," Chris reminds Reid. "We had an awesome time."

His turn completed, Reid drops the dice onto the center of the board and picks up his drink. "We did. I'm just being fair and going with someone else this time."

Ed smacks Chris's shoulder. "I'm more Reid's type. Remember that cute bartender he liked? The one with the curly hair?" He makes a show of pointing to his head and the mass of auburn curls there. "Tell me we wouldn't look great together."

"I can beat that." Alex brings up a foot to rest on the table and rolls up the hem of his jeans, flexing his calf muscle. "Reid is a leg man. Just look at these stems. I could spin you all around that dance floor."

Reid watches each of them, bemused. "I mean, technically speaking, *Millie* is my type. Being female and whatnot."

"Is it weird to anyone that this roomful of straight men is fighting over Reid and not me?" I ask.

Chris, Alex, and Ed seem to give this fair consideration before answering "No" in unison.

I lift my glass of wine and take a deep swallow. "Okay, then."

Finally, Reid stands, carrying his empty glass into the kitchen. "Millie, you need anything?"

"Other than tips on how to develop an alluring female presence?" I ask. "I'm good. Thanks."

At the counter Reid rinses his glass and bends to open the dishwasher, carefully setting it inside. It's something I've seen him do a hundred times, and I don't know if it's the talk of dates, or the wine, or if Reid is just looking particularly good in that dark gray shirt, but tonight, I don't look away.

I watch as he easily moves around the kitchen, picking up stray dishes near the sink and loading them into the correct tray. I can see the muscles in his back flex as he bends when he's done, rubbing a hand over the broad head of Chris's silver Labrador, Maisie.

I've had enough to drink that my limbs feel loose and pliable; my stomach feels warm. My brain is a little fuzzy around the edges—just enough to block out my tendency to overthink everything. Instead, my mind meanders around the fact that Reid doing something as mundane as loading a dishwasher and petting a dog is absolutely *fascinating*.

With the kitchen tidied up, Reid extends his arms above his head in a leisurely stretch. My eyes are like magnets and follow the lines of his body, the way the fabric of his shirt pulls tight across his chest and strains along the curve of his biceps. I get a peek of stomach.

Reid has a really nice stomach.

I bet he'd look great with that shirt all the way off . . .

Kneeling above me, arms outstretched, fingers wrapped around the headboard while he—

Whoa.

I mean . . . *WHOA. Where did that come from?*

I fix my attention down at the dining room table and it's a full five seconds before I dare to move again. I just had a *sex thought* about Reid. *Reid*. Reid Campbell, who always roots for the underdog in any sporting event, who pretends he enjoys classical music so Chris doesn't go alone to the symphony, who buys a new pair of running shoes precisely every six months.

When he returns to the table and sits down next to me, if the pounding of my heart is any indication, I do not look like I'm thinking about resuming our fascinating game of Monopoly.

I blink over to my empty wineglass, eager to point blame in the most convenient place. How many of these did I have? Two? Three? More? I'm not hammered, but I'm not exactly sober, either.

I'm the kind of tipsy where I should want to hug everyone, not pull my best friend's pants down.

GAH.

Strictly platonic best guy friend. Strictly platonic best guy friend.

Heat rushes to my face and I stand so quickly my chair teeters on its back legs. Four sets of curious eyes swing in my direction, and I turn, making a beeline for the bathroom.

"Millie?" Reid calls after me. "You okay?"

"Gotta pee!" I shout over my shoulder, not stopping until I'm safely inside the bathroom and the door is firmly closed behind me.

Normally I laugh when confronted with one of the dozen roosters we've given Chris over the past two years. But now? Not so much. The cock thing began as a joke—Chris complimented a giant rooster painting at Ed's mom's house, and she gave it to him on the spot—so of course every birthday, Valentine's day, and Christmas present since has been some form of rooster décor. But even the sight of one of my favorites—a RISE AND SHINE MOTHER CLUCKERS sign I got him for his last birthday—only makes me think of the cock joke, which makes me think of penises, which reminds me of the image of Reid naked, in my bed, on top of me.

Hands on the counter, I lean in to examine my reflection and, okay . . . it could be better. My cheeks are flushed, my eyes a little glassy. My eyeliner and mascara have converged in a dark smear below my lower lids.

Kneeling, arms outstretched, fingers wrapped around the headboard—

With the faucet on as high as it will go, I clean up and splash cold water on my face. It helps a little—cooling down my skin and clearing out the haze so I can think.

It's not that I find Reid unappealing in a sexual way—he's gorgeous and brilliant and hysterical—but he's also my best friend. My Reid. The guy who held my hand during an emergency root canal and dressed up as Kylo Ren when we went to see *The Last Jedi* on my twenty-ninth birthday. I'm close with the other guys, but for whatever reason, it's different with Reid. Not *that* kind of different, but . . . closer. Maybe it's because he always knows to find me in the true crime section of the bookstore. Maybe it's because he has a level of intuition that I've never known in a friend before. Maybe it's because we can be quiet together, and it's never weird.

I squeeze my eyes shut; it's hard to have an existential crisis when you're drunk. Part of me thinks I should head to the nearest exit, but the other part thinks we should just . . . hug it out.

There's a knock at the door and I step back just far enough to open it a crack. It's Reid, looking sweetly disheveled with a dish towel still slung over his shoulder.

God damn it.

I straighten, hoping I look more sober than I feel. "Hi."

"Everything okay?" he asks.

"Totally." I lean against the doorframe in an attempt to appear casual. All this really does is bring my face within inches of his, which somehow makes me feel drunker. "You know how I am with wine. Goes right through me."

I'm an idiot, but before I can regret what I've said, he's laughing. *Why does he always laugh at my dumb jokes?*

"Ed and Alex are headed out," he says quietly. "You can't drive. Can I take you home?"

"I'm not drunk." This statement would carry more weight if I didn't hiccup immediately after saying it. "And I wasn't going to drive."

He tilts his head and a piece of soft brown hair falls forward, curling over his forehead. My brain immediately sides with Team Hug It Out.

"Come on," he says. "You can control the radio on the way."

It's sunny and perfect in Santa Barbara at least three hundred days a year. We get most of our meager rainfall in early spring, and as we drive down Highway 1 at midnight—windows open and Arcade Fire blasting on the radio—it smells like a storm in the distance.

"Did you have a good night?" I ask, rolling my head to see him. It takes a few seconds for my eyes to refocus. The inside of the car is dark, his profile in shadow.

"I did."

"Does it feel different?"

He turns to me and smiles, the tips of his lashes glowing gold in the light from the dashboard. "What? Tenure?"

"Yeah. Knowing you can only be fired for incompetence or gross misconduct."

He laughs. "Define gross misconduct again?"

"Sexual harassment, murder, embezzlement . . ."

"You're kind of making it sound like a dare." He reaches for my hand where it sits on the console between us and squeezes my fingers. "You cold? I can turn on the seat warmers if you want to keep the window open for air."

"I'm good," I say, but he keeps hold of my fingers anyway. "Maybe with less time in the lab and more in the classroom, you can cut back a little. Have more time to yourself."

"To do what? Play pinball with Ed?"

"I don't know," I say, "explore new hobbies, find yourself, date. You work too much."

He turns to me again and grins adorably. "Why would I need a date when I already have you for the banquet?"

I roll my eyes. "I mean, like, in the general sense."

"Okay, Pot. When's the last time you went out with someone who wasn't one of us?"

I search my memory, counting back five . . . six months, and can't help but recall the veritable wasteland my sex life has become. I've been stressed with deadlines and family stuff and my brain is just looking for an escape pod, a little release. No wonder I'm having sex thoughts about Reid.

When it takes me too long to answer, he gives my fingers another squeeze. "Need me to get out a calendar? I think I have an abacus in my office."

"I think it was Carson? The barista who worked at Cajé."

In the dark I see his eyes narrow as he thinks. "Wasn't he younger than you?"

"A few years," I say with a shrug.

"*Seven* years," he corrects. "And he had a nose ring."

That was some impressive recollection, Reid. "Men date younger women all the time and get a pat on the back. Why does dating a younger guy automatically make me a cougar?"

He holds up a hand. "I am not calling you a cougar. Listen, if twenty-one-year-old college me had had the chance to bang beautiful twenty-eight-year-old you, I'd have done it in a hot second."

Wait, what?

A shiver moves down my spine and he notices, shifting to run a hand along my arm. "You have goose bumps."

"Oh." I reach over to close the window. "I guess it's chillier than I thought."

"So what happened? Between you and—"

"Carson," I finish for him. "Nothing happened. He was twenty-one. There weren't a lot of places it could go."

"You mean, it was just sex."

I'm thankful we're still sitting in the dark so he can't

see me get all blushy and awkward. "My muscle tone had never been better."

Reid barks out a scandalized laugh.

"I'm not lying. What about you? When was your last . . . you know?"

"Hmm." He taps his thumb against the steering wheel. "My last *you know*. I'm not sure. You probably know my life as well as I do. You tell me."

"You work all the time."

"Funny thing about that," he says with a grin. "It's probably how I got tenure."

I concede this with a dorky little nod. He turns down State Street, which, this time of night, is the quickest route to my house. I watch as we dart past the streetlights one by one.

"Does that make us lame?" I wonder. "That we've been single this long and nobody in our group is in an actual relationship? Ed and Alex date more than us, maybe even Chris, but it never goes anywhere. Is it possible we're all enabling each other to die alone? Are we turning into a weird celibacy cult?"

"We're definitely enabling each other."

"But should we be worried about that?" I ask. "One of the many, *many* problems I had with Dustin was that he wanted a good little wife. I'm not even sure I have that gene and haven't been with anyone long-term since him. You haven't since Isla. Does that make us failures?"

"I think it means the opposite, actually," he says, pulling into my driveway and shifting the car into park. He turns to face me. "Let me ask you a question. Do you love your career?"

I don't even have to think about it. "One hundred percent."

"Well, there you go. And even if we are enabling each other, who cares? You could never die alone, because you have me."

It's suddenly quiet in the car and I know I should go inside. I should wash my face and put my pajamas on and go straight to bed.

I should let Reid go home.

The problem is I don't want to.

"Come inside with me," I say, pushing open my door and already climbing out. The air is cool and smells like the ocean, but it's not enough to drown out whatever buzz is still humming in my veins or make me come to my senses.

I have no idea what I'm doing or what's happening between us, but when I reach the porch and pull out my keys, Reid is right behind me.

chapter two

 reid

've never hooked up with a friend before . . . is that what's happening right now?

I mean, it seems like it might be. Millie is being herself but a little . . . *more*. Giving me a shy smile while her eyes wander a lot more than I'm used to, then twisting her fingers in mine when I held her hand in the car . . .

It's like unlocking a window and letting the wind blow it wide open. If Millie is flirting, then what? Should I flirt back? This is a very *The Usual Suspects* moment—I had no idea Millie was this person.

Are we doing this?

I blatantly check out her backside when she ducks into

23

the fridge to grab us each a can of sparkling water. It feels nearly clinical the way I study her.

Objectively, it is a fantastic ass.

It's just that it's *Millie's* ass. Initially—briefly—she was known as Dustin's Millie. Later—and better—she was known as one-of-the-guys Millie, *Our* Millie. Now, it appears, she's Drunk Flirty Millie.

I've looked at her ass before, of course. I've looked at all of her, frankly, but I've done it in the dissociated way all guys look at women—almost without realizing we're doing it. Casually, too, and entirely due to the habit of proximity: while helping her out of her coat, while holding her beer as she takes off a sweater, while examining her outside a changing room when she asks whether she should buy a particular pair of jeans. Regardless, no matter how objectively pretty she is, Millie Morris has always been off-limits.

But mostly I think she's been off-limits because she's never shown any particular interest in any of us.

She clears her throat and I drag my eyes back up to her face. Which, it's fair to say, may be the best part of her: the enormous bright green eyes, the sarcastic mouth, the splash of freckles across her nose and cheeks. She's beautiful, yes, but I've never truly veered into *Is she sexy?* territory until tonight.

"I was checking out your ass."

"And?" She leans a hip against the counter and gives me a smile that's unlike anything I've ever seen from her. Most of her smiles are openmouthed, delighted, often given through a choking laugh as she quickly swallows a mouthful of beer. Other smiles are half-baked, amused at us while we try to get a rise out of her. The rare smile is triumphant—when she gives us the perfect amount of shit. They're rare only because she so infrequently shows her cards.

But this one is a little like being told a secret. She seems to agree, because she bites her bottom lip halfway through it, like she's trying to put it away.

I think she wants a rating on her backside, but it's probably clear from my expression that I'd give her high marks. "What's with you tonight?"

A bare shoulder lifts and drops. "I'm tipsy."

This makes me bark out a laugh. "'Tipsy'? I'd be amazed if Chris has any wine left in his house."

"Don't blame that on me," she says. "You're the one who went and got tenure. Besides, Ed took down two bottles by himself, and Alex was pouring mine."

"Ed's blood is ninety percent alcohol."

"And ten percent Cheeto dust."

She moves over to me, waters in hand, and the only

way to describe her gait is sashay-y. It's so dramatic it makes me start to laugh. We've known each other for more than two years, and I never would have predicted this playful, seductive side of her. But the sound is cut off in my throat when she puts the waters down on the end table near me and puts her hands squarely on my chest.

Anticipation comes alive beneath my skin.

"Mills."

"Reids."

Speaking through the pressurized air in my throat, I say, "What are you doing?"

"Seducing you." She lifts one hand and draws a pinky down the side of her face, pulling away a strand of auburn hair. "Is it working?"

I've never had reason to check myself around her before, and the answer easily slides out of me, unfiltered: "Yes. But why?"

Another shrug. "I haven't had sex in a while. You were doing dishes earlier."

"Dishes?"

"It was sexy. And you stretched. I saw stomach muscles and happy trail."

"Oh, well, of course we should end up here."

She growls a little as she stretches to press her nose into my neck, inhaling. "I like how you smell."

I freeze. When she says this, it feels a little like standing at the static center of a spinning room. Again: Millie. This is *Millie Morris*. Goofball. Colleague. Stealer of my Stanford sweatshirt. Woman who shares my exact tastes in beer. The glue of our circle of friends. "You do?"

"Yeah," she says, and blazes heat into me with the press of her mouth over my pulse point. "It's familiar, but I never realized until now how nice it is up close."

While she kisses up my neck, I'm dragged back two years, when Dustin brought her along with him to meet up with the rest of us for drinks. Chris, Alex, and I thought he seemed like a cool guy; maybe he'd be another colleague we could end up hanging with. Academia is hard as hell, and it helps to have a community of people who get the schedule, understand the pressures. But within a half hour, Dustin was playing darts with some surfers, and Millie got us all drunk on car bombs and dirty jokes. From that night on, Millie seemed more *ours* than *his*. I know they ostensibly broke up because their schedules weren't compatible, and they hit a plateau— also he was basically a dick—but I sometimes wonder how much her friendship with us contributed to the breakup.

It was a friendship that came at the perfect time. I was still reeling from Isla calling off our engagement, and only beginning to find my friend clan at the university. Chris, Alex, Ed, and I hung out, but it was spontaneous—never something we planned or assumed. As soon as Millie joined our little gang, though, being together became the default: barbecues at Chris's when it was nice out. Football at Millie's on Sundays with a big TV and the best furniture. Game night at Ed's. Inside jokes and familiarity. We fell into a rhythm and built a scaffold of community. Before Millie we got together when we randomly bumped into each other; because of her we now have lunch every Monday and Wednesday, and I can't imagine a week without it.

I fucking love all of them, but romance wasn't even on the table. Now it's just me and Millie here, standing so close our chests touch. I'm trying not to contemplate what the others would think right now.

When I focus again, it's hard to think of anything; Millie has been busy. One finger is tucked into my belt loop and her lips are hovering near my chin, skirting along my jaw. It's decision time. All I have to do is tilt my face down to her, and we'll be kissing. I'm already getting hard, and the question whether this is a great or disastrous decision is growing cloudier.

"Are we going to do this?" This time I say it out loud. Her breath, against my mouth, is sweet with wine and the apple Jolly Rancher she swiped from Chris's counter on our way out the door.

"I really, *really* want sex tonight," she admits. "Specifically, I'd like sex with you, but if you're weirded out by this, then it's cool if you leave and I dive into the drawer of sin in my bedroom."

I haven't exactly made up my mind, but my lips pass over hers once—just to see—then again, and it's not weird, not even a little. It's soft and easy. My pulse taps out an impatient beat inside me. "The drawer of sin?"

"Sex toys."

"No," I say, kissing her again, "I translated that. I mean . . . you have an entire *drawer* of them?"

"It's not a huge drawer." Her mouth comes over mine, firmer now, and then she grins into the kiss. "But yeah. It's full."

Wow, her lips are unbelievable—playful, soft, immediately addicting. It takes almost no time for her to transition from *Millie, my friend* into *Millie, sexpot*, and for a tiny flicker, I desperately hope that we can transition back just as easily.

But then her hands come up under my shirt, and I hope instead that time snags on this night, so it doesn't ever end.

Her palms are soft slides of heat, up over my stomach,

to my chest. Fingernails teasing, fingertips mapping every inch of me. Her sounds vibrate against my lips, into my mouth. My shirt is up and gone. Her hands work madly at my belt, my button, my zipper, until my jeans are a puddle of black at my feet.

All the thoughts we shouldn't have about our friends are unleashed—how she kisses, what sounds she makes, does she take charge, is she fun?—and by her grin I can tell the same thing flies through her thoughts. What a relief to find all the unexpected ways we're compatible.

I like her little gasp when she digs into my boxers and feels me. I like the sneaky smile that presses against mine. "Reid. I'm touching your dick."

"I know."

"I like it," she whispers.

"Coincidence? I do, too."

She giggles, pulling her hand out of my boxers and cupping her hands at my waist while she walks backward, leading me down the hall to her bedroom. She kisses my collarbone, my neck, my jaw.

Millie is easy to undress: just a tug of fabric up over her head, and then she's standing there in nothing but her underwear. I've always semiconsciously suspected she had a great chest, but now I get to confirm with my eyes, and hands, and mouth. I've always appreciated that she likes to swim, that she eats pretty well—but now I get to see the definition along her arms, her stomach, the strength of her thighs. Her hair is a mess; her mouth is a little swollen from me already. I haven't had sex in months, and I'm momentarily overwhelmed—a starving man at a buffet, unsure where to start.

"You're overthinking something," she says, and then moves closer, hooking her thumbs into the waistband of my boxers. "Don't think."

I twist a strand of her hair around my index finger. "Should we establish some ground rules?"

When Millie pulls away slightly, her eyes are dark and heavy. "If you want?"

"I just feel like we should."

Her lips return to my neck, sucking. "Okay, one, we both come."

I pull back and look at her. "Seriously? That needs to be said?"

A wry curve tugs at her mouth. "Oh, you'd be surprised."

"I've got you," I say, kissing her smile. "But my rule is we don't tell the guys." Ed is so genuinely optimistic, he'd probably be happy for us even if it's just one night of fun. But Alex is a smart-ass who would give us unending shit and Chris would be horrified.

It's her turn to pull back in surprise. "*That* needs to be said?"

"I feel like they'd be jealous, I guess."

"Of me, obviously. Clearly everyone wants to bang Reid."

This makes me laugh. "Clearly."

"So, you're not telling Chris? You tell him everything."

She's right, but he would never be on board for this kind of impulsive decision. Chris is the most intentional, cautious person I've ever known. "I swear I won't."

Her hand slides over my stomach, and a fingertip traces the line of hair above my boxers. "Any other rules?"

"I have condoms," I say. "But they're in my car."

"I have some in my drawer of sin."

I can hear the smile in her voice, but the blunt mention of something so physically related to the act makes her neck go warm under my mouth.

Her bra comes off with a little slip of my fingers, and I lose even more of my plan to savor this when I fit my hand around the warm curve of her breast. "What do you like?"

"Everything," she says, quickly adding, "except anal."

"Wow." I pull back, looking down at her. "Never mind. If that's off the table then I gotta go."

She pinches my nipple, laughing at my high-pitched shriek.

"I was kidding." I punctuate my point by pushing her underwear down her hips.

"I know." Her mouth slides over my shoulder. "But I wasn't."

"I'm not really into it, either."

"Really?" she says, and I love the genuine way she searches my eyes. I've never been this close to her before, and she's certainly never looked at me like this—with the combined tenderness of best friend and lover. "I assumed you were into everything."

"When did you assume this?"

Her hand comes around me, stroking slowly, and my mind goes all wavy. "You know. Just . . . random Reid thoughts."

"While we were at Gio's last week, you looked at me and thought, 'Huh. I bet he likes anal.'"

"I think it was when you were eating a club sandwich at lunch Wednesday," she jokes.

I laugh, and it fuses with a groan when she leans forward to drag her teeth along my neck. "I swear, Ed needs to never wear that shirt again."

"The white one?" she asks. "Chest hair extravaganza?"

"It's just so thin . . ."

I bend to kiss her throat, her shoulder, and then I forget what I was saying because she's pulling me down onto

33

the bed, and her nipple is in my mouth and she's stroking me and I probably couldn't remember my own name if asked.

"Is this weird?" I murmur into her skin. "Why are we talking about the guys while I'm doing *this*?"

"I like talking," she says, and digs her free hand into my hair. "I like talking to you while—"

Her voice falls away when I suck.

I half expect it to be like this the entire night—easy conversation like we've always had, but through kisses, touches, even through the sex itself. But when her hand finds a certain rhythm, it shifts something over inside me, something more instinct than conscious thought. I make my way down her body, she later makes her way down mine, and when she finally comes back up over me, on top of me, she looks directly into my eyes as she sinks down and I wonder during the first gasping burst of sensation why we haven't been doing this every day for the past two years.

I leave Millie's around two, when she's fast asleep and starfished across ninety percent of the mattress. I kiss her cheek when I go; it feels weird to leave after only half a night together—but I have to think it would be even weirder to wake up with your best friend naked in your bed.

I didn't have much to drink, but the next morning I feel hungover anyway. It's a cocktail of the light-headed relief that comes on the heels of a night of great sex . . . mixed with the nauseating anxiety over a fight with a friend.

Not that Millie and I are fighting. I mean, I can't even imagine Millie angry. She wasn't *that* drunk, but if there's anything that could piss her off, it'd be the perception that I took advantage of her last night.

Chris's office is in the building next to mine, and just inside the entrance closest to the campus coffee kiosk. This proximity means that he's lucky enough to be able to slip out and back in for coffee without running into fifteen colleagues in the hall, but it also means that people are constantly walking past his office, on their way to or from the kiosk, interrupting his workday.

Like I do now, stepping through the open door and into his office. "Hey."

For a chemistry professor, Chris keeps his office impressively tidy. There are no teetering stacks of dusty lab notebooks or piles of outdated textbooks being used as makeshift tables. He has a small plant on his desk, a jar of pencils, a few molecular models here and there, but—

much like the man himself—Chris's office is much more put-together than any of the rest of us seem to manage.

He looks up, pulling his glasses off and setting them down near his keyboard. "Hey. I assume you guys got home okay last night?"

I expected him to ask, but the way the question comes out so immediately feels almost accusatory—almost *knowing*. The answer bursts out of me, a touch hysterically: "Of course we did."

He stares at me a second longer before he reaches for the paper takeaway cup I've put down on his desk. "Cool. Thanks for the coffee."

Out of all of us, Chris is the most intuitive, and—because he and I first met in graduate school nearly a decade ago—he also knows me better than anyone else. If even a flicker of last night passes through my thoughts, he'll see it. But maybe that's exactly why I'm here. Millie and I drove a mallet into our easy rhythm, creating a fault line that will either lie dormant or break everything into pieces. I need to know I can still act normal . . . where *normal* means I pretend the fault line is not directly underfoot.

"You good?" Chris asks.

"Oh, yeah." I stare with intense focus at his bookshelves, specifically studying a worn copy of Wade's *Organic Chemistry*, and finally, the moment snaps free. "Just wanted to come by and say thanks again for hosting last night."

"Of course, man. I'm really happy for you."

My gaze swings higher up on his bookshelf, to some molecular models, some awards on small pedestals, and . . . "Nice cock."

He groans, standing so he can reach for the rooster-shaped stress ball and toss it into the trash. "You have my students in on this rooster thing now."

"A student gave you cock?"

He jerks his attention past me, out into the hallway, before giving me the expression that speaks to the mental murder happening inside his brain. "Think you could keep your voice down?"

I grin. "I can try."

"What do you have going on today?"

Checking my watch, I tell him, "I'm giving our department seminar in thirty. Wanna come?"

"No."

"Then I'll see you at lunch."

I'm halfway through my fifty-minute presentation on optic nerve inflammation when the back door to the theater creaks loudly open the way it always does when someone unfamiliar with it tries it from the wrong side. Heads turn, and my chest suffers a weird, painful hiccup as Millie steps in. Dressed in black jeans and a deep green sweater, she tiptoes down the aisle with a paper bag in her hand and a dramatically apologetic expression for the disruption of her entrance. Millie has never come to one of my seminars; given that I'm in neuroscience and she's in criminology, she'd have no reason to. How did she even know where to find me? Maybe she wants a word with me afterward . . . ? The thought makes me uneasy.

Last night was good, right? I mean, to me, last night was incredible. We had sex twice. We talked for an hour in between, about all the kind of stuff we always talk about: Ed's latest lab disasters, Millie's upcoming lecture at Princeton, whether Alex will get tenure this year. Nothing too personal, nothing deep. Eventually pillow talk turned into touching, which turned into me climbing over her and words falling away. Before last night, I couldn't have even imagined the quiet, rhythmic sounds she would make, but I can't seem to get them out of my head today.

Glancing at the slide up on the large screen, I find my place again. As the only retinal specialist in the department, I try to keep my presentations sharp, interesting, and accessible. Millie knows my biggest gripe—that the rest of the neuroscience department likes to forget that the retina is part of the brain—and I catch her grinning when an image of the central nervous system comes up, with the retina highlighted right up front. The smile unknots the seed of tension in me.

This is Millie. She's unflappable. Of course we're okay.

In fact, she meets me halfway up the aisle as everyone is filing out and pulls a small pastry box out of the bag, handing it over. Inside, there is a cupcake with a unicorn sculpted out of frosting.

"What's this for?" I look up at her. "We celebrated my tenure last night, and my birthday is still a month away."

Millie grins. "It's the morning-after cupcake." When I don't figure out a response fast enough, she adds in a whisper, "It's a *good job with the orgasms* cupcake." Pausing, she looks down at my hands. "And it's an *Are we okay?* cupcake."

This rare display of vulnerability tilts me sideways, so I close the lid and boop her nose with my index finger, the way she always does to us. "You know we're fine."

"Then come to Cajé with me." She tugs my hand. "I need caffeination."

"I already had some . . . with Chris . . ."

But she's already turned to head up the aisle. I should have led with the more compelling *I need to get into the lab* explanation, because to Millie, work always comes first, but there's no such thing as too much coffee.

Cajé is a coffee shop right near campus and it's generally populated by the scruffiest representation of our student body. I'd wager there are as many white people with dreadlocks outside on the patio as there are baristas inside. And, although I know Millie can slob it up with the best of them on the weekend, right now in her fitted jeans, heels, and cashmere sweater, she stands out like a spray of flowers in a field of dry grass.

Without even bothering to ask what I want—she knows, anyway—she leans in and orders two medium Americanos, extra hot, and then, in a rushed flurry, points to a miraculously empty table for me to snag.

I wipe the table off with a couple of napkins, trying to calm the unfamiliar anxiety I'm feeling about an upcoming conversation with Millie.

My best friend, Millie, who puts moisturizing facial masks on me while we watch our favorite 1990s gangster movies and generously eats all the melon in my fruit salads.

With two steaming cups in her hands, she walks toward me at the table, and I have to make a conscious effort to look normal, which I'm pretty sure negates any potential for success.

This is so weird.

I mean, it's impossible to ignore the way her jeans curve over her hips, and then I'm boomeranged into wondering whether I would have noticed this before last night.

Sitting wordlessly, she smiles, touching her cheek, and the motion catches my eye as she drags a few wayward strands of hair behind her ear. There's a new, bare honesty here, an unspoken awareness captured by eye contact and screaming, *We had sex!* My gaze slides down to her neck and trips over something there. I don't think I would normally spot the tiny red bruise on her throat if I hadn't been the one to inflict it.

She notices me noticing and covers it with a fingertip. "I'll put some more makeup on it before lunch."

That's right. It's Wednesday, one of two days each week we all meet at Summit Café, near the library.

"It's cool. It's small," I say. "I mean, sorry."

"Oh, don't be sorry."

The sex is front and center now. Millie stares directly at me and it's a lot, having her undivided attention like this; it always is. Only now instead of simply enjoying it, my mind toggles between the calming surety of her expression and the memory of her eyes falling closed in relief when she moved on top of me and found that buckling moment of pleasure.

"You sure you're okay today?" I ask.

She nods decisively. "One hundred percent. You?"

"Same." I wonder whether she's also having these disruptive flashes of recollection. I don't exactly know how to extricate us from this topic, but letting the words "It was really good, though" tumble out of my mouth is probably not the way to do it.

She could make this awkward—and it's absolutely what I expect her to do because making us uncomfortable is Millie's favorite pastime. But she's feeling generous, apparently. "Of course it was good. We're both amazing in bed." When I laugh, she adds, "But . . . we're still on the same page, right? About . . . us being friends?"

"We're on the same page."

And we are. For as good as last night was, I don't want to be with Millie that way again. At least, I don't think I do. I definitely shouldn't. We're too good at being smart-ass friends to be very good tender lovers. I can't really imagine Millie like that, anyway.

She reaches across, squeezing my hand. "You're my best friend, Reid."

"You're going to make me cry."

With a laugh, she shoves my hand away. "But seriously, I can't do the dating-a-colleague thing again. What a disaster he was."

"To be fair," I say, grateful for this easy entrance back into *normal*, "his name is *Dustin*."

She quickly swallows a sip of coffee to protest this. "There are some who might say *Reid* is an especially pretentious name."

With a hand to my chest, I feign insult. "*No one* says that."

Millie reaches out, curling her hand around the forearm of a passing student. "Sorry. Quick question. Is 'Reid' a douchey name?"

The guy doesn't even hesitate or bother to look at me. "Totally."

Millie releases him with a smug smile and brings her mug to her lips.

I mirror her movement with my own mug. "He just said yes because he was intimidated by the obvious, hot professor randomly grabbing him."

"Be my guest," she says, spreading a generous hand. "Ask someone yourself."

"Excuse me," I say, stopping a female student with a raised finger. "Would you say the name 'Reid' is pretentious?"

She's very pretty—soft brown skin, a halo of curly hair—and when our eyes meet, she flushes. "Is that your name?"

"It's immaterial," I say, softening it with what Millie calls my Flirty Eyes.

"I mean," the girl says, "*I* don't think it's a pretentious name."

I thank her and she wanders off when I turn back to Millie. "See?"

"Her answer sounded like a nice way of saying, 'The consensus is that name is douchey.'"

I laugh. "Her answer was a clear no."

"If it was a no, it's because she wants to fuck you."

The word *fuck* coming out of her mouth does strange things to my pulse. She says it all the time, but just last night she gasped it into my ear, right before telling me she was close.

Again.

I try to make my voice sound as wounded as possible. "I had no idea you think my name is douchey."

Millie is not falling for it. She grins over the top of my mug. "I don't, really."

We fall into an easy silence and I try not to think about Sex Millie too much or study Friend Millie too closely. She's completely rebounded. Millie really is as constitutionally solid as she seems.

And holy shit, she's just as fun in bed as I would have guessed.

"So," she says out of the quiet, "in the interest of returning to Best Friendship, we should probably find other dates for commencement."

"Looks like it."

chapter three

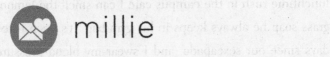 millie

Hey, Taylor," I say. "This is Millie. Millie Morris? I'm not sure if you remember me or not—we saw *Girl on the Train* together at the dollar theater last summer? You kept insisting that the new wife couldn't be the killer because she was a mother, and I argued that forty-two percent of children killed by a parent are killed by the mother, alone or with an accomplice. Um, anyway, I have this thing in June and I was wondering if you'd like to be my date. It's black tie and I have to RSVP, so if you could give me a call as soon as possible. And haha, I promise not to talk about mothers murdering their own children—"

The line disconnects. *That's weird*, I think, but I pencil

in a check mark on the MAYBE column next to Taylor Baldwin's name anyway.

"A 'maybe'?"

I jump at the sound of Reid's voice so close to my ear. Heat radiates off his skin as he tries to read over my shoulder. His hair is damp where it brushes my cheek; he's freshly showered and standing so close that even during lunchtime rush in the campus café I can smell the lemongrass soap he always keeps in his gym bag. It's been three days since our sexcapade, and I swear my blood pressure still hasn't completely recovered.

An elbow to his stomach sends him back into his own space and has the added benefit of allowing me to angle my date notebook away from him. "Do your feet even touch the ground when you walk? I didn't hear you."

He leans over the chair beside mine, catching my eye. "Were you really quoting murder stats while asking someone out? I may have some insight into why you haven't dated since the fetus barista at Cajé."

"Um, pardon me, sir. I was using that as *context* since I wasn't sure he would remember me by name. Maybe the guy sees a lot of movies." I erase my checkmark with an aggressive rub before sweeping eraser crumbs into Reid's lap.

Suppressed laughter curves the corners of his mouth and my eyes are snagged there, my thoughts drifting from mouths to lips to tongues, and all the things those parts managed very capably to do. I want to rub Purell on my brain. Trying to be cool about banging your best friend is a lot harder than I would have anticipated.

"I was just giving him some details to jog his memory."

"I can think of a handful of adjectives to describe you," he says, and slides his tray down next to mine and sits. "*Forgettable* is not one of them."

A tiny, hot bubble bursts in my thoughts, making me want to ask—*You mean, even in bed?*—but I make a show of scrutinizing my notebook instead, ignoring the embarrassed flush I feel warming the back of my neck. "Thanks. I think."

He unwraps a set of plastic utensils from a paper napkin. "You're calling guys in the middle of the lunch rush?"

"The noise is my camouflage! I can't do it in my office. What if Dustin walked by and heard me asking someone out in a voicemail? I'd have to suffer his smug face for a month."

Reid stares at me for a couple breaths longer before he seems to decide to give up on this. Or me. He digs a fork into his salad with one hand and thumbs through a scientific journal with the other. Despite my momentary short circuit a few minutes ago, things have been . . . fine between us. Normal. *Comfortable*. Did we manage to avoid the awkward sleeping-with-your-strictly-platonic-bestie thing? I can't possibly be that lucky.

I bend, picking at my own salad.

"So who were you calling?" Reid asks, nodding toward my phone.

I stab a piece of cucumber. "If you'd started your eavesdropping a little earlier, you'd have heard that his name is Taylor."

Reid takes a bite, chewing while he searches his memory. "Taylor. Why doesn't that ring a bell?"

I shrug, picking out the tomatoes and setting them off to the side. I'm not surprised Reid doesn't remember him. For starters, Taylor and I went out once, almost a year ago, and I'm not all that chatty about my love life, anyway. Reid and the guys might go on and on about their dates—or lack thereof—but it's never been my thing.

"How many have you called so far?" he asks.

"Three." I've called seven. "Are you going to hassle me?"

He holds up his hands, defensive. "Just making conversation."

"You know, at least I'm *trying*. How many have *you* called, Reid?"

He shoves a forkful of lettuce into his mouth and grunts something noncommittal into his salad.

I sit back. "That's what I thought."

He swallows before reaching for his bottle of water. "I had a lecture on optic neuritis to prepare and we need to submit a few abstracts for the Society for Neuroscience meeting. Plus, someone has to scour the pages of *Pinball Enthusiast* for Ed's next birthday present." He pauses just long enough to wave away my *I knew it* face. "I've been busy, okay? I'll get to it."

I raise my brows. "We're *all* busy."

The grounds crew is working outside the café, and when the door opens again it brings with it a gust of air fresh with cut grass. It also brings Chris, who is clearly agitated as he makes his way to our table.

"Do you have any idea how many available, reasonably attractive single women over the age of twenty-five I interact with on a daily basis?" he says in lieu of a greeting.

I blink. "Hi, Chris."

He sets an insulated coffee mug on the table and pulls out the chair next to Reid. "I'll fill you in: *two*. One is the lady who lives above me and walks her cats, and the other is you."

I stick a piece of lettuce to my front teeth and give him my cheesiest smile. "So, what you're saying is . . . I've got a chance."

Reid and Chris stare blankly at me for a lingering beat before turning back to each other.

"It's only been a few days," Reid tells him. "I think you're too stressed about this."

"That's what Chris does," I remind him, pulling the lettuce free. "He takes things very seriously and does them better than all of us."

Ed steps up behind Chris's chair, pulls out the last seat at our small table, and asks him, "Didn't you and Rebecca Fielding bang in the bathroom at the faculty Christmas party? You could ask her, since you've already dated."

Chris lets out an audible sigh, but it's Reid who answers. "Sex isn't dating."

"Either way," Chris says, "I've got nothing for this commencement thing."

"None of us do," I tell him. "But you have plenty of time."

"But do we actually need dates?" Reid asks.

"Wait." Ed wags his finger back and forth between me and Reid. "I thought you two were going together?"

Reid stabs another forkful of salad. "We decided not to."

"Why?" Ed looks understandably confused.

I have to be sending Reid a look that's half threatening reminder and half panic, but he doesn't look flustered at all.

"Because Millie is her own person and can find a date

by herself. It was a dick move on my part to call dibs like she's some sort of new toy."

I give Reid a patronizing *That's right, you chauvinist* smile, and he kicks me under the table.

Ed makes some kind of dismissive noise in the back of his throat. "It's Millie. It's not like you can offend her."

I start to argue this but then realize he's right. "Well, maybe I should have been more offended. But I only have one emotion, and it's hunger."

Chris, who has been noticeably silent, looks up from his coffee. "I've been thinking lately . . . what about a dating site?" He offers up the suggestion carefully, like he's aiming a shot into a very distant, very small basket.

A dating site? I scrunch my nose. "Ew."

Ed obviously agrees, because he's the first to speak up. Good job, Ed. "You want *these two* to use a dating app?" he says, pointing a thumb between Reid and me.

Chris looks on, as confused as I am. "It's how my sister met Ashley."

"Reid and Mills are the oldest thirty-year-olds I know."

Wow. Ed sucks.

"I'm twenty-nine," I remind him.

"And you watch *Murder, She Wrote* every night, alone, in bed."

I frown and throw a cherry tomato at his pouf of hair. "Because it's a good show and my bed is hella comfortable."

"And you still use the word 'hella'—"

"Ed," Reid says. "You're doing that thing again."

"What thing?"

"Being a dick. Something like forty million people use dating sites. It can't be that complicated."

Ed turns to us, his smile the expressive equivalent of a condescending pat on the head. "Why do you even know that kind of statistic? And, no, it's not complicated, per se. It's nuance. There's an entire language involved in these sorts of things."

"We have six degrees between the four of us." Reid looks back down to his lunch. "I think we can keep up."

Chris leans in toward Ed. "What kind of language?"

"Why do I already know this is going to be like teaching my mom to use the DVR?" Ed rubs a hand over his face. "Okay, for example, 'thirst trap' is someone posting intentionally sexy pics to get attention."

I shake my head. "Isn't that the point of a photo? To get attention?"

"Yeah, but this would be like, 'Look at my new watch,' but showing the watch just gave an excuse to zoom in on your boobs."

Chris reaches for my notebook and pencil, flips to a new page, and prompts Ed to continue, ready to take notes. "Okay. What else?"

"Nerds," I say. "We are nerds. And old. Ed, you're right. My God, we are too young to be this old."

Everyone ignores me. Ed leans back in his chair, eyes on the ceiling while he thinks. "Let's see . . . 'Ghosting' is when someone you're chatting with online just disappears. No reason or anything. As opposed to a 'slow fade,' where they start to respond less and less over time."

Chris is diligently jotting all this down.

"'Benching' is pretty self-explanatory," Ed says. "They like you but keep you on the bench so they can continue playing the field. 'DTR' means to define the relationship, so 'The Talk.' 'F2F' means they want to meet. Oh, and if you do meet, a 'half-night stand' is when you hook up, and leave when the sex is over."

Something inside me comes to a stop, and I work very, very hard to not look up at Reid. When I glance up, his eyes immediately dart away from my face.

None of us says anything. Chris is finishing his note taking. Reid and I are studiously not looking at each other. Ed is leaning in, excited now.

"Seriously, you guys want to do this?" he asks. "Like, Team Dating App?"

"Um," I say. "No? But . . . maybe." I glance at Reid. "If we must."

"Okay. Well, if you're all down, Tinder is pretty awesome," Ed says.

Tinder? When would he have time? Ed is either in the lab or playing one of the half-dozen arcade games he owns. I try to imagine a scenario in which someone is expecting a hot hookup, and they open the door to find Ed standing there instead. Like I said, Ed is good-looking in his own way, he's just . . . so *Ed*.

I guess he's getting more action than I thought. The reality of this slaps me into awareness. Ed has game because he *expects* to.

"*You* use Tinder?" I ask.

Reaching across the table, he pulls a discarded tomato from my salad and pops it into his mouth. "Sometimes."

"*And?*" I am suddenly dying to get the rundown on Ed's Tinder booty calls.

"No," Chris interjects. "No Tinders or Grindrs or any other hookup apps. We need *dates*, not sex."

I don't miss the way Reid's eyes flicker my way.

Ed pulls out his phone, swiping through his apps before turning the screen to face us. "We use it to find *matches*. We meet them, hook up, have fun—whatever, and *then* we ask if they want to go to the banquet."

"I love that the sex comes before the date," Reid says dryly.

Ed nods sagely. "Sex is just the bonus."

Chris's chin comes to an amused landing in his cupped hand. "Boy, in what universe is sex with you a bonus?"

"I have an IQ of one hundred and forty-eight," Ed says. "I'll let you connect the dots."

"Actually, being smart means you're probably having *less* sex," Reid tells him. "A 2007 study showed intelligence is negatively associated with sex frequency. In fact, only sixty-five percent of MIT graduates have even had sex."

"Pull up the plane, Reid," I say.

He laughs. "Okay, I guess what I'm saying is maybe Chris and Ed are right. Chris's sister is happy. I know a few people who've met their significant other online. Hell, I know lots of people who've met some of their best friends online. Maybe a dating site isn't the *worst* idea."

I slide my notebook back and point him to my neatly arranged columns. "I have a whole list of maybes. I don't need someone else to find me a date."

Reid gently takes it from me. "I think 'maybes' might be a tad optimistic."

"What if we don't all find matches?" Chris asks. "Then what?"

57

"Whoever doesn't have a date takes Millie," Ed suggests.

My voice tears out in a playful screech: "Why are we assuming I'm *also* not finding a date?"

Just over Reid's shoulder, I spot Avery Henderson waiting at the counter for her coffee and I stifle a whimper. Now a professor in the English department at UCSB, Avery was my little sister's college roommate at the University of Washington and, quite frankly, has always been in better touch with Elly than I have. Avery picked up on this about nine months ago, too, when she realized I hadn't heard that my sister was expecting twins, and since then, she loves to lord it over me when we run into each other at Saturday Pilates. But here, at lunch with my guys, I am unprepared for the ambush and try to duck into Reid's shoulder, hoping she won't see me.

Unfortunately, when the barista hands over her coffee, Avery catches my eye. I smell Reid's shirt to make it look like that's what I was doing all along.

"Can I help you with something?" Reid mumbles.

"I was—never mind, just be cool. *Be cool.*"

"Oh my God. Millie!" Avery shuffle-runs over to us. "I was going to call you this week to see how you're doing."

I smile up at her with as much easy calm as I can muster. "I'm doing well, how are you and Doug?"

She waves this away like I knew she might, indicating that she and Doug should be the least of my worries. Her voice drops. "I mean . . . with your dad."

I lift my chin, mentally sweating under the weight of Reid, Chris, and Ed staring at me with loud questions in their expressions. "I'm good. We're *all* great."

Avery falters. "But Elly mentioned——"

Abruptly, I stand and give her an awkward hug. "I appreciate you asking," I say. "I'll tell Elly you said hi!"

"Yes, please!" Thankfully, she looks at her watch. "Oh man. I'd love to catch up more, but I have a class at two. You'll call me with any news?"

"Of course!"

She shuffle-runs out with her coffee in hand and I take as much time as is reasonably possible to sit back down, lift my napkin, shake it out, and slide it back onto my lap.

"So." I look around the silent table. "Where were we? Tinder no, but another app . . . maybe?"

Reid shakes his head. "What was that about? Something with your dad?"

I shift a little under the scrutiny of his gaze. "It's nothing bad." It's terrible. "Just . . . parents getting older."

Just fathers getting diagnosed with Parkinson's disease.

I uncap my water and take a long drink, trying to push

the worry and sadness back into place, where they won't bubble up easily.

Ed pulls out a sandwich he's had tucked away . . . somewhere and takes a bite. "My mom had her gallbladder out last week and bitched at me for an hour last night on the phone because she can't have McDonald's anymore."

I give a sympathetic wince, internally relieved that I might escape this grilling. "Yikes."

But per usual, Reid is undeterred. "Wait, Mills. Is he sick?"

Here's where I'm stuck.

I don't share much about my family. I don't do it in part because I don't see them much, but also because my mom died when I was twelve and it sucked, and it's made me really hate talking about things that suck.

But I also don't lie, and I especially don't lie to my friends. Threading the needle here, I tell them simply, "He hasn't been feeling great, but he'll be okay." I hope my tone puts Reid's antennae back down.

It seems to—he pushes his salad around his plate the way he does when he's full but feels guilty about wasting food.

But nope, I'm wrong: "You know you can talk to us if something is going on," he says.

I see the little press there, the emphasis on *us* when

what he really means is *You can talk to me, your supposed best friend*.

Thankfully, Chris and Ed seem to have tuned us out, so I turn to Reid, lowering my voice. "If there was something to share, I'd share," I assure him. "Avery is just dramatic. She likes to make a big deal out of little things."

"But you make *no* deal about big things," he argues.

"Everything's fine." I give him a little chuck on the chin.

"You're really terrible about sharing personal shit. You know that, right?"

"So I've heard," I say. It isn't the first time he's complained about this, but I'm not sure how to do better. There just isn't much to say at this point—Dad has been diagnosed, is on medication, and we're handling it. Or, rather, my sister is handling it, and I'm trying to figure out the best way to be supportive from a distance. Talking about it with my friends when none of us have any control over it would just stress me out and make me feel more helpless.

Ed looks at his phone. "I have some cells I need to sort, so I should get back soon. Are we doing this? The dating app? Are we all in?"

Three sets of eyes swing in my direction, and I groan.

"Let's check a few out," Chris says. "We'll find the best one out there and put as little or as much info as you want."

"And you can quit anytime," Reid adds with a hopeful lean to his words.

I'm positive I'm not ready for this, but I am unwilling to be the wet blanket. "Fine," I say, "but the first dick pic I get is going to be each of your phone backgrounds for a week."

Ed shrugs. "I can live with that."

University of Santa Barbara Campus IM Box

Christopher Hill
So, turns out there are approximately one MILLION of these dating sites.

Reid Campbell
I found one for Western men who want to connect with women from Russia. In case that strikes anyone's fancy . . .

Millie Morris
Omg this one is called Bernie Singles and is designed for users who like Bernie Sanders. What even.

Stephen (Ed) D'Onofrio
There are people out there who want to date someone who looks like Bernie Sanders???
FE-TISH

Millie Morris
Wait for it . . .

Stephen (Ed) D'Onofrio
Oh wait. Ignore me. I get it.

Reid Campbell
Are you sure your IQ was 148 and not just 48?

Alex Ramirez
I'm still trying to figure out why I'm involved in this

Millie Morris
That'll teach you to miss a lunch again

Stephen (Ed) D'Onofrio
Dude, Gluten Free Singles, Mullet Passions, 420 Singles. Actually, let me bookmark that one for later.

Millie Morris
These names: Equestrian Singles. Marry Me
Already. Date My Pet.

Millie Morris
Ooh, Chris: Rooster Mate

Stephen (Ed) D'Onofrio
GOOD ONE, MILLS

Christopher Hill
. . .

Reid Campbell
Children. Can we stay on task?

Stephen (Ed) D'Onofrio
Are we sure we don't just want Tinder?
Users make 1 billion swipes a day for a reason.

Millie Morris
1 BILLION??

Stephen (Ed) D'Onofrio

If it ain't broke . . .

Reid Campbell

Hey what about this one? It's called IRL. In Real Life? That's clever. It's a premium site so we'd have to pay, but we can filter our browsing preferences, see when someone's viewed your profile and read or deleted messages, and men can read summary profiles and read/reply to contacts, but not make repeated contact or send photos until they're accepted.

Christopher Hill

Sounds efficient.

Reid Campbell

That's pretty great, right, Mills? No creepsters or unsolicited dick pics?

Alex Ramirez

Why would she ever solicit a dick pic when she has the three of us?

Millie Morris
I'm looking.

Millie Morris
I'll admit tit doesn't look completely terrible.

Millie Morris
GDI *it. Why do I always do that

Stephen (Ed) D'Onofrio
Because you have tiny hobbit hands?

Millie Morris
I'd call you a douchebag, Ed, but that would imply you could actually get near a vagina.

Stephen (Ed) D'Onofrio
Savage.

Reid Campbell
So do we all agree?

Millie Morris
Sigh. I guess so

Reid Campbell
Yessss. Everyone registers and we'll meet at
Millie's tonight to fill it all out. Go team

Alex Ramirez
HIGH FIVE

Christopher Hill
HIGH FIVE

Millie Morris
limp high five

Reid shows up around six, Thai food under one arm, a laptop under the other. The wine is noticeably absent. Thank God.

"Where is everyone else?" I take the bag from him and carry it into the kitchen.

"Ed had some samples fail and needed to redo them.

Alex might be over later, but I'll be honest, his interest in joining another dating site is flaccid at best."

"That's because Tinder clearly already works for him," I agree.

"Right. And Chris had a student emergency, which is sort of great because it means I could get that hot chicken he hates."

He follows me into the kitchen, pulling out plates and silverware while I open up the containers. He moves around my kitchen with the same comfort he had at Chris's, handing me a glass just as I've raised my arm to reach for it, and we're stepping around each other like we do it every day. The silence is easy. We fill our plates with drunken noodles, chicken, and curried vegetables. I fill each of us a glass of water from the tap, avoiding the cans of sparkling in the fridge entirely—too soon—and we carry it all into the dining room.

With food and laptops ready to go, we both create new IRL accounts, and after we confirm our email addresses, a pretty thorough questionnaire awaits. Most of the questions are easy enough: Name, age, job, the age range and location of match I'm seeking, a brief rundown of my appearance, and whether I have or want to have kids.

But the others are a little more in depth, and by the time I've gotten to favorite things, and the About Me and what I'm looking for out of life, I'm beginning to zone out. I've always been better at pulling details out of other people than I am at examining my own.

Next to me, Reid doesn't seem to be having any problems, and his fingers fly over the keyboard, the keys making an audible *click* each time one is depressed.

"It occurs to me," Reid says, finishing off the last of his noodles, "that this is an excellent way to get to know each other."

I look at him over the top of my glass. "You've known me for over two years."

"Yes, but you know how you can talk to someone almost every day and still not know some of the most mundane things about them?" He glances down at his screen. "Like number four: your favorite place. What *is* your favorite place? If I had to guess, I'd say Cajé, but only because you're there for coffee at least twice a day."

I hum. "I do like my coffee."

"I know you take it black, even though your sugary cocktail preference would give me at least three cavities. You'll read anything you can get your hands on but have a dog-eared collection of Agatha Christie in your end table, and a bunch of *Sherlock* fanfiction saved on your phone. You know almost every detail about my hometown and family, but I know next to nothing about where you grew up or whether you used to fight with your sister or when you had your first kiss." He tilts his head and watches me in a way that tiptoes the line that separates adoring and scrutinizing. "You're a mystery, Millie Morris."

"I grew up in Seattle—which you already knew. My dad and sister, Elly, still live there. Elly is married, she just had twins, and she used to call me Green Gables because my hair was more red back then."

"And your mom died when you were twelve."

I keep my eyes on the screen in front of me, trying to suppress the mild feeling of dread I get whenever this subject comes up. It isn't Reid's fault. It's just . . . I'm fine. And whenever someone wants to talk about it, they seem disappointed that I'm not more emotional. "Uterine cancer."

Reid reaches across the table and gives my hand a squeeze. "That must have been so hard. I'm trying to imagine little Millie back then." I can feel him waiting for me to elaborate; he's not pushy—he does it in the gentle, unobtrusive way he always has.

At Reid's place, there are framed photos of his parents and his sister, Rayme, and even pictures of himself at various ages. Of course, his parents also have pictures of Reid and Rayme from infancy to present day all over their house. Seeing Reid at every age makes it easier to feel like I really

know him—I know what he looked like as a chubby tod-
dler, as a toothless second-grader, as a goobery preteen, and
as a seventeen-year-old who still only felt his awkwardness
and none of his beauty.

So I understand his desire to see deeper into who I am
by knowing my past—I *do*—it's just that it isn't ever a
pleasant experience for me to revisit being a kid. The urge
to change the subject feels like a balloon filling, pressing
against the underside of my breastbone. Standing, I move
to the sink, turning on the tap and waiting for the water to
run cold so I can refill my glass.

"My dad was really great after Mom died, though. We
were lucky." I spill some water on the counter because I feel
so awkward and uncomfortable about what I'm saying. It
isn't false, per se—Dad wasn't abusive or mean or absent—
he just wasn't Mom. And that was never his fault, even if it
is his greatest failure.

"And favorite place," I say, feeling the tension ease in
my chest at the subject pivot. "Hmm. There has to be
somewhere better than Cajé, though they do have great
coffee."

"But, like, places to visit?"

"I love the Artist Paintpots in Yellowstone," I tell him,
continuing to uncoil.

"Are they like hot springs?"

"Sort of, but with mud." I sit back down in front of my laptop. "You walk on little boardwalks that are suspended a few inches above the ground, where you can see these gurgling little pools of mud and water. The color depends on how much sulfur is in the ground, and I think it changes depending on the time of year and the weather, but it's amazing. It feels almost prehistoric in a way. We used to go every summer when I was little."

On the outside Reid is totally cool—nodding and following along while I speak—but I know him well enough to understand that he's cataloging this scrap of information and slotting it into the gap in his Millie Bank where most of my pre–Santa Barbara history remains blank to him.

"What about yours?" I ask. "Your parents' vineyard?"

Reid leans back in his chair and scratches his chin—the questionnaire forgotten for now. And I love this about him—how his love for connecting with people makes him the easiest person to hang out with. I wish I were more like him in this way. "Maybe," he muses. "Or the drive to San Gregorio? It's hilly, and full of redwoods. Totally gorgeous—and even better if you can do it on a bike."

"Who did you do that with?"

"Friends in grad school, mostly. Chris and I did it once, and Dad met us on the beach with sandwiches and contraband beer."

"Is that when Chris and your father fell in love?" Chris and James Campbell have a famous bromance that makes Ed and Alex sick with jealousy.

Reid laughs. "Probably." But then he blinks, and grins at me like he sees through my deflection. "Next question," he says, lifting his chin to me. "First kiss."

"Hmm." I stand, gathering our plates and carrying them back to the kitchen. I feel Reid's attention on my back the entire way, and want to rub a hand down my neck or call him on his intense stare, but that might lead to him asking why it makes me uncomfortable, and what would I say? *It makes me uncomfortable to talk about myself because I've always been either tragic or boring?* Or maybe, *It makes me uncomfortable to talk about myself with you watching me, because I still remember the way you looked down at me in my bed and I shouldn't be thinking about you like that anymore?*

"I was fourteen," I tell him. "I had this weird worry about our noses hitting, so I just opened my mouth and spun my tongue around a few times. His name was Tim Chen and he looked a little confused when we pulled away but didn't complain." I grin over my shoulder. "I assure you I'm a much better kisser now."

"Oh, I know," Reid says with a hoarse laugh, and then seems to realize what he's said as soon as I do. "Shit, there it is." We go silent and he adds, "I made it weird."

73

My laugh is a sharp, awkward bark into the room.

"Okay, no, that noise made it weird," he says, rounding the counter and moving to stand next to me. "What was that?"

"A laugh?"

He sets his empty glass in the tray and when I look over I notice his lashes, and the feathery shadows they leave on his cheekbones. I've never really noticed things like eyelashes on Reid before, but now I'm remembering the way they looked with his eyes closed tight, head thrown back and the muscles of his throat straining.

I shut off the water. This tension is exactly the kind of thing the Morning After/Are We Okay? cupcake was meant to eradicate—it was supposed to provide sexual closure.

Get it together, Millie.

"We're always pretty weird," I say, using my metaphorical broom to gather all sexy thoughts and sweep them under the metaphorical rug. "The sex just made us weirder."

"Our *half-night stand*?" he asks, and his smile is an adorable concoction of self-deprecating and sweet.

I shake my head. Must resist the cute nerd. "Stop. You can't pull off internet lingo."

"Come on," he says, laughing, "you guys act like I'm my dad's age. I'm thirty-one! I *am* the internet."

Reid sidles up beside me, reaching back and gripping the edge of the counter. I swear my pulse rockets forward when I catch the scent of his soap. I'm not sure I've *ever* thought about sex this much—even when I've been in actual sexual relationships with other people.

"And I'm glad things aren't *actually* weird between us," he says.

I manage an easy smile of agreement.

Nope.

Not weird.

Not even a little.

He lifts a shoulder in a casual shrug. "It's different, but not weird. I didn't mean to bring it up again, though."

I reach out, booping his nose with my index finger. "Don't worry, I'm sure I'll say something way more awkward the next time I make us something with eggplant."

"You said eggplant, not baby carrot. I'm not going to complain."

"*Oooo-kaaaaay.*" I dry my hands and walk back into the dining room. "How about we finish these on our own and call it a night?"

Read: How about if you stop being cute and leave me to my vibrator?

Reid is obviously pleased with himself. "Too far? How about cucumber? No? White asparagus?"

I close his laptop and place it in his hands. "Good night, Reid. Thanks for feeding me. If you didn't bring dinner I would have been left to gnaw on a rind of old cheese."

"You are the frattiest woman I have ever met," he says.

"It's Manchego. I defy you to find a frat house with Manchego."

"You know I love you," he says, smile straightening as we near the door. My heart clenches a little at the sincerity in his voice. Reid is so good. I could never risk screwing this up over something as trivial as sex.

"Yeah," I say. "I do."

"Then you know there's nothing wrong with the two of us making jokes about what happened. Maybe it'll even bring us closer."

"Maybe." I tap his computer. "But if our goal is to meet other people, you need to finish this tonight and send it to me in the morning for approval."

He looks down at me with a goofy smile. Reid Campbell really is fucking cute. "Yes, ma'am."

I open the door and push him out. "And make sure the guys do it, too. I'm looking forward to judging you all."

"As you wish," he calls out. When he disappears out the front gate, I am free to disappear into my bedroom.

chapter four

 reid

Millie Morris
Dude. You guys.

Christopher Hill
What?

Reid Campbell
What?

Millie Morris
Your dating profiles suuuuuuck.

Alex Ramirez

There were approximately six hundred questions!

Millie Morris

I'm aware. I filled them all out, too. I'm talking specifically about your essay/intro portion.

Stephen (Ed) D'Onofrio

I spent like two hours on it!

Millie Morris

Really Ed? Two hours?

Stephen (Ed) D'Onofrio

Two . . . ish.

Millie Morris

I'm going to paste the best example in here, which was Chris's.

Christopher Hill

That's right, boys! Learn from the man.

Christopher Hill
Headed to a meeting so I'll catch up then.
Back in an hour.

[Christopher Hill has left the chat]

Millie Morris
He left before he realized that his also needs
to be rewritten.

Reid Campbell
Hey, mine wasn't terrible.

Millie Morris
Yes, Reid, it was T E R R I B L E. You essentially
had the abstract from your most recent paper
in there. Women don't need to know about
optic neuritis until, like, date four. Ok, here's
Chris's: *I am divorced, 29, six foot three, and a
professor of Chemistry at UC Santa Barbara.
I enjoy running, home-brewing, and Cal
football.*

Reid Campbell
He forgot to mention roosters.

Millie Morris

He forgot to mention, like, anything interesting about himself.

Stephen (Ed) D'Onofrio

Wait why is that intro bad? I don't get it

Reid Campbell

Ed, aren't you supposed to be helping Shaylene transfect her cells?

Stephen (Ed) D'Onofrio

Shit.

Alex Ramirez

lol the downside of IM'ing with your boss

Millie Morris

Chris took the less-is-more approach. Alex, you took the all-about-me approach. I can assure you that the execution is equally offensive for entirely different reasons. Ed, yours had like 700 typos.

MY FAVOURITE HALF-NIGHT STAND

Stephen (Ed) D'Onofrio
I hate to break it to you but so will 90% of the
profiles out there. Most people are doing all this
on their phones

Millie Morris
I am so old.

Stephen (Ed) D'Onofrio
Maybe you should write them for us.

Millie Morris
Uh, PARDON?

Stephen (Ed) D'Onofrio
You're good at this shit and you obviously care
more that they're well written.

Reid Campbell
Ed. Cells. NOW.

Millie Morris
I am not being the organized, well-spoken
woman to your male chaos.

[Stephen (Ed) D'Onofrio has left the chat]

Reid Campbell
I can't believe I'm saying this, but he has a point.

Millie Morris
UGGGGGGH

Reid Campbell
Please Mills? I'll buy you lunch.

Millie Morris
You owe me lunch anyway.

Reid Campbell
Two lunches then. You can wear your elastic waist pants tomorrow.

Millie Morris
No

Alex Ramirez
Please Millie

Millie Morris
No

Alex Ramirez
It's a good idea Mills

Millie Morris
No

I sense that victory is near—Millie is just about to break—but I'm called away from pressuring her when my phone rings. My smile fades at the picture of my mom lighting up the screen. In the photo, she's standing on the wide front porch of my childhood home, wearing her worn denim shirt and rubber boots up to the knees of her khaki pants. Her long gray hair is tied back with a ribbon. We've always had an easy relationship, my parents, Rayme, and I. But three months ago, at Christmas, Mom and I took a long walk through the family vineyards behind the house and—whether out of some strange mood or the impulsive decision that I was an adult and therefore ready to also be a confidant—she told me about nearly all of her marital woes. Not only did I have to hear her frustration that my parents barely have sex, and how Dad never tells her she's pretty anymore, but I had to talk her off the ledge of panic when she started speculating that Dad was having an affair with the woman down the street, a forty-year-old artist named Marla who creates sculptures out of only things found in her yard: twigs, leaves . . . rodents.

So these days, unfortunately, a call from my mother triggers mild nausea.

"Hey, Mom."

She doesn't seem to be in the mood for small talk. "What night are you arriving for the party?"

I take a few moments to figure out what she's referring to, vaguely staring at the still-scrolling chat screen on my computer. Finally: "What?"

"Your birthday," she says. "I assume we're celebrating it here?"

"I assumed I'd just have drinks out with friends, or whatever."

"It may be just a go-out-for-drinks birthday for you, but thirty-two years ago," my mother says, voice thin with emotion, "I pushed out the most—"

"Okay, Mom."

"—beautiful baby boy—"

"Yup. Okay."

"It took twenty-seven hours of hard labor," she reminds me. "You were nine pounds, fourteen ounces! Do you have any idea how big that is? Oh, how I *tore*."

I rub my temples. "Thank you for enduring that."

"So, if you think you're celebrating this day anywhere but with me?" She pauses, and when I don't reply she says simply, "Think again."

"Okay, let me check my calendar." I minimize the chat window, catching only a gif Millie sent of Kristen Bell pretending her middle finger is a tube of lipstick, and peek at my calendar. "April second is a Monday," I say.

"Come the weekend before. Bring Chris. And Millie."

Her words snag the last shred of hope I see to avoid this. "But if I bring Chris and Millie, I have to bring Alex and Ed." My mom *gently* tolerates Alex, who, among other things, somehow managed to turn half of her guest towels green, and Ed, whom my mom has accidentally seen naked on three separate occasions.

Mom sighs. "Fine. Just this time, no nude races in the vineyards."

Exhaling slowly, I give in. "I'll do what I can, but you know they're hard to control."

I think that's all I'll have to endure for today, until she says, "Hopefully your father has gotten his head out of his ass by then."

At a loss, I can manage only an "Oh?"

"I bought new lingerie, but he still—"

My internal organs tangle and the words burst out of me. "Oh, crap, I'm late to a meeting, Mom."

Untroubled by my abrupt departure, she kisses me through the phone. "Love you, Reidey."

It wasn't *entirely* a lie. I do have a meeting . . . . fifteen minutes after I end the call with my mom. Which affords me enough time to hit the coffee kiosk and swing by my lab to grab Ed.

He meets me in the hall, deliberately ignoring my pointed look as I catch him tossing his lab coat over the chair closest to the door.

"Shaylene all set?" I ask.

He nods. "They're fucking HEK cells, Reid, and Shaylene is super smart. She didn't really need help."

She may be "super smart," but Shaylene is a first-year graduate student in my lab, with minimal hands-on bench work experience under her belt. As someone who claims to aspire to be a career postdoc in my lab, Ed has taken on the role of mentoring the new graduate students. But he sometimes forgets that we aren't all born knowing molecular biology.

"Besides," he says, "I've got to work on this essay for Millie."

It takes me a beat to get his meaning. "The *dating profile*?"

He runs a harried hand through his wild curls. I catch a glimpse of sweat forming right at his hairline. "Yeah."

"Ed, I think you might be taking this a bit seriously."

He stops near the water fountain and bends, slurping. Coming up, he swipes at the water running down his chin. "Chris has me all stressed out, man. And look at you guys! What if it's just me who doesn't get a date? It's Chris—Mr. Deep-Voiced Chemist, and you—Mr. Lifeguard-Body Neuro-Geek, and Alex—the hot Latin lover who bangs women in that darkroom every fucking day. Then there's me. Seth Rogen but Somehow Even Pastier."

I start to reply that I think he's actually more Zach Galifianakis but do a double take as we pass the darkroom in question, noting the IN USE sign lit up on the outside. "Wait, what did you say about Alex?"

"Dude, everyone knows that's where he gets laid, like, all the fucking time." Ed waves me off and stops me outside the department conference room. "But what if I agreed to this, and you all end up with dates for the banquet, and those dates turn into more, and where does that leave me?"

I have a flash of realization that this really matters to

Ed, that deep down, this chubby science nerd really does want to meet someone and build something lasting. But since I don't think he'd appreciate the condescending vibe of this new awareness of mine, I clap a reassuring hand on his shoulder and go for glib: "You'll find someone. And if not, you've always got Cheetos and *Madden NFL 18*."

"Man, fuck you."

Thankfully, only one other person has arrived already to overhear this. Unfortunately, it's the neurobiology department chair, Scott Ilian. He looks up, but noting that it's just Ed, blinks back down to the journal article in front of him. "Gentlemen."

The faculty meetings are so tedious that even I, an admitted workaholic, often want to slowly bleed myself to death at some point during the back-and-forth. Each week, emeritus professors return to continue to feel valuable—but mostly to hear themselves speak, most often on new department policies they know nothing about and which will not impact their retired lives in the slightest. New faculty want to be seen and heard and will fervently advocate for technology the department has either already considered and rejected, or can't justify purchasing for use by only one or two labs. There will be a segment where a decision is being made, and everyone generally agrees but needs to make the point themselves, which results in ten people saying the same thing, just mildly rephrased each time.

Forty-five minutes in, and in the depths of the Rephrasing Phase, I take a deep, steadying breath and glance around the room.

Norm McMaster, our oldest faculty member, with ears the size of shoes, is asleep with his chin to his chest. Annika Stark, the department's only neuroendocrinologist, is staring daggers at her nemesis/fuck buddy, Isaac Helm, who is currently rewording Scott's point about the need for more stringent admissions criteria. Annika recently had to kick a student out of her lab for failing classes two terms in a row, and Isaac is clearly just poking the bear, hoping for a fight that may or may not end up as sex later.

Sitting in his normal spot toward the back of the room, Ed is surreptitiously playing *Clash of Clans* on his phone. My own screen lights up with a text from Alex, sent only to me and the other guys.

Dude, did you guys
see what Millie sent?

Chris replies a moment later.

These profiles are good.

I slide my phone onto the table, resisting the urge to check my email right now. Did Millie end up rewriting our dating profiles after all? And if she did mine . . . is that weird? What would she say? *My name is Reid Campbell, I'm 31, six foot two, and when I'm not being a workaholic idiot, I enjoy running, manning the barbecue, and having astonishing sex with my best friend?*

When I return to my office, I see that, in fact, it's far, far better than that.

From: Morris, Millie <Morris.Millie@ucsb.edu>
To: Campbell, Reid <Campbell.Reid@neuro.ucsb.edu>
Subject: FINE.

I wrote this because yours came into my head, and then I realized I had to write all of them because I am an enabler and way too nice to all four of you. If you don't like it, don't tell me. I just wasted like an hour on these.

-Mills

I was raised on a vineyard and live near the ocean, yet I know neither how to make wine nor surf. But I do love to be outdoors: hiking, sailing, even hanging on the beach with friends. My travel bucket list is a mile long. I have weekends where I'm kicking back at home, catching up on Netflix, and weekends where I take off on a road trip with friends to find the newest, greatest brewpub. I've run a few marathons, but can never resist cookies, or barbecue. I'm probably considered old-fashioned when it comes to dating—I think a first date is dinner, not just drinks—but I was raised by a woman who thinks a man needs to take his time and earn respect, and I agree. I absolutely love what I do for work, but am looking for someone to help me find adventure elsewhere, too. If you think we might be a good fit, I'd love to hear from you.

I reread it once, and then again. It's simple but . . . better than anything I'd come up with on my own.

I'm reminded of the day I showed up at Millie's last summer, in the impulsive mood to tear down the highway with the windows down and music turned up loud. We drove toward San Luis Obispo, and found a tiny new brewery there, had a lunch of messy burgers and tangy IPAs, and then drove home, quieter on the way back, with full bellies and the sound of flapping air and Tom Petty in the car. It was the perfect day with the perfect person.

And I remember when all five of us tried to surf, and only Chris managed to get up on the board while the rest of us gave up and watched from the warm sand of the shore. Millie was beside me, wearing a blue two-piece. She didn't bother to spread out her towel; her stomach and legs were dusted with coarse sand, her eyes closed and face tilted up to the sky. We were new friends; she'd only been out of the relationship with Dustin for a matter of weeks at that point, and it was the first time we'd really talked about it—after a decent amount of prodding on my end: about how distracted Dustin was, about how weird it felt to be single, about how relieved she was to no longer be living with someone with such a hot temper.

I see our moments in every line of this profile, except one: I don't know how she knows that I can't imagine going on a date with only drinks, that a first date over coffee seems odd to me. I wonder whether she sees deeper, too, to a place even I can't really access, and which understands better than my conscious mind does the ache I feel at the thought of Millie also writing a profile for *herself*, for others out there to read.

I'm unprepared for the way this hits me. The train of thought gives me a lurching nausea that resembles what I felt earlier, talking to Mom—the sense of something being *all wrong*. I press the heels of my hands to my eyes, and then open the IM thread with the guys.

Reid Campbell
Ok Millie's attempt at my profile is pretty good.

Christopher Hill
Let's see it.

Reid Campbell
You, too. Here's mine . . .

I paste it in, and then read theirs as they pop up on the screen.

Christopher Hill
My friends would call me the calmest member of our group, and although I think it's true, I sometimes feel like I have so much strident curiosity burning inside me that I'm not sure I'll ever be able to retire. I have a silver Labrador named Maisie, and she is the current love of my life, but there's absolutely room in there for more. Having married—and later divorced— my high school sweetheart, I learned not that relationships are treacherous, but that finding the right one isn't easy, and we are all constantly growing with the world around us. I am a devoted fan of Cal football, roosters in any form, road biking, and will drive a hundred miles to find the best doughnut.

Christopher Hill
That rooster line is going, but otherwise—it's pretty good.

Alex Ramirez
I love her so hard for slipping that in. Here's mine: *I see so many people around here emphasizing how laid-back they are, and I'll be honest: that's not me at all—I love to get out there and make some noise. I grew up racing dirt bikes in Huntington Beach, and now spend as much free time as I can mountain biking in the hills around Santa Barbara. I love to cook, I love to eat, and I love to dance my face off at weddings. But don't worry—I don't need to find someone who loves all the things I do, I want to find someone who knows who she is, is happy with who I am, and is ready to get out there and have some fun.*

Stephen (Ed) D'Onofrio
And by fun, you mean sex.

Alex Ramirez
100%

Reid Campbell
Ed, where's yours?

Stephen (Ed) D'Onofrio
I live in one of the most active places in California, but I admit to being a bit of a homebody. Don't get me wrong—I love being outdoors, but I prefer the quiet version: the beach at night, the shaggy coastline, the hills at dusk. Some people are happiest out and about— me, I'm happiest when I'm in the lab or with my circle of friends, enjoying a good meal, and cracking jokes. I may never be the first across the finish line, but I will be laughing the entire trip no matter what. Honestly, I'm just looking for someone who wants to be there, laughing right next to me.

Reid Campbell
Wow. These are good.

Christopher Hill
Has anyone seen Millie's?

Stephen (Ed) D'Onofrio
No.

Christopher Hill
I mean, if we're loading these now, we'll see hers soon right?

Stephen (Ed) D'Onofrio
Not necessarily because even if she posts it online, men can't see women's full profiles unless they're granted access to them. So, you'd have to like her photo and basic profile and hope that she gives you access.

Reid Campbell
But wouldn't she? With us?

Christopher Hill
I mean we're not planning to date Mills, so maybe not.

Alex Ramirez
Why not just ask her to send it to you dumbass

Reid Campbell
Ok, I will. Let me add her.

[Millie Morris has joined the chat]

MY FAVOURITE HALF-NIGHT STAND

Millie Morris
What up losers

Reid Campbell
These profiles are awesome

Millie Morris
I know! I'm really good at this.

Alex Ramirez
Let's see yours

Millie Morris
Alex, please. At least buy me dinner first.

Alex Ramirez
Oh, girl, I would buy you dinner AND dessert
if you catch my drift

Millie Morris
Well that escalated quickly.

Reid Campbell
In the darkroom, right Alex?

Alex Ramirez
What?

Millie Morris
What?

Reid Campbell
Never mind. Mills—show us your profile.

Millie Morris
Okay hang on. Then I've got to jet to class . . .

Millie Morris
Here tit is. Enjoy. *"It is better to light a candle than curse the darkness." ~Eleanor Roosevelt. I've always been drawn to the eccentric, the eerie, the unbelievable. I'm a lover of books and beaches, movies and mayhem. If you want to know more, just ask!*

[Millie Morris has left the chat]

Christopher Hill

. . . An Eleanor Roosevelt quote? Is Millie a lesbian?

Reid Campbell

Not that I know of, but now I'm questioning everything.

Alex Ramirez

Huh. I feel like that last sentence could take Millie's inbox to a lot of interesting places.

Reid Campbell

So I'm not the only one who was underwhelmed by this?

Christopher Hill

Are any of us surprised that it says nothing about her?

Stephen (Ed) D'Onofrio

Maybe she's anticipating guys being sort of gross so she's sharing less?

Christopher Hill
Maybe.

Stephen (Ed) D'Onofrio
Someone should tell her that sucked. NOT IT

Christopher Hill
Not it

Alex Ramirez
NOT IT

Reid Campbell
W O W.

Stephen (Ed) D'Onofrio
What? She likes you the most

Reid Campbell
Who doesn't?

Reid Campbell
So are we doing this? I have to get back to work.

Stephen (Ed) D'Onofrio

Mine is ready to go. I'm using that pic Chris took of me last summer.

Christopher Hill

The one where you're dressed as Grimace?
I think that's a bad choice.

Stephen (Ed) D'Onofrio

No, the one of me on your back deck, you dick.

Christopher Hill

Marginally better.

Alex Ramirez

Clicking submit in 3 . . . 2 . . . 1 . . .

Reid Campbell

Here we go.

Stephen (Ed) D'Onofrio

Oh, and "tits." Everyone notice she typed tits again?

Alex Ramirez
Classic Millie.

Reid Campbell
Focus.

chapter five

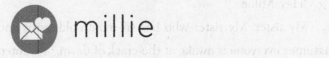 millie

My phone is ringing before the sun is even up.

   Well, *ringing* isn't quite right; it's buzzing incessantly from somewhere beneath my back. I try to roll away before realizing I'm tangled in the sheets and extracting myself feels like a lot of work—my arms are asleep, my head is foggy, and I'm not ready to leave this Chris Hemsworth dream.

Dream Me asked him to stay after class and he'd just stepped inside my office and closed the door. Normally I'd be horrified by that kind of student-teacher thing, but since Dream Me is dressed as Hot Teacher, and Dream Chris

Hemsworth is dressed as Thor (short-hair *Thor: Ragnarok*, to be exact), I'm willing to overlook it.

I pity the person who has the balls to tear me away from this escape from reality at—I squint at the screen—*five thirty*, because I'm going to kill them.

With fumbling hands I manage to answer, eyes still closed as I croak out a groggy "Hello?"

"Hey, Millie."

My sister. My sister who has six-month-old twins and assumes everyone is awake at the crack of dawn. "I wanted to get you before you left for class."

With a little work, I manage to roll to my side. It's not much of an improvement. "I don't have class until nine, Elly." I reach up and rub my eyes. "It's not even six yet."

"Oh, whoops," she singsongs. In the background I can hear water running and the sound of what I assume are dishes clanking in the sink. Elly is always on the move, always doing at least two things at a time, which is why I know she didn't call just to catch up. That's not really our thing, anyway. "Sorry about that. I was checking to see if you'd looked at your schedule yet, or thought more about what I said."

Guilt flares to life in my stomach.

Despite what I told Reid, Dad's Parkinson's disease has its claws dug in deep. Some days, he can barely get moving in the morning. His neurologist has mentioned he might need surgery to stimulate certain areas of his brain. With her two babies and a full life in Seattle, Elly needs help. She wants her single sister to do what she knows I can do: take the summer off and move home when Dad has the surgery, to give her a little break.

The problem is, moving home gives me this humid, panicky feeling in my chest, like I can't breathe. I don't want to go home.

Older than Elly by six years, I was always just a bit out of playmate range. I was Mom's little wacky duck—on my good days, I was silly and playful; on my difficult days I was obstinate. Elly, on the other hand, was quiet and studious—the dependable one. I wanted to host an *Unsolved Mysteries* reboot when I grew up; Elly wanted to be a nurse.

I was twelve when Mom died, Elly was only six, and suddenly I was the second-oldest in the house. Six years between us meant I was the babysitter, the cook, the maid, the big sister, the one Dad needed to step up. If I'd had Elly's temperament, it would have been so much easier—I get that now.

But I was also frantic with pain. I remembered every detail about Mom, and her laugh and her smile and her tight hugs. Frankly, I didn't know how to move about my space, my day, my life without a mother. Elly was almost too young to have such clarity, and it felt completely unfair that I should be expected to take care of her when I needed so much caretaking of my own. I could barely sort out my feelings, let alone help another child with hers.

Elly would ask questions about Mom—what happened, when was she coming back, did it hurt—and Dad would change the subject, so I'd try to answer as well as I could. I'd tell her that Mom got sick, that she wasn't coming back but that I was here. I'd tell her that it didn't hurt for long, and Mom loved us very much. Maybe Dad thought he was protecting us from the hard truth that Mom's death was fast and painful, or maybe it was just too difficult for him to face it himself. Either way, there was no oxygen in the house without Mom there, and over the next few years Elly stopped asking questions, and we all got really, really quiet. It felt like Dad was just waiting for us to be old enough to leave.

I can't explain it—that feeling of being so untethered to anyone. I used to dream that I was in the middle of an ocean and could see for miles in every direction, but there was no one else around me.

When I turned eighteen, I practically sprinted for the door.

Elly stayed in Seattle for school and got married, turning her loss into what she needed: an anchor and a family.

Was it different for her with Dad because he was her primary parent for most of her life? Maybe. But now, after doing everything for the past twelve years, Elly, my patient, gentle sister, is losing her patience with me.

"I'm not saying you should move home permanently," she says. "But you should at least come home *more*. Stay longer than for just a weekend. I think the summer could be really good—for all of us."

"I have to turn my manuscript in by the end of the summer," I tell her, "and need the time to make a dent in it." It's true, but it's also a very convenient excuse. Judging by her silence on the other end of the line, we both know it. "Let me see how much I can get done before then and figure out if it'll work."

"Thanks, Millie."

I can tell my sister wants to be happy for me, but disappointment hovers in her voice.

"I'll update you as soon as I know something." I roll to my back again and look up at the ceiling, at the way the blue-gray light from the window creeps along the walls. The muted color matches my mood. "How is he?"

"He's . . ." She shuts off the water and the silence grows while she formulates an answer. If I'm this anxious waiting to hear, what must it be like to live with it, day in and day out? "He's not great," she says. "Slower now, and less independent. His balance is terrible, so we're thinking of looking for a new house. Something without stairs."

Jared and Elly bought their house right after they were married. Things must be getting bad if they're considering selling it.

"I can help with that, too," I tell her, swallowing around the lump in my throat. "I'll have part of my advance by then, and it's all yours if you need it."

Two Cocoa Krispies doughnuts improve my outlook dramatically by the time I get to school, but the call with Elly sticks like a cloudy film on a window. I know I did my best as a kid, but I can't stop feeling like a selfish asshole now. Elly needs me. Dad needs me. But I would honestly rather walk across a beach of broken glass than spend the summer in my hometown.

Instinct carries me here: with a coffee in each hand, I use my foot to push open the door to Reid's office. He's finishing up a call, phone wedged between chin and shoulder, pen scribbling away at something on his desk.

The polite thing would be to wait outside or tell him to find me later, but Reid and I have never been particularly good at boundaries—obviously—and so I set his cup down in front of him and take a seat while he wraps things up. I'm not really in the mood to talk, but locking myself in my office isn't going to do anything but make me feel worse.

Given the fastidiousness of Reid's brain, his desk is a surprising mess. There's the usual detritus of files and assignments and books, but Reid is an obsessive note taker so there are Post-its and scraps of paper everywhere, notes tacked to the computer monitor, the window, the walls. A corkboard hangs just within arm's reach and it's so weighed down with bulletins and reports and random scribbles, I'm not even sure how it's still hanging.

The one on the side of his computer is a drawing of a brain—not just a doodle, but an actual anatomically correct illustration—with arrows and words like *limbic* and *superior colliculus*. This is exactly why we no longer play *Draw Something*—Reid goes way too deep. The Post-it just beside the drawing has the name *Lillie* and a phone number written in bubbly, heart-embellished script.

Do I remember him mentioning a Lillie?

"Sorry about that. You okay?"

I startle, sloshing my coffee on his desk. I didn't even hear him hang up the phone. "Shit. What?"

"You're . . . pouting." He sounds amazed.

My eyes flick to the tacked-up phone number, and

back to where I'm using my only napkin to sop up some of the mess. "Yeah. Totally. Just zoning out."

Reid eyes me with a curious grin before handing me a few tissues to help. He picks up his own cup. "Thanks for this. I meant to grab some before I started this morning but got called away."

"Of course."

He takes a sip, sucking in a breath when he burns himself.

"PS, it's hot," I say, and drop the tissues into the trash can next to his feet. "Long morning?"

"You could say that. I came in to get some papers graded and was cornered by a couple students begging for extensions. *But*, I'm glad you came." He looks at me again and then does a double take. "You sure you're okay?"

"Yes, Reid."

"You look . . . haggard."

"Wow. Seduce me, why don't you."

"Seriously, what's up with you?"

"Nothing, I swear."

He stares at me with flat skepticism for one, two, three seconds, before shaking his head to clear it. "Okay, whatever. I wanted to show you something." Reaching for his phone, he swipes the screen before turning it to face me.

I lean in. "Good God, Reid. You have ninety-eight updates to install? Amazon, OpenTable, Facebook . . . What is wrong with you?"

"Focus, Millie." He taps on a bright blue icon with a red notification bubble. "The IRL app. I woke up to eighteen notifications."

"Notifications for . . . ?"

He clearly thinks I'm going to figure it out because he pauses for a few lingering seconds before giving up. "Didn't you go through the app intro when you downloaded it?"

I spread my hands like he should know the answer to this. "Obviously not?"

Laughing, he says, "Okay, this means eighteen women shared their profile with me."

"Ohhhh." I fumble for my bag on the back of the chair and pull out my own phone. I hadn't even thought to look. "I filled everything out on the laptop." I turn the screen to him. "Oh, hey look, I didn't even download the app yet."

"According to Ed, you'll want to use your phone for everything else." He lifts his chin. "Search for it in the App Store."

"Whoa, whoa, slow down with this technical speak." My eyes are wide in faux-confusion. "Write that down for me, mansplainer."

"Jesus Christ, Millie."

"I do know how an iPhone works, Reid."

He leans back with a patient sigh and continues scrolling through his own messages. "One of them speaks French and is a scuba instructor," he says proudly, eyes widening as he zooms in on a photo.

Once the app has downloaded, I enter in the username and password I'd set up on my computer. "How does this work, exactly?" I ask. "There's no swipe right or whatever, is there? That sounds terrible."

"You know you were in the room when we talked about this."

I smile at him over the top of my coffee. "I probably wasn't listening. I do that sometimes when you speak."

"As I mentioned *before*, men can only see your basic info and summary, along with a thumbnail of your photo. They can't see the entire profile until you approve them. In which case you'll probably have some requests wanting to see more."

"But not eighteen . . ."

Reid ignores me and sure enough, an alert pops up signaling that I have unread messages. I'm surprised by the rush the little red bubble brings. "I have twelve requests pending."

Reid's brows climb up his forehead, impressed. "Not bad, Mills. Ed had four."

"You're comparing me to Ed now? Wait, what profile

pic did he use? Did he use the one of him in the bathrobe doing the Captain Morgan pose?"

Ed, who wanted to wear an *Animal House* toga for his faculty photo.

"Yes."

"And you're surprised I have more than him? Reid. Come on."

"I'm saying that with such limited information and only a thumbnail to see your pretty face, twelve isn't bad."

"What profile picture did *you* use?" I ask. "Were you wearing the FBI shirt?" I let out a short bursting cackle. I will never get over Reid having to borrow a shirt from Alex's trunk when his own disappeared from the beach, and all Alex had was one that said *FBI: Female Body Inspector*. We went right out for drinks that night, and, oh boy, Reid got some shit.

"Sadly, Ed spilled red wine on that one. I won't be able to wear it again."

"Well, that solves the problem of future commentary."

He leans forward, redirecting my attention to my screen. "The little percentage in the blue bubble at the top of the request shows—"

"Our compatibility, I know, I know. Seriously, how do you think I feed and bathe myself every day?"

"Just read through them and see who you want to share with."

With an odd mixture of dread and anticipation, I open the first message, wincing a little at the photo. I don't want to seem completely superficial, so I don't comment on the backward baseball cap or puka shell necklace, and start to read.

"'I might be the man your looking for. I've been a plumber for fifteen years and know a thing or two about cleaning pipes ;) I like to spend my weekends on the lake or at the barbecue, and am looking for a special lady to stand at my side. If you think your up to the challenge, drop me a line. I just might bite.'"

My eye roll must be audible because Reid looks up with a questioning glance.

"There's just so much here," I say. "Where do I even begin? 'Cleaning pipes'?"

"Virility is a sign of health."

"He wants someone to stand by him at the barbecue."

"I think that's kind of sweet—Don't look at me like that."

"Reid, he misspelled 'you're.'"

"You're always typing 'tit' instead of 'it.' It could have been an accident."

"Twice?"

"Okay," he says. "Let's look at the next one."

"'My name is Greg and I'm thirty-two. I'm a structural engineer because I live to figure things out. They say travel is good for the soul, and I firmly believe that. I studied abroad during college, and consider myself lucky enough to have seen the Eiffel Tower, Big Ben, the Colosseum, the Scottish Highlands, and the Parthenon all before I graduated. If you think you could be my next adventure, I'd love to hear from you.'"

This sounds too good to be true and so I pull up his photo. He's . . . wow, not terrible. Blond hair, tan, and leaning against a surfboard in the sand. I turn the phone to face Reid.

He leans in for a closer look. "Hmmm. He might—" He stops; his eyes narrow. "Is that a ring?"

"What?" I turn the phone back and zoom in. There's definitely something there. "Could it be a shadow?"

"I mean . . . it's gold."

I look again and he's right; there's a gold band on his ring finger.

"Maybe it's an old picture?" Reid says. "Does he say he's divorced?"

It takes a second to get back to his profile. Under relationship status, it says *single*. Under previously married it says *never*.

"Please tell me a person couldn't possibly be that stupid," I say. "Or gross. Why don't I expect people to be liars more often? I study criminology, for Christ's sake."

Disappointed, Reid holds out his hand. "Let me see your phone."

I slide it across the desk and let the full skepticism about this endeavor take root again. "I'm not one to say I told you so, but . . ."

He opens the next message. "Okay, this guy . . ." He stops, a scowl shaping his face. "Never mind."

"What?"

"He just . . . He had the word 'tits' in his bio, and I don't think it was your charming typo."

I wrinkle my nose.

"No, no. Let's keep going, they can't all be that bad." He opens one, and then another, and with each message his smile wilts further.

"I think this guy might be Dustin."

I groan. "Please tell me you're kidding."

"I'm kidding?" he says, and looks up at me.

He is clearly not kidding.

"That's depressing," I tell him. "How much faith can I put in an app that matches me with my ex? Good lord."

"I mean, maybe that means it's good?" Reid tries to be optimistic. "At one point you and Dustin—oh. God. This next guy has his penis as his profile picture. His actual penis. I mean, I hope it's his."

"Reid, you are too pure for this world." I take back my phone and go through the rest. One message simply says *Hey*. One assures me his dick is huge; one wants a full-body photo before he'll request access to my profile; and two want to know how much I weigh.

"This is it?" I wave my phone. "You got a French-speaking scuba diver and I got this? *These* are the kind of guys I matched with?"

There's a quick knock at the door before Ed is pushing it open.

"Here's the most recent FACS data," he says, and drops a few pages with scatterplots on Reid's desk. There are three strips of duct tape holding Ed's lab coat together, but I don't even bother to ask.

He considers the way I'm slumped in the chair, arms folded across my chest, and takes a bite of an apple he's pulled out of his lab coat pocket. I'm not even a scientist and I know that's disgusting.

"Hey there, sunshine."

I let out a growl.

He nods in Reid's direction. "Loverboy showing you his matches?"

I swing my eyes over to Reid. "He did."

Another noisy bite of apple, and Ed pulls out the chair next to me. "What about you?" He points to my phone.

"She has twelve," Reid answers for me.

Ed's eyes brighten. "Oh yeah? Any good?"

I open my mouth and then close it again. There's no great way to answer that.

"She got a bunch of weirdos," Reid explains for me.

Ed takes my phone and begins to scroll. "Maybe if you didn't mention you were into serial killers."

I should probably be concerned that he enters my passcode without prompting, but defending myself takes priority here. "First of all, I didn't mention anything about my job. Second of all, I'm not *into* serial killers."

"Yeah, but you said you're drawn to the eccentric, the eerie, and mayhem. Mayhem? Really? You used an Eleanor Roosevelt quote, Mills. Of course you got weirdos."

"*What*, I'm so boring that I need to lie?"

"You wrote a three-hundred-page dissertation on the 'Jolly Jane' Toppan murders and can't write a single interesting paragraph about yourself. Be more creative. You're not boring, your profile is. A *friend* should have told you," he says, pointedly in Reid's direction.

I glance between them before deciding I really don't care. "Thanks for the clarification."

Reid stands and walks around the desk, leaning back against the edge of it. He's wearing the pants I like, flat front and tapered. I've actually seen students check out his ass in these pants as he walks down the hall. Going on record that the front isn't too bad, either . . .

I probably shouldn't be thinking about this right now.

"You know I love you," he starts gently. I lift a single brow. "Don't take this the wrong way, but Ed has a point. Your profile said nothing about you."

"It said I like the beach."

Ed helps himself to my coffee. "Who doesn't like the beach?"

With a gentle finger under my chin, Reid turns my attention toward him. "Be honest, Mills. Do *you* think your profile was interesting? You wrote us these great, unique bios that said a *lot* with just a handful of words. I mean, you made Ed seem charming and interesting. *You* did that!"

Ed nods vigorously, if mockingly.

"But yours was just, I don't know . . . *meh*."

Back in my own office, I stare at the new profile on the screen.

Some people never go crazy.
What truly horrible lives they must lead.
~ Charles Bukowski.

You know that friend who's always planning
something, and gets a little too enthusiastic? That
would probably be me. I love birthday parties because
there's cake, any excuse to wear a costume, and
movies that I can't guess the end to. I'm looking for
someone who lives to laugh, who wants the wild,
chaotic mess that comes with falling in love, and
someone who could sit on the cliffs at Hendry's Beach
and listen to the crashing surf until the sun has slipped
into the ocean.

Not bad.

Call me a quitter, but rather than wade through the penis-dense marsh that is my old profile, I decide to start a new one.

I even give myself a new name: Catherine M. I would worry that I'm engaging in some sort of catfishing, but one, aside from the name—which is actually my middle name, and last initial—there are no lies in my bio; two, my photo is from the side and a little artsier than your typical profile pic, but it's definitely me; and three, I don't have any nefarious intentions. To double down on this, I make a solemn promise to the universe that if any rich, elderly gentlemen should happen to fall in love with me, I just won't respond. Easy.

It's a study of human behavior, I think, scrolling through the rest of my information. Market research, but for dating—and no different than restaurants using red or yellow color schemes to create the perfect setting that would entice a person to stop and eat. In this case I've put out a few stimuli meant to elicit a response. I'm still me— just *secret* me. I give my state rather than my city. I say late twenties rather than twenty-nine. I say *academics* rather than *criminology*. I may not be precise in this new profile, but I'm authentic.

This is good. This feels safe.

Without overthinking, I click SUBMIT and head for class.

My Research Methods in Criminology course meets at the end of the day, and by four o'clock the students are a squirrely bunch. It can be a fascinating course, focusing on crime mapping and analysis, but it can also be tedious. Aside from a looming research project, never-ending lectures, and countless stats and procedures to memorize, the students themselves can be their own worst enemy.

Like most faculty members these days, I'm in constant

competition with cell phones and laptops and all forms of social media for the attention of my class. Reid has explained that the ability to stay focused depends entirely on two neural processes: directing our attention to goal-related activities, and blocking out irrelevant distractions. Which I think in the simplest of terms means *The goal is to graduate, so turn off your damn Instagram*. It should be easy enough—but apparently there are days where even I am not immune.

With just five minutes left of my last class of the day, I hear a buzzing from inside the lectern. Everyone is mostly working, quietly cleaning up lecture notes and jotting down project time lines from the PowerPoint still on the screen behind me. When the buzzing comes a second time, I pause.

I've been mildly on edge since loading my new profile a few hours ago, ignoring most of the group chat messages and avoiding the coffee kiosk and the guys altogether. I realize they were right and my Millie profile really did suck. But what if it isn't just the profile—it's actually *me*—and even with a more genuine version of myself out there, I still don't get any good matches? Am I even going to tell them about Catherine—whom I've nicknamed Cat, and whom I absolutely plan to make much more emotionally healthy than Millie, and who easily discusses things like feelings and fears and long-term goals?

Surely I can do that much, even if it's anonymous.

Thankfully no one lingers after class and I'm able to jog-walk back to my office and solitude. It takes a moment for the app to load, but when it does, a red bubble with a number six appears on the screen. Six matches, and a couple of the guys have already requested access to see my profile. Just like that, a mixture of adrenaline and dread trickles into my bloodstream. I check the first one: an aspiring writer from San Francisco.

Pass. Writers are crazy.

The next is a pediatrician who recently moved to Santa Barbara. His bio is funny, his photo is great, and there's no wedding ring or wife accidentally snapped in the background. I press yes and share my profile with him.

But I never make it to the rest.

I'm not prepared for the next photo that fills the screen. *You have a new match. Would you like to show Reid C. your profile?*

It takes a second for this to sink in. I matched with Reid? Well, *Catherine* matched with Reid, but since her profile is more genuinely *me* than Millie's was . . .

I debate just ignoring the notification, but come on,

this is actually pretty funny. According to the match notification, Reid and I are 98 *percent* compatible. He will love this.

Decision made, I click ALLOW and type up a short message before I can change my mind. I guess the guys will find out about Catherine after all. Reid gets me like nobody else. A Monopoly joke? I mean, come on. It's so obvious.

chapter six

 reid

I wake to the standard barrage of late-night texts from Ed and Alex—this time, it's a debate about the best underrated comic run in the past couple decades. Ed is fiercely arguing in favor of *Hawkeye*, *Squirrel Girl*, and *Fence*. Alex is just as vehement that Thompson's *Hawkeye* is just as good as the Fraction run, and that Ed is being a sexist pig. Millie tells them both to shut the fuck up around one in the morning, and then the thread devolves into a string of increasingly filthy gifs ending with a video of a man dressed as a horse having sex with a woman. My friends, everyone.

Without studying any of the clips too carefully, I reply:

I'm so glad I passed out at eleven last night.

It's early—my alarm hasn't even gone off yet—and outside the sky is a hazy purple-blue. I'm on the very edge of falling back to sleep when I remember that I matched with another woman on IRL yesterday, and curiosity over whether I've got any new messages is a weird, anticipatory thrill that feels like a streak of caffeine into my bloodstream.

In fact, I have two new contacts. Two women, Catherine M., and Daisy D., have offered me access to their profiles.

There's a weird, low clench in my stomach at the sight of Daisy's photo: she's twenty-three, blond, and absolutely stunning. I can tell her profile photo was taken on the craggy rocks at the edge of Ledbetter Beach. Her extended profile tells me that she's a graduate student in education, originally from Texas. The algorithm connects us as an 82 percent match, but I'm willing to put the remaining 18 percent of incompatibility aside for the sake of what I'm seeing in her profile photo.

Her message is simple: Hi Reid! Your profile seems really nice. This is my first time doing this, so I'm not sure how it works, but I'd love to talk to you some more.

Catherine is a professor as well—and although she

doesn't specify which school, I don't know anyone with that name in the UCSB bio departments, so this doesn't set off any alarm bells.

Hi Reid, her message begins. Apparently, we're a 98% match (With odds like that we should take our wallets to Vegas or play Monopoly, I'm good with either).

This brief, easy introduction makes me laugh—and there's something so genuinely easygoing about it that feels immediately appealing. But it's hard to get an instinctive, physical response to her: her profile picture is only of her shoulder and neck; her head is turned away, allowing just a glimpse of her jaw. Since it's a black-and-white photo, I can't even tell what color her hair is.

Alex's voice rings in response: *Only ugly chicks go for the "artful" profile pics.*

I swear he's ruining us all one by one.

I'm in the lab all morning with Ed watching a demo of a new imaging system, but he's clearly been holding out on me: as soon as we get to lunch, he pulls out his phone and shows Millie the photo of a woman he matched with last night. I watch him for a lingering beat, aware again that he seems genuinely invested in all of this.

Based on Mill's reaction, the woman is either beautiful or hideous—her surprise really could mean either.

Alex sits down on the other side of Millie and leans over to look. "*You* matched with *her*?"

Ed gives a long enough pause that anyone but Alex might rethink his choice of word emphasis. "Yes."

"And you posted a picture of *yourself*?" Alex is immediately pelted with Ed's balled-up napkin.

Millie hands the phone back to Ed. "She looks nice."

"'Nice'?" Alex unwraps his sandwich. "She looks like she'd go down and eat a motherfucking *salad*, if you know what I'm saying."

"What am I even walking up to here?" Chris sits down and carefully slides his Cobb salad onto the table in front of him.

"Alex is being a goblin," Millie explains. "By the way, you all should know that I received a message last night from a man I thought I'd matched nicely with." She grins. "He gave me explicit instructions on how to milk his balls."

"*Milk* his balls?" I ask for clarification.

Alex opens his mouth to answer, but before he can, Chris gives a quiet "Dude. No."

Moving on without hesitation, Alex says, "This dating app sucks. No one has given me access to their profiles yet."

"Because you come across like Animal from *The Muppets*," I tell him.

Millie protests, "Hey! I wrote that profile. And it's all true, to be fair."

"It *is* true," Alex says. "My greatness may not come across on-screen, but is impossible to ignore in person."

"And that ego," Chris says.

Alex grins up at him.

I poke at my pasta. "*I* matched last night."

"Oh really?" Millie drawls.

I look up at her sly grin. "You don't believe me."

At this, she laughs. "Oh, I believe you."

"There were two," I say and, oddly, her smarmy smile tilts down at the edges. "A woman named Daisy, and one named Catherine."

I pull out my phone and open the app, handing it over to Chris when Daisy's photo appears. He gives a low whistle. "Shit, man."

Alex takes the phone from him and reacts the same way.

"So Catherine is hot?" Millie asks, reaching for it after Ed takes a glance.

I shake my head. "I can't tell from her picture. That's Daisy, and holy shit, *she*—"

"What do you mean you can't tell from her picture?"

I take my phone back from Millie and look up at her. Her eyes are doing the weird intense, unblinking thing she does when she's trying to work out a mystery or eat a hotter pepper than Chris without tearing up.

"Catherine's picture is, like, of her neck or something," I say, waving it off. "I can't see her face."

Alex performs as predicted: "So, she's ugly."

"Alex, come *on*," Millie protests.

"Well, who knows," I say. "But for sure I'll reply to Daisy and—"

Millie cuts in. "Maybe for *Catherine* it's about what's behind the curtain rather than the curtain, you know?"

"If she was hot," Alex reasons, "she'd show her curtain."

Ed balls up his burrito wrapper and tosses it onto his tray. "Maybe she's pretty but, for her, finding someone compatible isn't all about looks?"

Millie sits up, pointing at him with a mixture of enthusiasm and aggression. "What Ed said. *That*. Why is it always about looks?"

"What do you care?" Alex asks. "*You're* hot."

"My point is that *Catherine* doesn't care," she argues. "And thank you, Alex, for being smart."

Chris speaks around a bite of salad. "I mean, let's be real. Reid is the Zac Efron boy next door. He isn't gonna go for someone ugly."

This makes me laugh. "If any one of us is a boy next door, it's you, Chris."

"Man, come on. You think America is talking about a black dude when they say that?" He swallows, and points at Millie with a fork. "To a large degree, looks are gonna matter. If you choose not to show a face, there's a reason, right?"

Millie scoffs. "Like being *private*? I have about ten requests for my cup size on here. I can understand why a woman wouldn't want to share her face right off the bat."

"I mean, that's not a bad point . . ." I look to Alex, hoping for once he keeps his mouth shut, and when it seems like he will, I turn back to Millie. "Will you help me reply to her, Mills?"

"To Catherine?" she asks.

"To Daisy," I say, then amend, "Well, both, I guess. Maybe I could copy and paste what I write to Daisy into Catherine's box, for now."

Millie stares at me for a long, flat second, and then stands. "Sure, Reid. Send along their messages and I'll help you."

We all go very still.

"Are you sure?" I point to her narrow eyes and stiff posture, something we've never seen on her, other than the time we were playing cornhole at Chris's and Millie—the reigning, undisputed champion of cornhole—was briefly losing to Alex. "You look like you're going to kill me via decapitation."

She laughs but it's a weird *ha-ha-ha* laugh. A movie villain laugh. "I'm not going to kill you." Millie slides her messenger bag across her chest, hooking a thumb beneath the strap.

"I don't feel reassured," I admit.

"I just think you're being shallow."

The unfamiliar disappointment in her voice is cutting, and beyond that . . . another type of unease starts to worm its way through me. Is there something going on here? With Millie . . . and the prospect of me dating?

"Why do you care who I reply to?" I ask as carefully as I can. I'm a little out of my depth here because *Is she angry?* And what does it mean that I'm not really sure what angry Millie looks like?

"It's just a female solidarity thing," she says. "Why are we always expected to share the picture of us with our boobs out on the beach, but dudes can share the candid one with their slobbery dog?"

"I want to remind you," Ed says, "that this same group has had strong opinions about what photos *I* share, too."

"You're tripping because I didn't want you to look like a McDonald's ad?" Chris asks him.

"I wasn't going to wear the fucking Grimace costume!" Ed yells, and about fourteen people around us turn to look.

When I turn back to answer Millie, to tell her she's right, that I need to give Catherine more of a chance, she's gone.

chapter seven

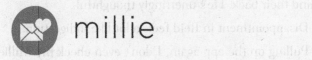 millie

I'm in a dramatic huff by the time I get back to my office. Seriously. *Copy and paste?* What the fuck, Reid?

Dropping into my chair, I reach for the bag of peanut butter M&M's I keep in my bottom drawer. No, it's not the greatest coping mechanism, but since I already finished the bottle of scotch I used to keep there, M&M's will have to do.

Shallow isn't a word I'd have used to describe Reid before today. Manipulative? Maybe. I mean, aren't we all a little? Even a tiny bit self-absorbed? Sure, I'm guilty of that one, too. But *shallow*? No. Which is why this feels like such a big thing, because more than angry about how quickly Reid prioritized his response to Daisy over Catherine, I feel disappointed.

It's not an emotion I'm used to where Reid is concerned. He's the one I called when I got a flat tire halfway to Monterey, the friend who will bring us each a smoothie the morning after a night of particularly heavy drinking, the person who refuses to speak badly about anyone, especially behind their back. He's unerringly thoughtful.

Disappointment in Reid feels a lot like indigestion.

Pulling up the app again, I don't even check my Millie profile, but stay logged into Catherine's. She has two new requests, one of which looks like a reasonably normal guy, and one I instantly delete.

Eric is a twenty-six-year-old makeup artist, and according to the app we're an 84 percent match. I'm not going to lie, the idea of dating someone who can do my makeup better than I can is pretty damn appealing, and so I click ALLOW to let him view the rest of my information.

Moving on, I open the profile page and click her—*my*—photo. It's a picture my sister took on my last trip home, and I picked it not only because you couldn't clearly make out my face, but because no one here has seen it before. I'd been watching the rain as it puddled outside the window, and I look thoughtful, almost serene. It's no Daisy on a beach with her smile and her boobs, but it isn't a *bad* photo. Certainly not one that warrants a copied and pasted reply.

The messages Reid received from Daisy and Catherine were both brief, and the differences in our matches were pretty big—98 percent versus 82 percent! I'm starting to think Reid is a fake scientist who doesn't care about numbers. Any preference he has for Daisy at this point is purely visual. What a dick!

Is it crazy that I'm suddenly determined to make Catherine the winner here? To teach them a lesson? Not just for my own vindication, but for like . . . *all of womankind*?

If I asked the guys, I'm sure they'd tell me my— *Catherine's*—first step should be to choose a new photo. Unfortunately, I can't show my face, and a close-up down the front of my shirt wouldn't be all that impressive, either, so I'll just have to make Catherine more interesting. This would be easier if I could be creative and tell a lot of stories, taking snippets I've heard from other people or gleaned from books, spinning them into details I could share with Reid. But since I'm being semishady as it is, I can't lie. Catherine's stories have to be my stories, which means I can't show him the easy, superficial stuff I've let him see before. I'll have to actually work for this and dig deep.

But first, Reid will need to reply.

He's already forwarded me the messages from Daisy

and Catherine. It only takes a few minutes to write something he can paste into each of their boxes—I am now literally writing letters to myself but *why the fuck not?*—and so I ping him in a separate window.

Millie Morris
I have your replies. Do you want them here or email?

Reid Campbell
You are a goddess. And here is good

Millie Morris
HUGE SIGH

Millie Morris
For Daisy → An 82% match? Not too bad!
You've read my profile, so you know I grew up in California. If I'm not mistaken, your profile photo was taken at Ledbetter Beach? I'm an Associate Professor at UCSB, just down the road from there. I've gone to a couple parties at the park, just off the beach, and even attempted a few surfing lessons there. It didn't go well. Let me just say that my pride, and my favorite board

shorts, are still floating around there somewhere.
I also see from your profile photo that you have
giant knockers, which must mean that your
fertility, and quality of life, are higher than those
around you.

Reid Campbell
I may leave that last sentence out . . .

Millie Morris
As you wish.

Reid Campbell
Mills, this is so great of you. THANK YOU.

Millie Morris
For Catherine → I assume a 98% match basically
only leaves our preferences for Coke vs Pepsi
(Coke FTW), our favorite of The Chrises (I'm
secure enough in my masculinity to admit that
bearded Chris Evans is a 10/10), and whether
Star Wars episodes I, II, and III can be skipped
entirely (the correct answer is always yes). To
see if we are in fact the same person: favorite
funny movie?

Dots appear in the chat window as Reid types, before disappearing again.

Millie Morris
Hello?

Reid Campbell
Sorry, I'm here. Daisy's seems a bit . . . idk, stiffer than Catherine's?

Millie Morris
Oh right, right. I know how you can fix that.

Reid Campbell
How?

Millie Morris
WRITE THEM YOURSELF

Reid Campbell
I'm sorry, Mills. Thank you. Who knew I was so charming?

Millie Morris
And humble!

Reid Campbell
Seriously, these are great. Do you want my login and you can just send?

Millie Morris
Am I going to be the one having sex with one of these women for you, too?

Reid Campbell
If you're into that, sure.

Millie Morris
I do not want your login. I also think you should write your own letters. This is weird, even for us.

Reid Campbell
Milllliiiiiieeeeeeeee. You're better at this than I am. This is clearly your thing.

Millie Morris
You'll get the hang of tit. Gotta run, class

[Millie Morris has left the chat]

It's almost nine by the time I finish up at the office and pull into my driveway. Just like every night, the neighbor's cat is waiting on my porch. I reach down and scratch behind her ears, wondering for the hundredth time if I should get a pet. I love living alone but can imagine it would be nice to have someone or something waiting when I walk in the door, too.

Alas, I'm never home. I'm never here, and—Elly's voice reminds me—I'm certainly never in Seattle.

I set down my things, order dinner, pour a giant glass of wine, and power up my laptop. I told her I'd firm up dates for a visit, and I'm going to do it before anything else drags my attention away.

How convenient, then, that there's an email from my new editor with a suggestion for deadlines, and some questions about my outline. I text Elly with a very loose window of dates for me to come visit, but I know one week—whether in June, July, or August, her choice—won't appease her.

The red bubble in the IRL tab drags my attention away

from my email inbox, and with a little grunt of irritation, I open it up, knowing exactly what it is.

A letter from myself, how exciting.

But my competitive fire reignites, and I hammer out my reply as fast as I should probably be writing the book I have due in four months.

From: Catherine M.
Sent: 7:39 pm, March 28

Reid,

I can't believe you went for The Chrises this early in our email relationship. It is both genius and brave. I was lucky enough to see Chris Evans at Comic-Con a few years ago, and you won't believe this, but he's actually better looking in person. I approve of your bearded Captain America man love.

Also approve of skipping Episodes I-III, aka *The Emo Awakening of Anakin Skywalker*. The others are non-negotiable, though. I'm a little freaked out about our compatibility, however: Both Pepsi and Coke taste like sugar gone to die. Who hurt you, Reid? If I'm going to have that many calories, there'd better at least be alcohol involved.

And funniest movie ... let's see. I'm not sure I can narrow it down to just one. A few of my favorites (and in no particular order): *Tommy*

*Boy, Anchorman, National Lampoon's Vacation,
Superbad, 9 to 5, Blues Brothers* ... I could do this
all day. *Revenge of the Nerds* gets a special mention
because my parents took us to an 80's night at a
drive-in once, and expected us to sleep in the back
seat during the show. Ok, Mom. I saw my first movie
boobs in that drive-in.

And I'll stop now so I don't get too chatty. You're
up: favorite movie and favorite quote? I'll go with
one from *Girls Trip.* "Girl, you can't get no infection
in your booty hole. It's a booty hole."

Did I just break some sort of online dating code by
bringing up butts in the first message? I'm gambling
that it's both genius and brave.

Bye, Reid.
Cat

I mean, for fuck's sake. If he doesn't get that it's me
from the butt reference/anal sex joke, there's no hope for
this boy. Plus, I made him see that movie with me three
times—*in the theater!* Come on, Reid!

The doorbell rings and I stand from my laptop, pressing
SEND before heading to the door, wallet in hand and salivary
glands standing up and anticipating pizza.

It's not pizza.

It's Reid, on my porch, and he brushes past me before I have a chance to stop him.

"Do you have any food?" he says, already halfway to the kitchen. "I'm starving."

"Then you should have more than a salad for lunch."

"I like salads!"

Oh, he's hangry.

He steps into the kitchen and holy fuck my laptop is still on the counter with the dating site up.

"Reid!" I call out, and thank God, he turns: he's standing *directly* in front of Cat's profile and her "artsy" black-and-white photo on the screen.

"What?"

In my socks, I skate gracelessly across the room and nearly fall onto my ass at the transition from wood floor to kitchen tile. "Pizza is on its way!" I lunge past him and slam the computer shut.

Reid turns to me slowly, wearing a puzzled grin. "What . . . was that?"

"Porn."

His eyes light up with scandal and he reaches for the laptop. "Let me see."

I slap his hand. "No! It's sick porn."

Oh *my God*, Millie.

Of course, now he's *really* interested.

"For work." I wave what is supposed to be a nonchalant hand. "You know."

Reid doesn't look very convinced. "I hope the FBI never has reason to check your search history." God, me too. "Your job is super weird, Mills."

"Hey, I'm not the one dissecting cow eyeballs, okay?"

To my immense relief, he seems to move on and takes a seat on the stool right in front of my laptop. "So, hey," he says more quietly. "Are we okay?"

A new kind of unease trickles through me. "Yep, all good. Listen, I was about to head to bed."

"Didn't you just say you had pizza coming?"

"Right." *Shit.* "I mean, I'm going to bed right after pizza. And the porn." I offer an encouraging nudge toward the door. "So maybe we can talk tomorrow?"

"But if there's pizza, I want some." He gives me a winning grin. "I'm hungry, remember?"

"Then take some to go?"

The muscle in his jaw ticks, and there's the tiniest tilt of his head. "Are you sure everything's okay? You were annoyed with us today."

"I—what?" I'm having a moment where I register how natural Reid is in situations like this—situations where friends are having a conversation about emotions and conflict—and how, by contrast, in those same situations I turn all jerky and monosyllabic.

"Mills."

"Okay, I was a *little* annoyed," I hedge.

He rests his chin in his hand, listening attentively. This is a huge admission for me—that I'm feeling something negative—and his blue eyes crinkle with an encouraging smile.

"But I got over it," I say, pointing to the counter like my emotions were dropped there with my keys when I got home. "I mean, obviously. I sent you the messages for your women. I wouldn't do that if I was pissed."

That . . . might be a lie.

Reid sits up a little, and with him sitting on a stool and me standing, he's just slightly shorter than I am. It's a distracting angle for many reasons. He could pull his knees apart and bring me between his legs. He could lean forward and kiss my throat. I could straddle his lap.

Shut up, sex brain.

"Well, I'm glad you got over it," he says, "but if you hadn't, it would've been fair. I was being a dick, and you called me out. Thank you."

I'm listening to his words, but I'm thinking of his lemongrass soap and the way it smelled on his neck and chest and stomach.

I clear my throat. "Well, you know I'm always happy to help your moral development."

"By the way, I sent the messages you gave me," he says.

"Oh?" Stepping away, I take in a huge lungful of Reid-free air and move to the fridge to grab him a beer. I'm torn between wanting to extract more information and needing to change the subject entirely. No good can come from us chitchatting about my not-totally-fake profile.

"Yeah. I haven't heard back from them yet."

I pause, and then glance over my shoulder at him. "Huh."

After accepting the bottle with a quiet "Thanks," Reid pulls out his phone and swipes to the home screen. "Yeah, I—oh." He looks up, beaming. "I got one."

The doorbell rings, and I make a beeline for it, throwing money at the pizza guy and carrying the box of heaven into the kitchen. I need a change in topic. I want to talk about whether he also notices how *into* all of this Ed seems to be, or listen to Reid babble about scienceness, or gossip about Dustin also being on a dating site and whether we agree he wants to have a significant other specifically to help his chances of becoming dean.

Basically, I need Reid out of my space. Not because I *want* him out of my space, exactly, but because I'm feeling the same way I felt the night of his tenure party—like it might not be such a terrible idea to invite Reid into my bed, and I'm thinking these things while he's reading a message from another woman.

Who is actually me . . .

Hello, twenty-first-century predicaments.

But maybe when he reads Cat's last message, he'll figure it out and we'll laugh and I can stop thinking about this entirely. That would fix all of this.

Right?

I hold my breath as I watch him scan it, and then his eyes light up and he turns the screen to face me as he bursts out laughing. "Catherine—Cat—just quoted *Girls Trip*. She's your *twin*, Mills!"

I let out a jarring guffaw that makes him do a bemused double take, but then I can't think of a single thing to say to look less like a shrill maniac.

When he turns his phone back to read it again, I ask lamely, "Sooo, nothing unusual?"

"Unusual? No. She's super funny." Now I'm torn between insulted that he didn't realize that *I'm* super funny, and swooning that he's talking about me and doesn't even know it. Holy shit, this is both incredibly sweet and incredibly fucking stupid.

I open my mouth to tell him *It's me, you idiot*, but then he looks up at me with this goofy smile, and my heart does a weird swan dive in my chest. He seems genuinely excited.

"What should I say?" he asks.

I shrug because I'm not supposed to know what Cat said, so he reads the message out loud. I don't really have to listen because I reread it about seven times before sending—not to mention I have a terrible poker face—so I busy myself instead with putting pizza on plates.

"Not bad, right?" he asks once he's done.

"You're right, she sounds amazing."

He stands, finally, taking a plate of pizza. I watch him lift a slice, fold it in half, and take about a foot of it into his mouth in one bite. He wasn't kidding about being hungry. After he swallows, he says, "I'm really glad we did this. The whole dating thing. Feels promising."

I nod as I chew, silently encouraging him to go on.

"I've been thinking about what you said that night"—he takes a meaningful pause before adding—"on the way to your place . . ."

Oh. Another nod.

"I wonder if maybe you were right."

I pick up my pizza and bring it to my mouth. "I mean, you'll have to narrow it down a little. I'm right all the time."

"About the five of us enabling each other. I don't know,

maybe we were getting too comfortable. Maybe we did need to shake things up."

I take a bite, and nod again.

"Work has always been my priority, and for the first time in my life I'm seeing that there should be more. Dating someone was an obstacle I had to work around—it meant having to explain my hours and my time away, and just never seemed worth it."

"And now?"

He picks at his pizza and shrugs. "I think for the first time in my life, I feel like something is missing. I want both."

"There's nothing wrong with that. You might just be growing up, Peter Pan."

Reid smiles at me from across the counter. "What about you?"

"Me?"

"Yeah. I know you haven't had the same . . . experience so far with the app. But—"

"Let's not get ahead of ourselves."

"I'm serious."

I straighten and wipe my hands on a napkin. "So am I. I thought about getting a cat today. That's a solid step into the commitment zone."

Reid reaches for another slice and I pick up my wineglass, taking a long gulp. We eat in silence, and only the occasional sounds of Reid's chewing and my wine chugging fill the silence. Finally, Reid places each of his elbows on the counter. "I hate when you're upset with me. Even if you won't admit it. And especially if we're going to be trapped together all weekend at my parents' place. You're still good with that?"

A weekend with Reid? SOS.

"One, I'm not upset with you. Two, you know I wouldn't miss a weekend with your mom's cooking."

He tugs on a piece of hair that's escaped my bun. "Or someone's birthday cake."

"It's your mom's birthday?"

Reid rolls his eyes before leaning in to press a kiss to my forehead. "All right. I'm out." He lifts a third slice of pizza to indicate he'll take it with him, and turns for the door, stopping just short. "I know you're tired of talking about this, but did you ever change your profile?"

Panic stabs me in the chest. "My profile?"

He gives me another few seconds before saying slowly, "On IRL."

Ah. The account he knows about, full of boob requests and popped collars.

"Oh! Millie. Right. No." I abruptly quack out a string of words.

"You should," he says. "It sucks."

"Thanks."

"Thanks for listening to me. You're so fucking great." He turns for the door again. "I envy the man who gets you."

I have the feeling I should respond to this in some way, but my brain has become a solid brick of Styrofoam. Even if I were emotionally mature enough to have a good reply, he's already halfway down the front steps. So, I suppose the only thing to do is loudly yell, "Same!" to his retreating form.

Reid's wave over his shoulder—he doesn't even turn around—tells me exactly how stupid that was.

Five minutes after he's gone, the words *You are perhaps the best man alive and deserve more than any of us to be happy* swim into my head. But I don't know what to do with them, so I flop down on the couch and turn on the television, wishing I had that cat.

Midway through my inexplicable *Grey's Anatomy* binge, my phone pings on the coffee table. I practically roll off the couch in my lunge to get to it.

From: Reid C.
Sent: 11:15 pm, March 28

Cat,

Coke tastes like sugar gone to die? And we could have been so perfect! You remind me of my best friend. She hates soda because it's too sweet, but then orders the most sugary cocktails I've ever seen.

We've got another thing in common with favorite funny movies, or maybe all intelligent people love *Blues Brothers*? I'm also adding *Caddyshack* to that list because it's hilarious, but also for the nostalgic factor. I was a caddy for a few months when I was sixteen, though I'd say my time following old rich golfers around was a lot less entertaining than in the movie. There were no raunchy sexcapades that I was aware of, and no rich businessman ever offered me beer from a secret tap in his high-tech golf bag. I did see somebody streak across the driving range one day, but it was more *Cocoon*, less *Animal House* than you're probably imagining.

I'm not sure if I mentioned it or not, but I'll be out of town this weekend. You know I grew up on a vineyard, and a couple of my friends are driving up for a few days. I'm already imagining what kind of craziness I'm in for, especially with copious amounts of alcohol around.

I don't come home as often as I should, and I'm not really sure why. The vineyard is great, everything is blooming and it's this peaceful place where you can unplug from the world, but I always get a little anxious about bringing everyone there. My parents are ... well, parents. I guess that pretty much sums it up. Lately it seems my mom is always ranting about this artist woman that lives down the road, or attempting to tell me something that will scar me for life. I'm not sure at what age moms start to feel like their son/daughter is old enough to become their new bestie/confidant, but I've definitely reached it. Your thoughts and prayers during this difficult time are appreciated.

And don't ever worry about being chatty, that's the point of all this, right? I didn't realize I'd enjoy it so much, but it's sort of nice getting to know someone this way.

Favorite movie quote ... all I can think of right now is from Zoolander: "What's this? A school for ants?"

Reid

From: Catherine M.
Sent: 11:37 pm, March 28

Zoolander. See, I've never seen that movie because my ex-boyfriend, who had promised to wait until I got back from a trip to see it with me, saw it with his dude friends and told me it was sooooooo funny he never laughed so hard in his entire life omg. Obviously I never watched it ON PRINCIPLE.

~Cat

From: Catherine M.
Sent: 11:43 pm, March 28

I can see how that last message looked a touch vindictive and I should probably dial it back since we're so new to each other, but this is one instance when I'm pretty content living up in my Petty Castle on the hill.

~Cat

From: Reid C.
Sent: 12:04 am, March 29

I will never judge you for your petty grudges. I'm
still pissed off at my track coach in high school
for putting Tucker Ames—the biggest asshole on
the team—in the anchor spot on our 4x400 relay
against Pacific Beach High.

From: Catherine M.
Sent: 12:21 am, March 29
Please tell me you called him Fucker Ames behind
his back for this unforgivable offense.

From: Reid C.
Sent: 12:26 am, March 29

You know, I didn't, but that's because when I was
16, I was 6'2" and weighed approximately 70 lbs. I
feared that if I even thought something shitty about
Tucker he'd know and the fear alone of him hitting
me would break my legs like toothpicks.

———

From: Catherine M.
Sent: 12:29 am, March 29

My dad never gave me the birds and bees talk,
but he did pull me aside when I was thirteen and
show me how and where to throw a punch. I didn't
use this knowledge until an unfortunate night (one
which we shall not discuss again) where I had a bit
too much to drink and throat-punched a guy for
cutting in front of me at the shuffleboard table at
a bar. Which is why I'm banned for life at the Goat
Hill Tavern in Costa Mesa.

———

From: Reid C.
Sent: 12:36 am, March 29

It's hard these days to find a woman who takes her
shuffleboarding seriously.

———

From: Catherine M.
Sent: 12:43 am, March 29

I'm selling myself pretty hard tonight. Does this
explain why I'm on a dating app? Maybe.

—————

From: Reid C.
Sent: 12:59 am, March 29

No, look. Back when I was in grad school, there were a million single people my age. Now that we're settling into our careers, our worlds are getting so much smaller. Throughout the day, I see maybe a handful of the same people, and unless I do something like this, or join an intramural softball team, or take sailing lessons, I'm unlikely to meet someone new. Dating apps don't make us lame, they make us modern and technologically savvy. Right?

—————

From: Catherine M.
Sent: 1:04 am, March 29

Right! And I didn't mean it like that. But I think it is fair to say that I tend to focus on, shall we say, the low-hanging life-fruit: getting my turn at shuffleboard, grading this stack of assignments, meeting friends for beers. Rather than, say, doing the emotional heavy lifting that I know I should be doing on a daily basis.

I wonder whether I'm single not because I haven't met the right person yet, but because *I'm* not the right person yet. The other night, I had the most terrifying thought: Who would I be a good match for? Like, I honestly can't imagine who that man is. Someone who likes to watch television from 2004 and drink beer and make fun of each other? Okay, sure. But is that the stuff that lifelong relationships are made of? I honestly don't think so, but I don't even have a cat to ask for input.

chapter eight

 reid

There's a standard set of warnings I have to give Ed and Alex whenever we begin the final approach to my childhood home. First, do not hit on my little sister. Second, the downstairs toilet runs, so make sure to toggle the lever after you flush. And third, please don't ask my dad if you can try on his prosthetic arm.

The first and third situations have happened each of the dozen or so times my friends have accompanied me home. Dad lost his arm in a machine accident out on the vineyard when he was seventeen; for whatever reason, the prosthetic fascinates Ed and Alex. It's got a hook at the end that opens or closes depending on the angle, and the first few times they visited, Ed and Alex spent about three hours taking turns trying to pick up random things around the house. To be fair, Dad half pushes it on them because he thinks it's hilarious—probably also because it drives Mom crazy.

And although she's my sister, I am aware that Rayme is beautiful—it's impossible to be *unaware* of this. At twenty-five, she's six feet tall and could give Wonder Woman a run for her money in terms of both fitness and unguarded charm. Every guy friend—and a fair share of female friends, too—has had a crush on her at one point or another. Ed wants to marry her, Alex has far less honorable intentions, and even Millie has admitted that if she were a lesbian, she would one hundred percent hit on her. Only Chris seems unaffected by her dark hair and startling gold eyes—which I'm sure is directly related to why Rayme seems to try just a little harder to earn his attention.

There's also the No Streaking reminder, but, honestly, you'd think by this point that one would be *implied*.

We hit the soft dirt road, and Millie jolts awake next to me. Dragging a forearm across her mouth, she mumbles, "Was I snoring?"

"Yes." I glance briefly at her adorable just-waking-up face. Her eyes blink slowly, heavily over to me. Her mouth is a little swollen.

"And I drooled." She turns, looking over her shoulder out the back window at the other three following us in Chris's car. Because my car is in the shop, we decided to take Millie's Mini Cooper, which meant that Chris is scowling behind the wheel of his Acura while Alex and Ed appear to be singing loudly with the windows down.

I can feel her looking at me, and flash her a quick smile before turning back to the road. "Good nap?"

She nods, stretching. "I haven't slept well this week."

I let out a sympathetic grunt. I haven't, either. The last few nights, I've been up until one or two messaging Catherine and, less frequently, Daisy. It's the sort of addictive rush I haven't felt in years. It feels a little like being a teenager again.

Millie lifts her chin when we pass the Pine Grove Road sign that signals we're less than two miles from my house. "Almost there." She runs a hand through her hair and it spills like a sunset over her shoulders. "Want me to call Chris?"

She knows the drill.

"Sure."

Chris answers on the first ring through his Bluetooth, and it's a few seconds before I hear his voice over the sound of John Waite singing "Missing You" with the loud accompaniment of Ed and Alex.

"Get me out of this hell," he says by way of greeting.

Millie clears her throat. "Just calling with the reminders."

"Rayme equals no-no!" Alex yells.

"Prosthetic arms aren't toys!" Ed says.

And then Chris rounds it out: "Downstairs bathroom still broken—got it!"

Mom's already out on the porch, pacing as she waits for us, and she jogs down when we come to a crunching, dusty stop in front of the wide, outstretched farmhouse. When I climb out from behind the driver's seat, I know better than to expect a hug immediately—she goes to Millie first, then Chris, then me. Alex and Ed get the last hugs, the sort of *Oh, fine, come here, you idiots* embrace that I imagine most people give them.

Ed is notoriously awkward with all parents, but within three minutes Alex will have Mom charmed enough to forget why she was annoyed to begin with.

And in about eight hours, I'm sure he'll do something to remind her.

"I'm making ribs," Mom says, and grins at Millie, who pretends to swoon. A few visits back, Mom made ribs and

Millie ate them so enthusiastically that she looked like the Joker when she finally came up for air. It's the kind of culinary zeal my mom lives for.

"Sharon. Are you trying to make me move in here?" Millie asks her.

"Don't tease me." Mom pops a kiss to the side of Millie's head, then walks ahead of her into the house, calling out, "James! They're all here!"

Dad yells from upstairs, "You think I didn't hear that crap music booming down the driveway?"

Chris grins up at Dad as he descends into the living room. "Alex and Ed chose the emo eighties theme for this drive."

"Who was driving?" Dad asks, laughing knowingly. He doesn't bother to wait for an answer. "You are too goddamn nice, Chris."

The two of them disappear immediately to do who knows what. Discuss the weather almanac or the biochemistry of grape fermentation, probably. Alex and Ed look around, hoping to find Rayme, I'm sure, and I smile proudly when Millie reaches out to either side of her and shoves each of them in the shoulder.

"She's not going to be here until about five," she says.

I start to agree before remembering that I didn't know this. "Wait, what?"

"She texted me," Millie says, all innocent round green eyes and flirting freckles.

"Rayme texted you?" She didn't text *me*. Millie didn't mention it, either.

"Uh, *yeah*." Millie follows Mom into the kitchen and I'm left with Ed, whose hands are shoved deep into his pockets—safe, he won't break anything this way—and Alex, who saunters over and sits on the couch, kicking his feet onto the coffee table.

"Alex," I say.

He drops his feet.

"Want a beer?" At their nods, I turn and head into the kitchen. Mom and Millie are staring into the oven and moaning over the sight and smells of the roasting meat.

"Christ, that looks good." Millie's gravelly voice rockets a gallon of blood down my body and toward my groin, before I remember that she's talking about my mother's cooking.

Mom heads out the back door to pick vegetables for the salad, and Millie leans against the counter, smiling at me. It's a quiet smile, a real one, where her mouth curves but doesn't open, and her eyes move all over my face, cataloging, almost like she's reading a news story for the latest update.

"Hey, you," she says.

It feels like everything finally goes still. With the tenure party, the spontaneous sex, and this last week of cycling work/dating-app adrenaline/sleep/repeat, I realize we haven't just been *us* in days. It doesn't sound like a lot, but Millie is a fixture in my life. When I don't get time with her . . . it's weird.

"Hey, yourself."

"What's new?"

I shrug. "Work's been bananas. How about you?"

"Same." Millie pulls a hair tie off her wrist and bundles her hair on top of her head. "I got started on the book."

"That's awesome." I reach for a high five. Her hand is a soft slap of warmth against mine. "How are things going on the dating front?"

"Meh." She looks down to the floor. "There's one guy I'm talking to a fair bit."

"That's awesome! See, I told you they weren't all losers." She shrugs noncommittally. "Is he cool?"

She nods. "What about you?"

Tension rises like steam in the room, and it feels like every other sound falls away. "Yeah. Same. Well, the two still, really. But Catherine and I stay up late messaging lately. It's . . . nice."

Millie gnaws at her lip for a few seconds, and I can't read the reaction. Is it jealousy?

"Is this the one whose picture you didn't like?" she asks.

I groan. "Come on, this again?"

She grins. "Tell me about her."

There's a flash of annoyance when I realize how easily she's managed to turn the conversation back to me. She deflects before I realize she's done it.

"Well," I start, leaning back against the counter and choosing my words carefully, "I'm not sure what department she's in, but it sounds like she's faculty at UCSB. She's funny—I told you that—and laid-back, but shares these amazing stories. Apparently in college she went to Africa for a month and got into a car with the wrong driver and ended up, like, two hundred miles away from the town she was supposed to be in, but she just got on a bus and went back."

Millie smiles faintly. "Wow. How cool."

"She has a sister and—like you—her mom died when she was younger." I pause, looking at her closely. "You two would probably get along really well, actually. If things don't work out with us, maybe I just found you a backup best friend for when I'm out of town."

Millie bites her lower lip, looks at my mouth, and then takes a sharp, deep breath, turning away toward the sink.

"Did you notice that neither of your parents have said happy birthday to you?"

A breath comes out of me as a laugh. "It's not my birthday yet."

She turns back around to face me. "But isn't that why we're here?"

"Only sort of," I say. "Mom just wanted everyone here so she could brag that I spent my birthday with her."

My mother has three sisters, and they are notoriously competitive about how great their kids are. Some children have pressure to go to an Ivy League school, some are pressured to become physicians. Rayme and I are pressured to do all the things specifically that Aunt Janice's kids won't do, like visit regularly, send thank-you notes, and celebrate Mother's Day.

"Do you know what I was thinking earlier?"

She's looking at her feet when she says this, so I can't read her face to see why the tone has shifted. "I have no idea," I say.

"That we had sex only three weeks ago."

This sometimes happens with Millie. She's not exactly forthcoming about her thought process, and the sudden change in topic is so disorienting that for a breath I think I've misheard her. But I haven't, because she blushes.

"We did," I agree, wondering how she got from birthdays to here.

She lets out this strange, breathy laugh. "What were we *thinking*?"

"Probably that we were drunk and sex would be fun?"

"*You* weren't drunk," she says.

"No."

"I was." She considers this. "A little."

"Are you sure you aren't drunk now?" I smile and walk to the fridge, less to get a beer and more to cool down the entire front half of my body. We haven't talked about this again since the next morning, at Cajé—and it's pretty daring to do it here when Alex and Ed are only a room away. I realize, too, that she's wearing the same dress she wore that night. Is that what made her think of it?

I can't help but wonder if she's wearing the same thing underneath, too.

"Not yet, unfortunately. What I'm saying is, I could totally write you a letter of recommendation for one of your . . . lady friends. You know, if you need it."

I give her a smarmy bow. "I genuinely appreciate that."

Kicking off the counter, she walks to the fridge, opening it with comfort and pulling out a bottle of white wine. I don't even need to tell her where the glasses are; she finds one in the cabinet near the stove, fills it unselfconsciously, and then returns the bottle to the fridge.

It trips an old memory, one of how Isla came here again and again with me, but even on her tenth visit, needed Mom's permission or prompting for nearly everything.

Come on in.

Make yourself comfortable.

Would you like something to drink? Water? Wine?

Here, honey, sit next to Reid.

You two'll be sleeping in the room down the hall.

Yes, honey, you can stay with Reid, you're adults.

She never felt at home.

That isn't Millie. It's not that she's presumptuous or callous in any way, it's that she heeded the cues from her first visit here—the unspoken communication from Mom and Dad that my friends should all genuinely make themselves feel at home (except for racing naked in the vineyards). And here she is. She stretches, one arm over her head, then switches the hand holding the wineglass. Her torso elongates, breasts press forward.

Here she fucking is.

She's watching me watching her now, leaning back against the counter and sipping her wine. "What're you thinking?"

She knows what I'm thinking. She knows I'm thinking about the sex we had.

"Just watching you." I know her so well, and yet in some ways she's such a mystery to me. Even though what happened between us was fun, and hot as hell—in my opinion—I realize I still can't really know how she views it. As something fun we did, or as a mistake we made but managed to smooth over without incident. But since it's Millie, it occurs to me that she could be full of horrified regret, and I might never know, because she's shoved it so far below the surface.

On instinct, I scratch at her surface a little, digging: "Get any new messages today?"

Millie tilts her head from side to side. "I got one from my guy last night. I haven't replied yet."

My guy. The reference makes my stomach shrink about two sizes, my heart balloon about three until it is this envious, thundering beast in my chest. How weird is it that it didn't occur to me until we were standing right here that if Millie meets someone, I won't have free, unlimited access to her anymore? Without entirely realizing it, I've become the most important man in her life . . . and I *like* it.

"You're all pinched," she says, "like some new lab tech messed up the hematoxylin stain." She grins at me. "That's the easy one, right? See how I pay attention?"

I give her a proud smile, but my mind is turning this around, distracted. How honest should I be here? Millie isn't the most touchy-feely friend, but we've also never been *here*: no longer *just friends*, but never going to be more, either. "It just occurred to me that one or both of us could be in a relationship at some point soon."

She lets out her trademark husky laugh. "That *just* occurred to you?"

"Yeah. I know what I said the other night, but I don't think it felt real yet."

"If we were just doing this for the gala, you and I would still be going together. But Obama wouldn't want that. Obama would *want us to have sex lives*, Reid." I laugh, and she continues, "At some point, if we kept going the way we were going, we'd all be seventy and doing crosswords together in Chris's backyard."

"I mean, that doesn't sound completely terrible," I say.

"Come on," she says, shrugging and then taking a sip of her wine. "We both like sex." The whole lower half of my body explodes into heat when she says this. "I'm not entirely optimistic, but it might be nice to have someone that I'm close to, and who wants sex with me on a regular basis. And kids, maybe. Someday. And, like, a shared life of adventure."

"You know," I tell her, "if there was a way to translate

that kind of openness and sincerity to your profile, you might get more legitimate interest and fewer dick pics."

"Why you gotta be a hater?"

"Why you gotta be such a secret?"

She twists her mouth a little at this, narrowing her eyes at me. "Hitting me where it hurts."

So she knows she's bottled up. Interesting. "Seriously, Mills," I say. "You keep everything so close to your chest. Are you secretly a spy?"

She absorbs this with a smile. "You got me."

"Okay, no more jokes." And suddenly sincere curiosity burns through me and out: "Why? Why don't you tell me more?"

She opens her mouth to say something, and for a beat it feels like a revelation is going to pour down over me. Something about how it felt to lose her mother so young, or how she wishes her relationship with Elly were different. Something bare-wire honest about me, or her, or—fuck— even Dustin. But she presses her lips together again and just smiles at me.

"There," I say, pointing at her, "right there. What were you going to say?"

Alex steps in, swiping my beer from my hand. "She was going to say that Benedict Cumberbatch looks like an un- circumcised penis."

"I thought you were getting beers?" Ed looks forlornly at me, and then Alex, and then the fridge.

"Shit. I forgot."

Ed frowns like I've genuinely let him down.

"Ed," I say, "there are two six-packs in there. Just grab one."

He peeks around the corner like a guilty teenager, as if he's making sure that my parents aren't going to catch him stealing alcohol, and then does an open-grab-slam maneuver so fast that the condiment bottles rattle in the fridge door when it rockets shut.

"Is Chris still out with your dad?" Alex asks.

"Yeah." I grab a new beer for myself. "I swear he won't leave Mom for the younger woman down the road; he'll leave her for Chris."

"I don't think Chris is into dudes," Ed tells me, helpfully.

"He was joking, Eddie," Mills says with a gentle fist to his shoulder.

Ed downs about half of his beer and then burps. "Clearly I'm not firing on all cylinders. I need more beer."

Alex tilts his head to the side, indicating the living room. "Ed just got a message from Selma."

"The hot one?" I ask.

Ed nods, trying to look breezy about it. "It's going pretty well. I asked her if she wants to meet up next week."

"Already?" Millie asks.

"Millie," Alex says, laughing, "people on Tinder meet the same day they match."

Millie shrugs. "I know, but I guess IRL seems to emphasize taking things slow." She glances to me and quickly away. "Which I like."

"I'll meet her whenever she wants." Ed shrugs and then studies the beer in his hand. "I should cut down to, like, three beers a day. I need to lose weight. I'm tired of being brave at the beach."

"Isn't that why we get into relationships?" Millie asks. "To start eating and drinking again?"

Alex points his beer bottle at me. "What about you, Reid? What's up with your ladies?"

"I still really like them both."

"We need to think of a tiebreaker," Alex says.

Millie steps forward, slightly flushed as she looks at him with genuine scorn. "Has it occurred to you guys that Daisy and Catherine are probably talking to multiple men, too?"

I blink. I am such an asshole—and realize it the second she says this. "Is it terrible if my answer is no?"

Ed and Alex say, "No," at the same time Millie shouts, "Yes!"

I give a tiny apologetic wince. "It just seems crazy that

Cat would be having this kind of interaction with someone else."

"But aren't *you*?" Millie asks, genuinely annoyed. "With Daisy?"

Conceding this with a nod, I say, "I mean, yes, though I probably talk to Cat more frequently, and openly." When silence stretches for a beat, I say, "So when should I ask to meet them?"

"Maybe ask for more pictures first?" Alex says.

Millie gasps. "Don't do that, that's douchey!"

We fall into a contemplative silence.

Millie is normally unflappable, and can hold her own against us in every way. Is she worried she'll lose me to another woman? That the friendship we have will suffer?

"Okay," I say, "it's someone else's turn to be in the spotlight. It's not like I'm the only one who is on this app."

"Chris matched with one of his old TAs the other day," Alex says, and we all turn to look at him in shock. "I was giving him shit about it, but then I got on the app and saw that I'd matched with my *sister*." Our shock deepens into horror, and Alex shivers violently. "I feel like she's seen me naked now, okay? Maybe you can understand why we're hoping your story goes more smoothly, Reid."

We marinate in this for a few more silent beats, and then everyone turns their optimistic attention back to me.

"Well, I like them both," I say, "but I feel weird about dating them both in person because I've never really worked that way."

"So just ask Daisy out already," Millie says with vinegar on her lips.

"I like Catherine a lot, though," I say. "She's funny and we interact a lot more. It's hard to find funny."

Millie gapes at me, offended. "Excuse you! I am *hilarious*, you dark stain on humanity."

"I am forever calling my brother that, from this day forward."

All attention sweeps to the door to the living room, and a hush falls over the group as we all take in Rayme in unison. My little sister has always had a flair for exotic outfits, but right now she's wearing a loose-fitting sequined tank top and . . . I'm not even sure whether the bottom half qualifies as a skirt.

"Rayme, what on earth? It's *forty* degrees outside," I say, probably too loudly.

My sister is trying to kill Ed and Alex.

Or win over Chris.

"Wow," Alex says, tongue rolled out all the way to the floor.

"Alex, close your face," I say. "Rayme, go put some clothes on."

I think she's coming in for a hug, but she veers over to Millie instead, throwing an annoyed "*Excuse* me?" over her shoulder.

"Are you trying to murder them?" I point to Drooling Thing 1 and Drooling Thing 2.

She hugs Ed next and the contact turns him into a bright red statue, his arms stiff at his sides.

Millie gives me a reproachful glare but doesn't say anything. We both know my sister can fight her own battles.

"They are grown-ass men," Rayme says. "If they can't handle a skirt, they shouldn't be out in public."

In response, Alex throws his arms wide for her, and gives her the Latin-lover dimpled smile. Rayme approaches with understandable caution.

"Where the hell is Mom?" I ask. *She* would have my back here.

Millie twists, glancing out the kitchen window overlooking the expansive backyard. "Talking to your dad and Chris. She went out for a few tomatoes, and I think caught them on their way back." Squinting, she adds, "I think they were smoking *pipes*."

My parents, everyone: pipe-smoking hippies.

"Like hookah?" Ed comes alive.

"Like Sherlock Holmes," Rayme says with a laugh, and he goes still again under her attention.

Everyone from outside comes in, and indeed the cool air that blows in carries the warm spice of pipe tobacco. All smiles, and without taking a break in their conversation, Dad and Chris each grab a beer, walk toward the dining room, and don't spare any of us a glance. Rayme pouts, and Millie catches my eye. I try to think back on my sister's interactions with Chris from more than a year ago, but I swear even when she was nineteen, twenty, twenty-one, I didn't see Rayme as a human who would go on dates. Just like I'll always be twenty in my head, she'll always be fourteen and gangly, a young horse that hasn't grown into her limbs yet.

She follows Dad and Chris, Alex and Ed follow Rayme, and Millie helps Mom get dinner onto the table. I try to help, but they eventually shoo me away because apparently stealing bites of food isn't helpful.

My parents have an enormous farm table stretching most of the length of the dining room. The room, which is far longer than it is wide, has an expansive window overlooking the rolling hills of our family vineyard, and is easily the most spectacular view in the house, other than the one from their bedroom, which has the same view, just from higher up. Tonight, Mom has decorated the length of the table with a garland of flowers snaking around and between simple white candles. Ed sits down in front of his full place setting like he's at the White House: eyes wide, hands unsure where to land.

"Ed," Millie says, noticing it, too. "What's with you? It's like you've never seen flatware before."

Ed picks up a salad fork. "Growing up, we felt fancy if we put the plates on the TV trays."

Thankfully, Mom manages to swallow her sympathetic gasp. Instead, she says, "We're just here celebrating Reid's birthday this weekend, nothing too fancy for us. James, would you like to say a few words?"

We all swing our eyes to Dad, who looks at her like she's suggested he stand up and break-dance for us. "Sure. Uh, happy birthday, Reid. Thirty-one is . . . a good age."

"He's turning thirty-two," Millie says with a grin.

Dad lifts his wineglass to her in thanks. "Also a good age. And . . . let's hope for more rain, and that we can pull those soil nitrogen levels back up this spring, eh?" With that, Dad reaches for the platter of ribs.

"There's your birthday wish," my sister says with an amused tilt of her head.

To be fair, my father is not the most gifted orator. He does much better when he's coaxing miracles out of the earth.

"So tell me about this dating app thing," my mom says.

Rayme is visibly delighted. "Dating app? What? I definitely need to hear this."

"It's not that Grind Up I read about, is it?" Mom adds.

My eyes go wide as I look at them both from across the table. "First of all, *Grindr* is for gay men. So, no. And which of my dear friends here told you about any of this so I may properly thank them later . . . ?"

Chris, Millie, and Alex all swing their gazes to Ed, and I'd punch him if he weren't so far away, and also holding a butter knife.

"What?" he says, mouth already full. He swallows around a bite, and at least has the decency to look remotely apologetic. "Your mom asked if I was seeing anyone"—he aims a smile in Rayme's direction—"which I'm not, if anyone was wondering. I didn't know our Find a Date for Commencement plan was a secret."

At my side, Millie drains half of her wine, but doesn't come to my assistance.

"It's just for fun," I assure them with a small wave. "The administration is going all out for the Obama visit, and we thought it might be a good reason to find dates. Simple."

My mom shakes her head. "It certainly doesn't sound simple. In my day, we actually went *out* and met people. Dances, blind dates, drinks. For God's sake, you could be talking to one of Millie's serial killers online."

"I don't actually know any serial killers," Millie clarifies.

"Here's the thing," Rayme says, drawing an air circle that encompasses Chris, Ed, Alex, and me. "I get why they're doing it. It's like a conveyor belt of ladies they can scroll through while they play *Overwatch* or circle jerk or whatever it is they do. But Millie? Ugh. Dating sites are like the second circle of hell for women."

Millie lifts her glass again. "Not wrong."

"It hasn't been too bad," Ed says with a shrug. "I've had a good match. So has Reid. He's talking to *two*, actually."

Wow. Ed is *really* getting his ass kicked later.

"Reid," Mom says, tone disapproving. "I do not want you out there stringing anyone along."

Rayme pipes up next to her. "Yeah, *Reid*."

"It's not like that," I assure them, stepping on Rayme's foot beneath the table. "We're just getting to know each other."

"I don't understand what computers have to do with sex," my dad says. "Why not just go down to Rita's—it's that little place just off the highway. You remember that, Reid? Thursday night is ladies' night and beers are only two dollars. Place is *full* of women."

"Dad—"

"Oh my God, Jim," Mom cuts in, delighted, "do you remember when Reid was seventeen and tried to sneak in?"

"Got picked up by the sheriff for a fake ID!" Dad barks out a laugh and slaps his prosthetic arm on the table, causing the silverware and glasses to jump with the impact. Of course, every Campbell, as well as Chris and Millie, is used to it, but Ed and Alex both visibly startle in their seats.

"Point is," Dad says, "you should give it a try while you're here."

After I promise my parents that I'll give Rita's a shot, the rest of dinner is fine for the most part. Dad and Chris continue to speak quietly about phosphates and calcium concentrations in the area. Rayme joins in, and for the first time, I see Chris's eyes light up when she mentions a new cover crop they're going to try to bring up the pH of the soil. Alex and Ed give up on trying to lure Rayme into a conversation and end up listening as Mom loudly shares stories about the woman who makes weird art down the road, every now and then looking up to check Dad's reaction when she loudly enunciates the name *Marla*. The subject of my dating life is thankfully dropped.

To my right, Millie nudges me with an elbow. "You get enough to eat?"

I nod. This is the semiquiet part of the evening. Once the wine is really flowing, all hell breaks loose around here. "Just enjoying the calm before the storm. And by storm I of course mean board games and drunk nudity."

She stretches, and in a very un-Millie-like action, kisses my cheek. "Thanks for always including me."

True to form, shit really does hit the fan after dinner and cake. Alex and Rayme pull out a deck of cards and get swept up in a rousing game of Kings. Mom joins in, and at least three glasses of wine are spilled, but four bottles are consumed, so I'm not sure anyone notices.

Twister is brought out, and only then does Mom put her drunken foot down and suggest that Rayme put on shorts, at least. After I nearly break my leg trying to keep my right foot on red and my right hand on green, the other six drunken adults gather around the coffee table to play Bullshit with six sticky decks of cards, and I go in search of Millie, who disappeared about a half hour ago.

I find her bundled up on the back deck, changed into a sweater and jeans, reading on her iPad. She has the thick comforter from her bed wrapped around her, and has found one of Dad's wool caps to pull over her mess of hair. It's chilly out, but not freezing, and as soon as the door inside closes, the quiet falls like a hush over the deck. The vineyards stretching out ahead of us are an invisible sea of black.

"Hey, you." I sit in the lounge chair to her right, facing her. "You're missing Ed's recounting to Mom the time he was nearly run over by his ex-girlfriend, the fire breather from the carnival."

She grins up at me, joking, "You can only hear that story so many times before it's just another story, you know?"

"What're you reading?"

Millie tilts her iPad toward me. "*I'll Be Gone in the Dark.*"

"My adorable true crime fanatic."

She nods. "It's so good."

I want to talk to her a bit about the conversation we had before dinner, but feel like I should leave her to the book. She turns back to the iPad and I stretch out on the chaise, crossing my feet at the ankle. I like it out here— it's quiet and crisp . . . and relaxing. Millie is so calm all the time—being near her is a little like sitting in front of the fireplace. I pull out my phone, checking my work email before habitually opening the IRL app to see whether I have any new messages. In fact, I have two. One from Daisy, and another from Cat, to whom I'd mentioned my ambivalence about a weekend at home with my parents.

MY FAVOURITE HALF-NIGHT STAND

From: Catherine M.
Sent: 11:43 pm, March 31

When I was in the fifth grade, I had about seventy pounds of hardware in my mouth and could never get over the lisp from it. I mean, it was a terrible, cartoon-level bad lisp.

There was a girl, Tessa, who was an enormous asshole about it. She would raise her hand in class to answer a question, and do it with a lisp, and the entire class would fall apart laughing. It finally bothered me enough that I went to talk to my dad about it, and he gave me these "replies" I could use when she was mean.

Let me be frank right away: They were terrible. They were, like, "Tessa, I really don't appreciate it when you make fun of me this way," or "Tessa, you might think it's funny to make fun of my lisp, but it hurts my feelings." I mean, not only would saying both of these sentences with a lisp just send her into further hysterics, but these comebacks would not make any ten-year-old feel remorseful.

I figured my dad was just terrible at comebacks, and added that to the list of things that Mom Would Have Done Better, but then one day I came home crying, and went straight to my room, and about an hour later I heard his voice downstairs, and it got louder and louder until I finally heard him yell, "Look, I don't know if you feed her sand, or you make her sleep in a small, dark closet, but just keep your dumb bitch of a bully away from my daughter from now on or I'll come say it again in person."

Needless to say, Tessa never bugged me again.

I'm not really sure what my point is, but sometimes we think our parents are lame and then they totally surprise us by being awesome. I hope that this weekend is like that for you.

C.

I read it again, laughing, and then type a quick reply:

From: Reid C.
Sent: 12:02 am, April 1

OK, I just laughed out loud reading this. We're actually having a pretty good time. Mom made ribs and mashed potatoes, and only mentioned The Woman Down The Street about seven hundred times, but I don't think Dad noticed. My friends got her drunk so that she won't be mad when they run naked in the vineyards later. It's chaos in the house, but I'm outside with my best friend, which always makes me ... calmer. It's quiet and nice and I'm glad I came home. You were right.

I hope it doesn't sound too forward for me to say
that I'm really glad you wrote me tonight.

More soon.
R.

I open the message from Daisy.

From: Daisy D.
Sent: 9:15 pm, April 1

Hi Reid!

Omg I bet it's so pretty up there! Happy birthday!
Mine is in July. It always sucked to have birthdays
in the summer because no one was around! Let's
definitely plan a time to get together when you're
back! Have the most fun!

Daisy

I read this one again, struggling to find a thread of anything I can reply to here. Granted, I tend to overthink
things, but having conversations with Daisy online is a little
like playing Candy Land. I know some people are better in
person, and I thankfully get that sense from her. I type out
something, and then delete it. Honestly, I could just decide
to not reply, right?

I look over at Millie, whose screen looks like she's also reading a message on IRL, and with a faint smile on her face. That odd surge of jealousy is back, but I press in on it, forcing it to collapse into nothing.

Finally, I settle on a simple note to Daisy—Thanks! Have a great weekend!—and hit SEND just when Millie stands and moves so that she's hovering over me, with the comforter cocooned around her shoulders, cap low on her head.

"What are you up to?" she asks quietly.

"Was just replying to Daisy."

She goes quiet, and I look up at her face. It's lit with the warm light coming through the windows behind us, her head is tilted to the side, and she's frowning a little—the way she does when she's working out something in her head.

"You okay?" I ask. I feel like I've asked her that a lot in the last few days, but I suppose that's why it's inadvisable to have sex with your beautiful-but-closed-off best friend.

"Yeah." She reaches down, takes my hand. "Want to go upstairs?"

"Good call, I'm beat."

"I mean," she says even quieter now, "*upstairs*."

Her fingers tighten around mine meaningfully.

Holy shit.

"*Upstairs* upstairs?" I ask, leaning on the innuendo.

"Yeah."

Any intelligent thought process falls away, and I am wiped clean of any reaction but lust; after only one night she has me trained to alternate from concerned friend to eager lover with just the tone of her voice. "Like for sex?"

She laughs, a low rumble, and hesitates for only a moment before gifting me with a shaky "Yeah."

I stand, and we're so close I can feel the heat emanating from her body. I have a wild urge to kiss her, like I need to confirm that she's serious. It's short, just a brush of my mouth over hers, but she chases it a little, eyes heavy. Anyone inside would only have to turn and look out the window to see us, so it isn't smart to do this here, but I'm too thunderstruck to be cautious.

The first time was the last time, at least that's what I thought. But has she been wanting this again, and only just worked up the nerve? It doesn't sound like Millie. Or is it an impulsive thing, to be hosed down tomorrow and put away in storage inside of us again?

Right now I'm not sure I care.

chapter nine

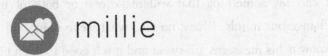 millie

After the briefest brush of his lips, Reid takes a step back, leaving what I assume is a platonic amount of distance between us. But I'm a little woozy from both the wine and his proximity so I chase him, stopping only when his eyes swing to the picture window where the rest of our group is congregated inside, loudly playing cards.

Right. Witnesses.

Reid takes my iPad, turning it over in his hands. I send up a silent prayer that I closed the app before locking the screen. For a second, things get too quiet; I think he's going to gently remind me that we're not doing this again.

That we should definitely *not* do this again.

But then, he looks up at me and half grins, eyes dark. "Why don't you head up first?"

Static fills my bloodstream. "Okay. My room?" At the end of the hall, it makes the most sense.

Nodding, he says, "I'll follow in a few minutes."

I take my iPad, grab my blanket, and head inside before I can say something that will make one or both of us change our minds. I have no idea what we're doing. All I know is his messages are sweet and it felt good to open up a little. His family is amazing and his house is so relaxing and I like spending time with him more than with any other human on the planet. He likes Cat, and Cat is me, and we're going upstairs to have sex.

I'll worry about everything else tomorrow.

Inside, I'm hit with a wall of sound as soon as I open the door.

"Oh good." Ed's face brightens when he sees me, and he steps forward, gripping my arm and pulling me into his conversation. "Mills, tell them about that girl I met on the cruise. The one with the leg," he says, and motions for me to take the floor.

His cheeks are pink from what I can only guess is a case of beer, and he's got that cartoonish grin plastered on his face. I don't have to see Reid to know he's watching me with amusement from outside, wondering how I'll extricate myself from happy, tipsy Ed. Once he gets going it's almost impossible to get away.

Fortunately, or unfortunately, I have to get in and out before anyone notices I have my *I'm about to have sex!* face on.

I frown. "Actually, I think I'm heading to bed." I rub my stomach. "Feeling sort of . . . *oof*."

Sharon stands, and the look of concern on her face is so similar to her son's, I'm momentarily thrown. "You're not feeling well, honey?"

I wave her off, wishing I'd been stealthier when sneaking in. In hindsight, hopping the fence to come in through the front door seems a lot easier than this. "I just *really* enjoyed the ribs, I think."

Ed's face falls, and Rayme sticks out her bottom lip in a sweet pout that is thoroughly catalogued by every nonrelative male in the house—including, I notice, Chris.

"But you're not really even drunk yet," she says.

I point to Ed. "He's drunk enough for both of us. Can't let that one out of your sight."

With that, I'm allowed to make my escape.

Unfortunately, victory is short-lived, because once I'm in my room, panic descends: what tripped my mood wasn't just how sweet Reid was being, it was the sudden, heated flash of awareness that if Daisy and Reid hit it off, *Daisy* will see Reid naked.

I may not have a clue what I want beyond tonight, but I certainly don't want anyone else to see Reid naked but me.

And then there's the reality that he agreed so easily. Has he been thinking about doing this again and waiting for me to take the initiative? Am I going to make an enormous knot of confused emotions with my best friend?

I am immediately distracted by something equally pressing. "Oh my God." I haven't shaved my legs in . . . *ho boy*.

Trying to triage this appearance situation—and knowing I don't have time to shave all my parts before Reid gets here, even if he does get waylaid by Tipsy Ed—I pull my hair out of its bun, fluff it, but then tie it up again. I throw off my clothes and pull on my pajamas, but then start to put all my clothes back on again so I don't seem too . . . eager? I manage to get my shirt on before I catch my reflection in the vanity mirror, noting the eyeliner situation currently pooling beneath my lids.

I pull out a makeup wipe, trying to scrub away the mess, but then Reid knocks, walks in, and does a mild double take in reaction to the mess of my mascara all around my eyes.

"Wow. What's up, Rocky?" His eyes drop to my shirt,

which I've put on backward, and my bare legs beneath. "You . . . okay?"

"Shit." I scrub at my eyes. "Yes."

"Aww, Mills. You're primping for me."

"Am not."

"You're freaking out." He comes up behind me, looking over my shoulder and meeting my eyes in the mirror. "Aren't you?"

"I'm . . . no." I turn around and face him. "Not freaking out. This is not the face of someone who is freaking out. This is the face of someone who . . ." *Just realized that she's a petty, jealous asshole and really wants to have sex but is also worried about the consequences.*

"Who what?"

I blink up at him. "Wait. How did you get up here so fast?"

"I witnessed your ambush and went through the garage." He stops short as his eyes travel down my body again, and he takes a step closer.

I cannot express how much I like intense, about-to-get-laid Reid.

Gripping my hip, he teases the elastic waistband of my underwear. "Here I was thinking I'd get to undress you."

Even through the fabric of his clothes, I can feel the heat of his body against my stomach, where the fronts of his thighs rub against the fronts of mine. "I didn't shave my legs."

We're so close; I feel his quiet laugh more than hear it. "You keep tampons in my bathroom and once used lube you found in my dresser to unstick a zipper. I don't think a little leg hair is going to shock me."

"I know, it's just—that's one of the things you do when you're planning to have sex. Shave your legs, brush your teeth, wax your . . ."

His brows go up. "You should know that I don't care about any of those things." He runs his nose along the curve of my jaw before straightening again. "Okay, except the teeth brushing part. We can continue to prioritize that."

"Noted," I say, eyes closing when his fingers trail lower, tracing my hip bone. I feel the way he smiles against my chin, along the column of my throat. "Everyone's downstairs." Open mouth, breath hot against my skin. "Should we do something else until they go to bed?"

My head falls back against the wall and I very clearly identify with the phrase *short-circuited*. I'd like to think there's at least one rational thought still bouncing around inside my cranium, but I'm incapable of retrieving it.

"Something else?" I say, voice a little wavery. "Like play Go Fish?"

His hands move up, dragging my shirt over my head before sliding my underwear down over my hips. He touches me like every part is worth something immeasurable.

His voice is a whisper against my shoulder. "I've never had sex in my parents' house before."

This catches my attention. "*Never?*"

He smiles again, moving lower, and dropping open-mouthed kisses between my breasts and over the cotton of my bra. He sucks on my nipple through the fabric and I arch into the touch. Big hands move around my ribs to my back, getting rid of the bra altogether with a casual flick.

Finally, he shakes his head in answer. "Never. Isla was always too nervous they'd hear."

My fingers twist in his hair. "I assume sex at your parents' house is the same"—I gasp in a breath as he opens his mouth against my skin, sucking—"only quieter."

Reid looks up at me, wearing a smug, devious grin. "I'm not sure I can do quieter."

Every single neuron in my body is firing, I swear it. "Oh."

Reid straightens to his full height and I have to look up to meet his gaze again. I'm completely naked—bra on the floor, panties pushed down—but Reid is still dressed.

"Should we stay here? Maybe against a wall . . ." he says, bracing one hand near my head to cage me in. He nods back over his shoulder. "The bed might squeak."

The idea of the mattress squeaking, of being able to *hear* what we're doing, causes heat to explode through my body.

I stretch to kiss him, and push against his chest to send him a step back. Then another, and another, leading him to the small double bed beneath the window.

There are suddenly too many clothes between us. I slide his shirt up his torso, stopping when he gets the hint and tugs it off himself. I've seen his body before. We swim together and go to the gym, not to mention that Reid *knows* what he looks like and struts around shirtless all the time. But it was pretty dark when we had sex, and I was a little drunk. Right now the lights are on and I am mostly sober. I'm going to look and touch and enjoy every inch that I can.

"I can be quiet," I tell him.

"That's good," he says, amused as I struggle with his belt. "Otherwise my dad will think it's the pipes or something and we'll have an audience of at least one."

"Ugh, no dad talk right now."

I graze a nail over his nipple and he sucks in a breath. "Okay, then my mom. Or Alex—God knows he'd probably pull up a chair and give me pointers—"

"I swear to God I will leave—"

I'm stopped by the grip of his hand on the back of my neck and the press of his smile against mine. His lips are as soft as I remember, but less frantic, more experimental as he takes his time. I shove him down to his back so I can straddle his legs, and he groans into my mouth.

"God, you feel amazing." He chases my bottom lip, sucking a little before pulling away and searching my face. "Are we really doing this again?"

The sound of his zipper lowering cuts through the silence. I guess that's answer enough. We both laugh at the insanity of this entire thing, quietly shushing each other at the sound of Ed's voice floating from downstairs.

"Not really the person I wanted to hear right now," Reid groans, rocking slowly up against me, the hard parts of his body molding perfectly against the soft parts of mine.

"This is vacation sex, right?" I say, breathless as his teeth graze my ear.

"Exactly." He pulls away long enough to lift his hips and help me push his jeans down his legs, before returning to my mouth. "Sex is like calories."

Kiss.

"Doesn't count on vacation."

Kiss.

To be fair, we should probably be giving this more discussion, but Reid's hands seem to be everywhere at once: on my breasts and between my legs, on my lips, my neck, my waist.

His reasoning makes perfect sense.

I'm not sure if it was in his pocket or in a drawer—I don't even want to think about where it came from—but one second there's a condom in his hand, and the next it's on him and he's staring up at me, waiting.

I move so slowly, careful not to call his name or rock the bed; it's almost hard to breathe, like the air is being pushed from my body to make room for his.

I don't want to examine too closely that this is Reid, and that doing this with him is somehow just as easy as doing anything else together. The way he smiles up at me is the same way he always looks at me: like there is nowhere else he'd rather be. There's no awkwardness or tentative touches. It's just us.

His hands map a circuit from my hair to my arms and thighs and everywhere in between. I watch his face, noting when sensation becomes too much and he has to close his eyes and twist his fingers in the comforter. I want to see more, to see him rattled and undone.

"You are," he says, breathless, "the best . . ."

And I shake my head, leaning forward to kiss him. I'm sweating and my muscles shake; I'm so tightly wound that I'm practically burning. I keep my movements small so we don't move the bed too much, but then he makes this quiet sound of relief and I'm not sure I care anymore. I'm so close to that feeling that might overflow and drown us both.

Reid's hands move from my breasts to my hips and he grips me tightly, moving with me. Sweat pools in the hollows of his collarbone, down the center of his chest to where our bodies meet, and I want to stamp the image on the back of my eyelids, frame it, and hang it on every wall in my house. His face is flushed with the exertion of holding back.

I see the exact moment he breaks. His mouth opens on a gasp, on a sound he can't make, and he falls, pulling me down with him.

I wake up alone.

I don't remember when Reid left, but when I think back on everything we did last night, I'm not surprised he needed to go crash in his own bed. The second time, we were . . . *enthusiastic*, to say the least, and I was exhausted by the end of it. My last memory is of falling to pieces with Reid behind me, and I swear I must have just passed out as soon as I returned to orbit. I'm no expert, but I'd call that a success.

Well done, Reid.

It takes some work to sit up and get my feet under me and—oh yeah, everything hurts. The bed doesn't seem to be faring much better: most of the blankets are piled on the floor, a couple of pillows are by the window, and the sheets are barely hanging on.

I have no idea where my underwear might be.

At least my jeans are where I left them, and after a quick stop in the bathroom, I fish my phone out of one of the pockets. There's just enough juice left to show that Cat has messages waiting.

Sheets straightened and pillows and blankets accounted for, I sit on the bed and open the app. I'm honestly surprised when I see one is from Reid; it takes me a minute to calculate when it could have shown up. There wasn't anything when I came upstairs last night, so he would have had to have written it while he waited on the deck (before heading up to have sex with me), in bed while I slept (after having sex with me), or back in his own room (again, after having had sex with me).

My finger hovers over the unopened message. What does it say that Reid still wrote Catherine after deciding to or actually sleeping with me? The point was to get him to like Cat more than Daisy, so am I happy he possibly wrote fake me while sex-drunk naked real me was sleeping in the same house? Maybe the same bed?

But did he write Daisy, too?

Straightening, I stop the mental spiral. Reid isn't a player. At all.

Still, knowing this about him doesn't really make me feel any better; he still slept with me and then left to go write another woman. The fact that I'm upset only compounds the knowledge that this whole alter ego thing is A Big Mistake. Sleeping together again is An Even Bigger Mistake, and will most likely end in a train wreck of mighty proportions.

Okay, okay, all that said, it doesn't make that flashing notification any less interesting, and since I've already screwed things up . . .

I look down at my phone. It's dead.

Unfortunately, my phone cord is in my purse, and my purse is in the kitchen. All the way downstairs.

With a deep breath for bravery, I throw on the pajamas I'd meant to wear last night, grab my dead phone, and tiptoe out of the room.

But the thing about old houses is that they're loud. The heat clanks its way up the ductwork, steel expanding and contracting before being silenced by the hiss of warmed air.

The windows stick, the frames protesting being separated from the sash. The floors creak with every step, particularly when you're trying to be quiet.

I've spent enough weekends here to know which boards squeak, and which steps to avoid, but Bailey, the Campbell family's schnauzer, is clearly not up to speed on the Sneaking Around plan. I manage to tiptoe past a row of closed doors and make it as far as the landing before Bailey comes barreling down the hall, almost knocking us both down the stairs.

We end up at the bottom a lot faster and a whole lot noisier than I'd intended, but when I strain to listen, I don't hear a thing. No footsteps or voices, just the faintest sounds of snores from upstairs.

Sweet.

My purse is where I left it, and rather than risk Bailey and the creaky stairs again, I pull out a chair, plug in my phone, and quietly settle in at the dining room table.

It takes a moment for the screen to come to life, but when it does, the notification is still there, waiting. I take a quick look around like I'm about to commit a crime, and open Reid's message.

From: Reid C.
Sent: 3:14 am, April 1

It's late right now, too late—or too early—I'm sure, to
be writing, but I really couldn't sleep, and I wanted
to thank you for your lovely message. First of all,
your dad sounds like an amazing guy, I'd love to
hear more about him. And I hope this doesn't show
too much of what a terrible human I am, but I hope
that Tessa is waitressing in a polluted truck stop
somewhere now.

You're right about parents surprising us. Back
when my parents were newly married, there
weren't many houses nearby. Coming here was
the first time my city-slicker mom had ever lived
in what she considered to be country, and she
was completely out of her element. She's nothing
like that now, but Dad likes to tell stories of her
screeching at the sound of a coyote, or running at
the sight of a raccoon near the garbage bins. She
also knew that accidents happened on farms all
the time—my dad lost his arm here when he was
a teenager—and so she worried about having two
small children at home, and us being so far away
from a hospital. When my sister was still just a baby,
Mom would have me do these drills to prepare
for an emergency. What would I do if Rayme got
bitten by a spider? What if she fell down the steep
stairs? What would I do if I didn't know where Mom

was? Of course, "I would find the candy bars you hide in the cupboard and eat them before you came back" wasn't what she was looking for, so we memorized my dad's cell phone number together, and practiced calling 911.

Even then I thought it was silly, but one day I found Rayme on the floor, and her lips were purple. I ran to my mom in a panic. In the calmest voice she's ever used, she told me it was okay. She called 911 and turned Rayme over on her lap, carefully hitting her between the shoulder blades and softly telling her to come on, breathe.

Turns out, Rayme had swallowed one of my Legos, and only once it was out and Rayme was crying again did my mom burst into tears. I must have been nine at the time, but I never looked at my mom the same way again.

That was a much longer story than I'd intended, but being here, with my parents and my friends, I'm glad I remembered that. I feel like I've been giving Mom sort of a hard time lately, and maybe I needed to remember how badass she was when I was little.

Speaking of my friends, I can't tell you what it's like being here with them again. I think it's easy to become complacent and maybe forget how important people are to you. I'm not sure if I gave

you Millie's name or not but we've been hanging out
a lot and . . . she's the most amazing and confusing
person I've ever known. It's late now, but maybe
I can tell you about her next time. Thanks for
listening, C, and I hope you have a great end to
your weekend.

R.

I sit back in my chair. I don't even know what to call
this emotion in my chest. Fondness melted with anger and
hurt. This wasn't just a quick note after he was with me.
This is a *letter*.

I bend, cupping my forehead. How much leeway do I
get here to be mad? On the one hand, we'd just had sex—
twice—and then he left to go write another woman. On the
other hand, *I* am that woman, and am lying to him every
time I pretend I'm not. Neither of us is innocent here, but
at least *I'm* only sleeping with Reid and writing Reid. He's
sleeping with me and writing two other—!

I scroll back through his message again, zooming in.

"Uh, what are you doing?"

I swallow a scream when I turn and see Ed standing
over me with a leftover rib in his hand. His eyes are glued
to my screen.

"Working!" I shove the phone into my pocket, hoping he doesn't notice the way the cord is stretched taut between me and the wall. I rest a casual elbow on the table and absently twist a piece of my hair. "I just needed to get my laptop."

Ed makes Disappointed Seth Rogen Face at me. "So where is it?"

"Where's what?"

Frowning, I track him as he walks to where my laptop bag is still hanging by the door, and back as he sets it on the table. God damn it.

Ed pulls out the chair next to me and sits. He takes a bite of rib, chews, swallows, thinks. "It's funny because it *looks like* you're pretending to be Catherine, and it *sounds like* you had sex with Reid last night."

I bark out a laugh that echoes in the empty kitchen. "*What!* That's insane! How much did you have to drink?"

I stand and move to step around him, only to be stopped short by the cord jerking me backward.

"Mills," he says, "I'm in the room next to yours, and in case you haven't noticed, the walls are pretty thin. I heard all about some 'spot' you wanted him to 'keep hitting.' I hope you both refreshed with electrolytes afterward, because"—he whistles—"*wow.*"

"I . . ." My eyes dart around the kitchen, hoping the

correct response will materialize on one of the community flyers on the fridge. "Okay, there's a good explanation for all that."

Ed scoots back, propping his feet on the edge of the table. "I'm ready when you are."

Defeat and panic make me insane. I grab Ed by the shoulders. "Don't tell him I'm Catherine," I say in a burst. "If he finds out . . . I . . ." I shake my head and start again, "He . . ."

To his credit, Ed doesn't seem to be taking much joy from my mortification. He sits up and holds his hands out in front of him. "What were you thinking? That you didn't want him to like Daisy?"

"Yes?"

"But you wanted him to like Catherine?"

I nod emphatically. I know the answer to this one. "Yes."

"But there *isn't* a Catherine."

"No. I mean, yes. It's my middle name . . ."

Ed rolls his eyes. "Well in that case, it's totally okay. So what happens if he does like Catherine? Won't he eventually want to meet her? I mean, you? Since *you're* Catherine."

I glance back over his shoulder and hiss, "*Can you stop saying Catherine so many times?*"

He glares at me. "Do you like him?"

"Reid? What? *No.*" I double down on this answer, even though it feels a lot like lying. "Not like *that.*"

"I love how offended you look, considering what I had to listen to last night." He stands and walks to the fridge, opening the door and pulling out a beer. "I am not drunk enough for this yet."

"Ed, it's like seven in the morning."

He wheels on me. "*I will not be judged by you!*"

Holding up my hands in defense, I tell him through a laugh, "Fine, sorry, sorry."

He cracks the bottle open and returns to his seat. "Now you. Out with it."

"Okay." Deep breath. Calm down. "I started an account because you guys gave me shit about how boring mine was, and also I was getting matched with a lot of assholes. But then Reid somehow matched with me—as Cat. I thought he'd figure it out because I made some stupid crack about Monopoly. And *Girls Trip*. And cats. But he *didn't!*"

I wait.

Ed blinks. "You are not blaming Reid here for being too dumb to know he's talking to you online."

Yes. "*No.*" I groan, dropping my head to my arms on the table. "When you guys started talking about how Catherine must be ugly, I guess I got a little competitive."

"Well, at least it sounds like you had a proportionate response. What could possibly go wrong?"

"Shut up. I know."

"We were all doing this together," he says. "Am I the only person taking this dating plan seriously?"

When I sit up again, he's looking at me with Sad Ed eyes, and I can barely stand it. "I'm taking it seriously. I promise. It just . . ." I flounder. "Once I started being Cat it felt—I don't know—easier to be more open? Is that weird?"

"Not really," he admits. "I think I get why you'd want to keep it to yourself. But . . . it's Reid. You know? You're lying to *Reid*. That's like lying to your dad or something."

"No, Ed, it's nothing like that. Please don't put Reid and dads—"

"It's bad, is what I'm saying."

"I know how bad it is," I hiss, and the truth rolls out of me without warning, "but it's also sort of nice."

He tilts his head down, staring up at me through thick eyebrows. "It's 'nice'?"

I feel my cheeks heat. My explanation comes out meek: "I like being able to talk to Reid like this. Is that terrible?"

Ed stares at me with gentle pity. "You are a mess, you know this, right?"

I sit up. "You won't tell him, will you?"

I can't even fathom what I'd do if Reid found out. Am I

in too deep? I mean . . . it doesn't feel like a runaway train yet. It feels like we're getting to know each other, like a sweet entrée into . . . a different place for us. But the idea of Ed saying something to Reid before I can figure out how to fix this so thoroughly nauseates me that it chases away any residual hurt-anger that Reid left my bed to go write Cat. I am, without a doubt, the bad guy here.

Ed runs a hand through his hair and looks around the room. "I won't say anything. But this kind of thing is sort of hard to juggle, Mills."

chapter ten

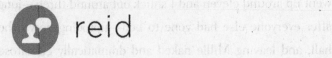 reid

Millie has to walk past my bedroom to get to the stairs, and I hear her passing by around seven in the morning. I know it's her because I hear her shushing Bailey and cleverly avoiding the squeakiest spots in the hallway—something Alex and Ed would never think to do.

It's hot—Mom habitually overheats the house—too hot to stay under the covers, even too hot to stay in my own skin with the cacophony of thoughts skidding around inside my head after last night with Millie.

Once was a fun accident.

Twice is two data points, and my brain scratches around trying to find a pattern.

Both times we were hanging out with friends.

Both times there was alcohol—although neither of us was drunk last night.

Both times there was—what? Mention of dates, other people, or the lack of partners in our lives?

And last night wasn't even a single quickie, in and out, back to our respective rooms. It was a *night together*. We went up around eleven and I snuck out around three—long after everyone else had gone to bed—tiptoeing down the hall, and leaving Millie naked and dramatically comatose on her bed as if a storm had blown through.

Was leaving a bad idea? Or would it have been awkward to wake up in bed together? Especially if we had to explain it to anyone else. I feel faintly nauseous, like this could go very bad very quickly. I know conversations about relationships and feelings aren't in Millie's wheelhouse, but in this case I feel like we need to have one.

Downstairs, only Millie and Ed are up. I heard the murmur of voices, but they've since moved to the back patio, and when I join them I wish I could say I'm surprised to find Ed with a beer in his hand at seven thirty in the morning, but I'm not. Millie is staring out at the vineyards. Ed is so intensely engrossed in Dad's morning delivery of the *New York Times* that he doesn't even look up when I step out onto the back patio.

"Mills," I say.

She turns her face to me, giving me a bright smile. "Morning, sunshine!"

I draw back reflexively, jarred. The greeting is too loud, too over-the-top. Especially considering that the last real sound I heard her make was a long, relieved exhale before she passed out face-first into the mattress.

Her eyes flicker over to Ed, and then back to me. "What's up?"

"Wanna go for a walk?" I ask, lifting my chin to indicate the tidy rows of vineyards that seem to stretch for an eternity.

She looks down at her bare feet, thinking it over for a few seconds, and then hops up. "Sure!" Again, too loud. "Just a sec. I'll throw on some shoes."

Ed still hasn't looked up at me, and I bend, trying to catch his eye. "Hey, Ed."

Eyes down, brow furrowed in deep concentration, he says a gruff "Hey."

"Thirsty?" I ask, nodding to his beer. "Coffee wasn't cutting it?"

"Uh-yup." Very seriously, he turns the page of the newspaper, reaching the crossword puzzle and folding it up like he might actually start doing it.

"Don't." I hold my hand out. "My dad would murder you. He waits all week for the Sunday puzzle."

217

Ed unfolds the paper and, instead of making conversation, starts reading an article on some new graffiti artist in Queens.

"What's with you?" I sit at the edge of the chaise longue where Millie was lying before I came out. "Both of you, actually. She's Merry Sunshine and you're Very Monosyllabic."

"Nothing." He glances up at me, and then away. "Seriously, just . . . readin' the paper. Relaxin'. Drinkin' some beer."

"Okay then, Pauly Shore, keep on with your relaxin' and drinkin'."

Millie comes out and smiles more calmly at me this time, and I'm relieved Ed is acting so off it isn't even weird for us to not invite him along with us.

I let her lead me down the back porch and through Mom's garden, which transitions to vineyard after about thirty feet, allowing us to practically disappear into the foliage and the fog. But although we aren't in view of the house any longer, the silence doesn't immediately vanish.

After a minute or so of listening only to our footsteps tromping through dried leaves and soil, I say, "So, hey."

Beside me, she laughs knowingly. "Yeah. Hey." She glances at me. "I'm so sorry, Reid."

This draws me up short emotionally; it's an effort to keep my pace walking. "You're *sorry*?"

She stops, turning to grin guiltily up at me. "I don't know what gets into me sometimes."

There's an obvious joke to make there, but I ignore it, in part because I'm immediately irked by her flippant tone. "You didn't exactly have to drag me upstairs last night, you know. Clearly you were going somewhere I was willing to go as well."

"But should we go there?" she asks, wincing. "I mean, you're talking to all these women online and at some point that will turn into something and we'll need to stop anyway."

I pull us farther back in her sentence, hung up on the phrasing. "'All these women'?"

She shrugs, and I swear there's a weird curl to it, something defensive beneath her nonchalant exterior. "Yeah."

"There are *two*."

"Well, both Daisy and Catherine seem sort of serious, right?"

Is she digging?

"How serious can it be if I've never met them in person?"

"You seem, I don't know. *Invested*. That's all I'm saying. You're writing them frequently, right? And recently?"

I nod carefully and she continues, "I don't want to put a wrinkle in that with our . . . friends-with-benefits thing."

I study her face as she squints out into the vineyard, trying to read between the lines here. A twist of guilt works its way through my torso, and I'm immeasurably glad that she doesn't know I wrote Cat after leaving her bed last night. If she did, I'm sure a simple "I couldn't sleep" explanation wouldn't cut it.

"Do you," I begin, unsure of what I want her answer to be, "want me to *stop* . . . talking to these other women?"

"I mean, only if *you* want to."

"To be fair, you have someone you're calling 'my guy,'" I remind her.

She doesn't move. "Yeah."

I laugh, feeling my chest start to tighten with unexpected disappointment. Last night was fun. Something new and a little scary is expanding in my chest, and it's hooked to the memory of Millie above me, her eyes closed, neck arched. If she'd asked me to stay, would I have? "I have no idea what is going on right now, Mills."

"Nothing is going on." She says it more calmly, back in control. She returns her focus to me and puts a warm hand on my arm. "Really, Reid. At least, not with me. I'm good."

Without asking me anything in return, she pushes on ahead, her pace picking up. A flock of sparrows pass overhead, and she looks up to the sky. "Man, it is so beautiful out here."

With that, the conversation about last night seems left behind us and I feel . . . slightly untethered.

"It really is," I say quietly.

Millie starts talking about the weather, which leads into a story about this time she was hiking with a friend in Yosemite and her friend almost died trying to take a picture of a sign that described the risk of death on the trail. I listen, hopefully making noises at the appropriate moments to let her know that I'm still paying attention, but inside I'm sort of shredded. The truth is, I'm curious whether I'll have better in-person chemistry with Daisy than I do over messages, and I'm interested in the possibility that I'll have just as good chemistry with Catherine in person as I do over messages. But after last night, I think my heart got ahead of my brain a little. If the twist in my chest is any indication, I *think* I wanted things with *Millie* to grow deeper.

Watching her in superficial storytelling mode, I honestly begin to wonder whether she's capable of that. As a friend, she's fun, and loyal, observant, and thoughtful. Her quiet depth comes out as humor, and reveals how unbelievably brilliant she is. She's wild in the best ways while still keeping her life drama-free—all great things in a friend. But I don't want a buddy for a lover—I want a lover who goes deeper than Millie ever seems to want to go, and the realization that this isn't ever going to evolve makes me oddly—surprisingly—sad. Odd, that is, given that until this morning, it wasn't even a conscious goal to get us there.

She stops, staring out at the rolling hills, and I give it one last chance. "Tell me about this guy you're talking to."

Blinking over to me, she gives me an easy grin. "Maybe there's more than one."

Ouch. "Okay, then, tell me about the one you're calling 'my guy.'"

Millie takes a deep breath, pulling her shoulders up to her ears. "He's pretty great. You know how you just get a good vibe from someone in writing?"

I nod. I know exactly what she means. Cat's black-and-white profile photo swims through my thoughts.

"He's funny and . . . open about things," she says carefully, and that part stabs a bolt of pain through me because, honestly, I'd be more open with her in person if she ever took the bait and engaged in that kind of conversation with me. It's depressing to realize that the last time we talked about anything very deep was at the beach, nearly two years ago, after she left Dustin, and told me in simple, bare terms how hard he was to live with. But after a few minutes, she went quiet and then started talking about how much she loves watching the waves crash on the surf.

"Are you going to meet him?" I ask.

"It's weird because I feel like I know him already," she says, still not looking at me. "What if I do? What if we know each other from somewhere? Would that be awkward? I think so. So, part of me is like, 'Yeah! Let's set up a date!' and part of me is like, 'Um, that's the worst idea ever.'"

"But you haven't *really* met him," I say. "I mean, wouldn't you know if you had? What's his name?"

She waves a hand. "Just . . . Guy."

"His name is Guy?" I stare at her, my smile slowly breaking wide. "You're going to go from dating a Dustin to dating a *Guy*?"

"Maybe it's not his real name," she says, flustered. "Who knows. Maybe it's Dougal or Alfred, and Guy is just a nickname."

"You're so weird," I say, pinching her cheek.

She looks up at me, glowing in obvious relief. "*You* are."

Mom has made her famous lemon-ricotta pancakes by the time we get back, and Millie and I fall into our chairs at the table with a sort of desperate, haven't-eaten-in-ten-years vigor. Breakfast is a loud, mimosa-filled affair, with a sticky syrup bottle winding its way up and down the table, a giant bowl of fat berries with cream passed from hand to hand, and a huge platter of bacon slowly emptying until we are all groaning, hands clutched over our too-full stomachs.

Alex eyes the couch in the other room like he's desperate for it to sprout legs and walk in here to pick him up, but before he can muster the energy to go there, Dad stands, shuffles to the couch, and falls onto it. Rayme works up the nerve to lean against Chris's shoulder, and I watch it happen in slow motion—from the decision she seems to make as she leans to her left and the gradual tilting until she makes contact with him. Chris may finally be aware of her: his eyes go very wide, and he goes very, very still.

Ed, to my surprise, stands and begins clearing everyone's plates before starting the dishes in the kitchen. Mom watches him go with something like fondness in her eyes. Apparently no one ended up naked in the vineyards last night, and Ed has figured out how to please my parents: simply by keeping his pants on.

I feel the soft pressure of a foot over mine, and look across the table at Millie, whose eyes are closed and whose head is tilted back, relaxing after what was, without hyperbole, the best breakfast ever cooked. It seems like an accident at first, but then she nestles her feet more firmly against mine, like she's trying to get warm. Opening one eye, she peeks at me, stifling a grin, and then feigns sleep again.

An ache—*desire*—is tempered with a flush of irritation. I don't want to be the safe friend she can touch and flirt with if she's only going to erect a new boundary every time something intimate happens. No matter what she or I have said before, we're in a weird limbo, and we need to get the fuck out of here as soon as possible, or risk ruining what is without question one of the best friendships of my life.

Breaking Mom's house rule, I pull my phone from my pocket, and open the IRL app at the table. I'm a little disappointed to see that Cat hasn't written back . . . but at least Daisy has.

From: Daisy D.
Sent: 10:29 am, April 1

Hey Reid,

I hope you're having an awesome time at home! My weekend ended up being pretty dull—a friend who was supposed to be in town flaked last minute, so I've basically been in my pajamas all weekend, bingeing old seasons of *Big Brother*.

I'm not sure what you're up to this week, but do you think you'd be willing to meet in person? For dinner? See! I remembered you don't do first dates over coffee or drinks. I sort of like that a lot about you.

Let me know if you're up for it.

Talk soon,
Daisy

I glance up at Millie, who is still resting with her eyes closed. It's time to push past this uneasiness in my gut and just . . . get out of this weird friend-lover zone with Mills.

Gently pulling my feet out from under hers, I sit up a little straighter, opening our text box. She sits up, too, looking groggy as I type out a message to her.

> Sleepy?

When her phone vibrates in her back pocket, she leans to the side to pull it out. I watch her read my text, and grin as she replies.

> Someone kept me up late.

I wipe a hand down my face. Enough with these mixed messages.

> I just got a note from Daisy.

> She wants to go out.

I watch Millie absorb this and nothing in her expression shifts—not a single muscle.

> Are you going to?

> > Would it be weird?

> For me, or for you?

> > For you.

Her eyes meet mine over the table, and she gives me a tiny frown before looking at her phone, typing.

> I told you, Reid, I'm fine.

I'm beginning to hate the word *fine*.

> > Cool.

If Millie is okay with this, then I'll just have to work on being okay with it, too.

I pocket my phone and stand, following Ed into the kitchen to help him clean up. He frowns as he slides the plates into the sink to begin rinsing them, and his weird silent treatment is starting to annoy me.

"What's with you?"

Startling, he looks over his shoulder at me. "Nothing. Just full."

"Of beer and pancakes?"

Finally, he gives me a real smile. "And mimosas and bacon."

We start to work in tandem as I bring in dishes and he rinses them and slides them into the dishwasher.

"Everything okay with you and Mills?" he asks.

"Yeah, we're good. Just catching each other up on the dating stuff."

Ed looks at me with interest. "Yeah?"

"Did you know the guy she's talking to is named Guy?" I laugh. "Is that even a real name?"

His expression droops strangely. "Huh. No, I didn't know that."

"What about you?" I ask. "How's sexy Selma?"

"She hasn't responded yet." He pushes his sleeves up and digs his hands into soapy water. "I asked her to meet, and she never replied. Usually she responds within a couple hours."

A feeling like heavy clouds rolling in passes through me. I want this experiment to go well for Ed, and if he's chatting with someone who is dishonest, or vanishes without explanation, I'm going to be pissed.

"Maybe she's just swamped at work," I offer.

"She's a bartender."

Yeah, I've got nothing.

I look up, relieved to see Chris coming in, carrying the mostly empty platter of bacon. "I think I might die of pork overdose," he says.

"What about you?" I ask him, then give him more context. "You're being extremely tight-lipped about your dating adventures."

He slides the platter onto the counter, then leans back. "I don't know, man. I know it's working for you, but it might not be my vibe."

"You could just ask Rayme out," Ed says without turning away from the sink.

A heavy curtain of silence falls, and Chris's eyes meet mine. Instead of looking away, he holds my gaze as if he's reading me. When I met Chris, he was married to Amalia; they divorced a couple of years later. I've seen him with a few women since then, but he's never been particularly effusive when it comes to sharing details about his love life. So it takes me a few beats to register that he's reading my reaction to see whether I'm horrified by what Ed has said. Strangely, I am not.

"You could, you know," I tell him quietly.

Chris scowls, but I know him well enough to know he's covering. "Man, she was fifteen when I met you."

I shrug. "Yeah. *Ten years ago.*"

He opens his mouth to reply, but is cut off by the appearance of Rayme and Mills next to him.

"What was ten years ago?" Rayme asks.

"Nothing," I say, too quickly, sounding extremely suspicious.

Millie slides her knowing eyes around the room, landing eventually on me. "What's going on, weirdos?"

"They were talking about us," Rayme guesses in a dramatic stage whisper, and the two of them turn and saunter out of the room.

This has all become officially too much for me. It feels like we're in a van, teetering atop a cliff. If we lean one way, we slide back to safety. If we lean the other way, we catapult headfirst into a canyon.

The problem is, I have no idea which direction to lean to get us safely to the ground.

chapter eleven

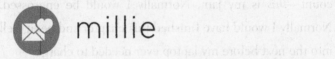 millie

I f you were a murderer in the nineteenth century, it's likely that poison—most commonly arsenic—was your weapon of choice. Used for everything from killing rats to removing hair and controlling insects, arsenic was cheap, easy to acquire, and kept in abundance in most Victorian homes. If you were a desperate woman with an abusive or rich husband you'd like to kill, arsenic was a relatively easy way to do it.

As you might have guessed, the section of manuscript I'm working on—and that I should have finished hours ago—is about poison. More specifically, it's about women throughout history who've been tried for using it. Nannie Doss—dubbed the Giggling Granny—murdered husband after husband, and always wore a smile, even after admitting to killing four of them. Anna Marie Hahn lured rich, elderly men to their deaths, though not before taking them for everything they had. Blanche Taylor Moore's life was a scandal of dead family and husbands and extramarital affairs, and even inspired a made-for-television movie.

Mayhem, calculated murder, history, and a body count—*this* is my jam. Normally I would be engrossed. Normally I would have finished this chapter and been well into the next before my laptop ever needed to charge.

But today, nearly a week after Reid and I had sex (again), I have the attention span of a teaspoon. It doesn't take a genius to understand why.

Since I love torturing myself, I pick up my phone and reread my texts with Reid.

> Dinner tonight? I was thinking pizza and gossip about Chris and your sister . . .

Nothing tickles me like hassling him, but he didn't take the bait.

You are way too easy.

Pepperoni sound good? We'll
fancy it up with the two bottles
of wine your mom gave me.

Correction: the two bottles
my mom caught Ed putting
in your purse.

Details. Should I text everyone
and order?

It's been fifteen minutes and Reid has yet to reply, but just as I'm about to put my phone down, a new one comes in:

Actually I can't.
The date's tonight.

Date?

Did we make plans I'd forgotten about—

Then it hits me.

Daisy.

He's referring to the date he'd texted me about, when I had promptly lied through my teeth, or through my fingers.

So Reid is going on a date. But I'm fine.

I can't think or concentrate for more than ten consecutive minutes, but it's cool.

Emotions are live wires, and mine are DOA.

If things go well, they could have sex tonight.

I'm definitely not fine.

Gathering my things, I push away from the table and carry it all outside, in desperate need of some air.

I don't have a huge yard—this *is* California, after all—but it's lush and shaded during the summer months, and full of golden colors in the fall. A full-grown ginkgo blots out most of the fading sun, leaving just enough spikes of sky visible where there will soon be stars. Its branches creak overhead and I take a seat on the patio swing, using one foot to gently rock in time with the breeze.

It's cooler out than I expected, but the overcast weather seems appropriate considering my mood. Reid is going on a date and I'm here, just like I am every night and will be every night in the future because I'm doing nothing to change it. What does it say about me that rather than looking at my own profile, I want to look at Catherine's? What does it say that I want to write him, even now? In the slim hope he might read it during his date and possibly think about me. Er . . . *Catherine*.

The swing squeaks, a gentle reminder of when Reid

helped me hang it. Dustin and I had just broken up, and I'd mentioned needing an extra set of hands. Reid volunteered before it had even occurred to me to ask. He helped lay the pavers that wind their way to the garage and replaced the smoke detector after an unfortunate Thanksgiving incident. And when I wanted to release a paper lantern on New Year's Eve—somehow setting the fringe of my scarf aflame in the process—he was there to put out that fire, too.

But if things go well with Daisy . . . will he still be?

I glower at my laptop and don't bother listening to the tiny professional voice in my head—it's immediately over-shadowed by the possessive one telling me to ignore the manuscript I'm supposed to be working on and open up the IRL app to reply to his last letter.

From: Catherine M.
Sent: 6:48 pm, April 6

Reid,

Wow this is becoming a regular occurrence. Do we officially qualify as pen pals now? I'd always wanted one when I was a kid, but never went anywhere or did anything—what would I possibly have to say?

Thank you for your last letter. It was so honest and sincere, and I want to tell you how much it meant that you shared it with me. Do me a favor and give your mom a big hug when you see her next. She won't know exactly why, but something tells me it will make her day. Fingers crossed that there was no late-night streaking in the vineyard.

So, as pen pals we're supposed to be honest and tell each other things we might not otherwise say, right? I know the goal here is to find people we like. I like you, Reid. I know that means that I should put my best foot forward, but I'm in an odd mood and I seem to have lost my filter. Besides, wouldn't it be better to be brutally honest? I feel like we meet people in life and want so much for them to like us that we suck in our stomachs and pretend we don't fart and tell them a bunch of things we think they want to know. If it works they fall for the person we want to be, and not for the person we are.

So in the interest of honesty: My dad is sick. He's sick and I haven't told anyone because I'm sad enough about it without making everyone else around me miserable, too. Isn't that insane? I have the most kind and understanding friends in the world, all of whom would do anything to help, and I've kept this from them because I don't want to be a drag.

Which leads me to my next bout of emotional diarrhea (and if you write me back I promise not to ever use that term again). I'm lonely. I'm lonely because I don't tell people what I need or what I want, and then get hurt when they don't figure it out on their own.

Is it possible to be a highly functioning adult with a successful career, awesome friends and a lovely family, and still be a Level Five Hot Mess? I may be living proof.

And because I can't leave with the phrase "emotional diarrhea" this close to the end (okay, NOW I'll never use that term again), here's an embarrassing little tidbit about myself to cap off this dumpster fire of a reply. When I was sixteen, I had such a crush on a guy named Leslie. Rather than—I don't know—actually talk to him, I came up with elaborate reasons to pass his locker at least six times a day, and would covertly just happen to show up wherever he was going to be.

One weekend in October, I heard a bunch of his friends were going to the local corn maze and haunted house. I love all things scary, but for some reason can't stand the idea of ghosts. Still, my lust for this boy had clearly clouded my judgment because I threw together a costume and dragged my best friend along with me.

Everything was fine at first, I managed to make tit halfway through the attraction without peeing my pants or otherwise embarrassing myself, but I still hadn't seen him. Unfortunately, my best friend had, and she wanted to make sure he saw me. Her brilliant plan involved telling one of the workers that it was okay to scare me and grab me from behind. I'm sure in her head I would scream in this really adorable way, Leslie would see me, and we would slip off to make out and probably end up engaged. What happened was slightly different.

The guy did grab me, and I definitely screamed, but while attempting to flee, I ran into a faux-serial killer with a prop chainsaw and somehow managed to slice my left shoulder open pretty bad. SIX STITCHES. Leslie did see me, but covered in my own blood and only as I was being carried out on a stretcher.

Funnily enough he stopped by my house a few days later, and we did actually make out.

He was a terrible kisser.

C.

My Uber drops me off a few buildings down from the Sandbar.

With a giant smile, I walk to where Ed is waiting.

Strangely, after sending that insane note to Reid, I feel better. Maybe the best strategy here is to scare him off Catherine with boatloads of honesty, and hope that Daisy is a dud . . . oh, and also figure out my own shit.

Like, what does my jealousy mean, and are these spasms in my stomach what most normal people describe as love? Or is it the Indian food I had for lunch staging a mild gastrointestinal coup?

"Your smile is weird," Ed says when I reach him. "Like you're farting."

"Trying not to."

He rolls with this easily. I love Ed. "Do you want to sit inside or outside?" He points to my stomach. "Maybe outside, better air circulation?"

Downtown Santa Barbara is lively this time of night, with bars and restaurants that line the sidewalks, and brightly lit patios with seating that spills out toward the street.

Although the inside looks warm and inviting, with pin-tucked leather stools and a wide-open bar, it's quieter on the patio. Plus, he's not wrong about the ventilation. I'm still not sure what to name this feeling in my belly.

"Three for outside," Ed tells the hostess. It takes my brain a moment to catch what he's said.

"Wait. Three?"

Like a hot Latin Dementor, Alex materializes at his side.

I turn on Ed. "You brought Alex? I told you I needed to *talk*."

Alex snags a chip off the tray of a passing waiter and pops it into his mouth, talking around it. "Why would you need to talk to *Ed*?"

I frown at Ed. "Never mind. It's nothing."

Ed gives him a conspiratorial tap on the arm to get his attention. "Because she's Catherine," he whispers, and then leans in, adding, "Oh, and she and Reid are sleeping together."

Thunder booms inside my skull. "Oh my God! Ed!"

"What? You said I couldn't tell Reid," he says. "You can't expect me to keep something like that to myself. It's bad for my skin."

Alex's eyes go wide. "I'm sorry, what the fuck did you just say?"

I'm saved from having to respond when a pretty waitress appears to lead us to the patio. Because both Alex and I are locked in place, Ed gives us each a shove and we reluctantly follow.

She takes us to a round table with a low, flickering fire in the center, and hands us our menus before leaving. An awkward silence settles between us as Alex is probably attempting to wrap his head around what he's just heard, and I file through my vast bank of knowledge to narrow down how to most efficiently murder Ed. Arsenic seems like a good choice.

"So . . ." Ed says, casually perusing his menu. "How is everyone?"

Alex stares blankly at the paper in his hand. "I don't even know where to start."

I couldn't agree more. "That makes two of us."

"I heard the entire thing through a paper-thin wall, so if you'd like I can start there," Ed tells him. "Perhaps a dramatic reenactment?"

I wouldn't have thought it was possible, but Alex's eyes widen further, and I see the moment he puts two and two together. "At his *parents'* house?"

I sink into my chair.

Across from me, Alex calls back the waitress and gestures to the rest of us at the table. "Yeah, we're gonna need some *drinks.*"

If you want to get as drunk as possible for around twenty dollars, a Blackout Beach is a pretty fancy way to do it.

After loosely explaining the situation to Alex, I look at

him over the top of my giant drink—a potent concoction of vodka, rum, blue curaçao, peach schnapps, *and* a shot of 151, served in what can only be described as a fishbowl. I'd bet money no good decision was ever made while holding a drink this size.

"So you're the ugly girl," Alex says, and I debate whether I would feel better drinking the final third of my Blackout Beach or throwing it in his lap.

"It is not an *ugly* photo," I say, and settle on throwing a tortilla chip at him instead. "What was I supposed to do? I can't actually show my face."

Alex vaguely motions to the general vicinity of my boobs. "You could show your—"

Ed cuts him off, reaching to cover Alex's mouth. "Even I know you should stop talking."

Alex pushes him away. "Let me get this straight. You're writing to him as Catherine, but having sex with him as Millie?"

"Yes. But we're not *having* sex," I say. "We just *had* sex."

"Okay, so just the once, then," he clarifies. "I mean, that's different."

"Well . . ." I say, taking a long pull on my straw while I pretend to think. It tastes like candy gasoline. "Maybe twice."

Alex leans back in his chair, arms folded across his chest. "Maybe?"

I sigh. "Fine. Twice."

"So far," Alex suggests, and Ed takes a break from shoveling in chips and salsa by the handful to bark out a laugh.

I glare at them both. "There's no *so far* about it. It was a weird little accident. It won't happen again."

Alex laughs now and his eyes are devilishly bright in the light from the fire. "Do you know what an accident is, Mills? Spilling a glass of water is an accident. Cutting someone off in traffic—that can be an accident. As much as I would personally enjoy using it as an excuse, I don't know how person one would *accidentally* put their penis into person two."

"Well, theoretically, depending on the circumstances, the angle of your fall, and the velocity—" Ed stops and looks around the table. "Carry on."

Alex clears his throat before turning his attention back to me. "Not even getting into the fact that you confided in *Ed* about this and not me. Does Chris know?"

"Hell no, Chris doesn't. And I didn't *confide* in anyone." I poke at my drink with the straw, glaring at Ed. "I only admitted it to him because he basically caught me."

"And let me tell you," Ed says, straightening, "I don't think the amount of insulation they have in those walls is up to code. I might as well have been in the same room for the things I heard. I almost took a shower myself."

"If you don't plan on doing it again," Alex begins, "then why are we here? Why did you need to talk to Ed? I mean, I'm surprised to hear about the Catherine thing, but not really the rest. You and Reid are . . . different with each other. I'm frankly surprised you haven't banged long before now."

Ed narrows his eyes, and I swear it's like watching a cartoon lightbulb go on above his head. I'm already wincing when he says, "He's out with Daisy, isn't he?"

I push my drink away, unsure whether my stomach can tolerate any more black booze. "He is. But what I wanted to tell you is that I don't think we need to worry about the Catherine thing anymore."

"Why?" Ed asks, shifting when the waitress arrives with our food and another round of drinks.

I gladly trade my Blackout Beach for a water, thanking her before she steps away again. "I did my best to scare him off."

Alex is already shaking his head. "I don't think that's possible."

"Trust me," I say, and unroll my napkin to place it in my lap. "If he hasn't blocked me by tonight, he'll definitely do it by morning. I was sort of having a moment, and did an emotional purge in his inbox."

Ed pauses with a taco halfway to his mouth. "I'd kind of like to see that."

Alex seems to be similarly surprised, and I look at each of them in turn. "See what?"

Ed sets down his food, leaning forward with his elbows on the table. "Come on, Mills. We all know you keep your cards close. It's nothing to be embarrassed about, but it would be cool to know more about what you're thinking, you know? I could always be wrong, but . . . I've known Reid for a long time. If your plan was to scare him off by letting him get to know you—or Catherine—you might want to think of a plan B. Reid is an emotionally intuitive dude. He *likes* feelings."

The problem is that I know, and it's one of the things I love about him. He's sensitive and able to express himself in a way I've never been able to. Reid moving on from Cat would be the easiest conclusion to this mess, but that's sort of the problem. I can't deny how good it felt to unload all that today. It felt good to tell him some more about my past, and how I'm lonely, and how that loneliness is almost entirely my own fault.

"You look like you're going to fart again," Ed says.

Alex wrinkles his nose. "Millie, drop it on the other side of the patio."

"I'm not going to fart, you jackass. I'm thinking about how many chances I've had to tell Reid the truth, and how I'm selfish, and never do."

"Not to oversimplify things," Alex says, "but we're all sort of selfish. *I'm* letting you pay for my dinner—"

"Wha—"

He holds up a hand before I can correct him. "Reid is talking to two women at once, and thinks neither of them knows it. *And* he's having sex with you. Reid is doing just fine." Alex winces a little before this next part: "But if sex with Daisy happens tonight, I'm guessing he'll need to rethink some things."

chapter twelve

 reid

The minute I see Daisy in the restaurant, all coherent thought slips out of my head. Her photos don't lie: even from across the room there's something almost magnetic about her. She's beachy-casual in a sleeveless shirt and skirt; she seems cut from the pages of a catalog. Even so, Daisy shrinks a little under the focused attention of the number of men who turn and watch her while she searches for me. I told her I'd be wearing a blue-checked dress shirt, and I'm relieved to see her eyes light up when she spots me.

I get a slight sour tang in my mouth because as she approaches, I feel that ever-present shadow of Millie in my thoughts—and the sex we had last weekend—and the twin shadow of Cat and the authenticity I find in those messages that I can't honestly find anywhere else.

I'm not a juggler—I've never been a juggler—but the easy attraction and fun I have with Millie seems to crumble when we try to talk about real things. I can't tell if Cat and I would have the same level of chemistry in person, even if our conversations feel infinitely deeper.

And then there's Daisy. Sweet, *beautiful* . . . and right here.

I reach to shake her hand but she embraces me instead, pulling me in for a tight hug. Her breath is warm on my neck, her blond hair tickling across my cheek. "I've been so nervous!"

"Absolutely no need to be nervous." I smile at her as I step back.

"I know." She pulls out her chair. "I guess I'm just so glad you were telling the truth and you're not, like, eighty and *enormous*."

This bounces around inside my cranium. I can only say, "No . . ."

The waiter approaches, and Daisy orders a rosé, I order a scotch, neat, and my stomach slowly climbs into my throat while I wait for all my opening questions to come back into my head. But all I can hear is the mental peanut gallery of Ed protesting Daisy's fat phobia and Alex reminding Ed that Daisy has nice stems, and Chris ignoring all of it. Mental Millie is gone; she must have disappeared as soon as I registered my own relief that Daisy was indeed beautiful.

We start speaking at the same time: "I hope traffic wasn't too bad," I say, just when Daisy says, "I heard this place is *so* good."

And then we do it again. "It is really good," I say, just as she says, "No, it was fine."

"Oh," she says, "go ahead."

I clear my throat awkwardly. "No, no, I was just saying that they do have good food here."

She nods, smiling around at the maritime décor. "Cool." Daisy unrolls her napkin and puts it in her lap. "I used to have a beach theme in my bedroom, like shells and stuff."

"Oh?" I take an enormous gulp of water, cooling down the path from tongue to stomach as it begins to dawn on me that Daisy and I have zero chemistry whatsoever.

"Like, when I was a kid. Some fish nets, shells—I already said that, oh my God—and, like, everything was painted blue. Blue walls, blue bed." She pauses, looking at me like it's my turn to speak. I have no idea what to say. Finally, she adds, "Blue dresser. I wanted to be a mermaid."

"Oh." I nod, smiling as I struggle to shush the part of

my brain that wants to point out that a mermaid probably wouldn't surround herself with nets. Or a dresser. I mean, if mermaids were real. I clear my throat. "I bet that was . . . fun. I had the same boring red comforter from when I was seven until . . . well, it's still in our guest room at home." I try to ease the tension with a joke. "Maybe I wanted to be a fireman."

Okay, that didn't work.

Silence stretches a mile in every direction. Mental Millie returns, lifting up her cocktail for a sardonic toast and letting out a long, throaty laugh. She says saucily, *Oh, I'm* familiar *with that comforter.*

"So." I desperately tread water. "You're a student at UCSB?"

"Early childhood education," she tells me, and then thanks the waitress when our drinks are delivered. "I'm almost finished and will work at the Bellridge Preschool Academy starting in the fall."

I have questions about a "preschool academy" but let them go for now. I mean, at least she seems focused, directed. "You've already got a job lined up?"

Daisy nods. "I know the owner, she's really great. Tons of hot dads there, too," she says, and then laughs.

"Oh . . . that's . . ." I lift my scotch, take a slow sip. "That's good."

Daisy chugs a few gulps of her wine. "I don't know why I said that." She throws her hands in the air. "I'm on a date with you, talking about hot dads."

I wave a hand. "We've all done it."

Daisy laughs again and shakes her arms out. "I haven't been on a first date in a while."

"That's okay—"

"I didn't mention this before, but I broke up with my ex, Brandon, about six weeks ago, and I swear he's probably dating every girl he meets, but I was never like that. I think that was part of what drove him crazy, that he thought I was really social—because we met at a party?—but really I just don't like big crowds, or whatever, and he always wanted to go out and rage. I'm so over that, it feels so undergrad, you know what I mean? We were together for four years though, so."

I dig around in the mental fracas, searching for something to anchor to here so I can craft a decent reply, but Daisy continues before I'm capable. "Anyway, I tried this IRL thing and it's so easy to, like, talk online but then being here in person and you're like—ahh!" She mimics being surprised, with wide eyes and a round mouth. "Like you're so *hot*." She takes a giant gulp of her rosé and then speaks after a rushed swallow, "But also sort of quiet?"

I feel like I've been run over by the train in this wreck,

and it takes me a second to register that this time she really is expecting me to speak. "I'm quiet?"

"Are you? I mean, you seem quiet."

"I'm not usually. Just . . ." I let the thought fade out. I'm floundering. I've never had to put someone at ease so . . . *actively*. I almost want to just tell her maybe we should try this another time.

"Brandon was the talker in our relationship," she says, her face glowing pink. "Or, I mean when we were alone we both talked, but when we were out he did the talking and it was sort of nice. Not that I don't like to talk. I do. I'm just bad at it." She laughs at herself, and then looks helplessly down at the table, maybe like she might find a Xanax there. "Obviously."

"You're not bad at it." Holy shit, I could not sound more disingenuous if I tried. Gesturing to our menus, I ask, "Should we take a minute to figure out what we want to order?"

Daisy looks a little mortified. "Sure."

The two minutes that we peruse the menu in silence are torture. Absolutely the most awkward, loaded two minutes of my life. I can feel the pressure building in Daisy, almost like she's going to explode without conversation happening.

The waitress comes to take our order, and afterward

Daisy immediately excuses herself to use the restroom. I am praying that she's texting a friend to help get her out of this date.

I pull out my phone, texting Chris.

> Zero chemistry.

What?

> With Daisy. I mean, it's immediately clear why she's single.

God, that sounds terrible.

> I just mean—she's incredibly nervous and talking a lot about the ex.

Man seriously? That sucks.

> She's hot. But there's just no vibe at all and she's so nervous it's weird.

> OK gotta go.

I expect her to be right out, but I wait a couple of minutes, then five. Our waitress brings bread, and I absently nibble a slice, waiting.

Another few minutes pass, with no sign of Daisy.

With twitchy fingers, I reach for my phone again. Other than a final message from Chris, a simple Later, there's nothing. No emails. No voicemails. My thumb hovers over the IRL icon.

I open it, drawn to the red 1 beside my inbox.

It's from Catherine.

Slowly and covertly, I scan her latest message. It's long and personal—and a little rambly—but once I finish it, I go back and start again.

It's like word vomit, but even so it's pretty fucking endearing. Am I really this hungry for such bald honesty? Probably a little. I love my friends, but sometimes feel like we don't go very deep, and whenever I read a message from Catherine, I feel like I'm gulping down water, or shoveling chips in my mouth. I devour it.

"Reid?"

I look up, and the schmoopy grin on my face cracks, fading. I've been sitting here reading a message from one woman, on what I'm pretty sure is visible as the app where I met *this* woman, and I have no idea how long she's been standing at the side of the table.

With her purse slung over her shoulder.

Quickly, I stand, too. "Daisy. Are you okay?"

She shakes her head. "I'm not feeling great. I think I just got myself so nervous about tonight."

I look for the lie, but don't find it. Anyway, if she wanted to lie she probably would have said her friend needs an emergency pickup, or her dog had a seizure.

"What can I do to help you feel less anxious?" I ask her, and I can't tell if the urge to calm her is because I was busted reading a message from Catherine, or because she looks so genuinely vulnerable. "I get it, I do. I've been out of the game for a while, too. But I'm the same guy you've been talking to online."

"You're the same guy who's been talking to a lot of women, I guess." She nods to the phone still clutched in my hand.

"Aren't we all?" I ask her, gently. "I mean, we're all on these apps . . . dating . . . But I'm sorry. *That*—checking my phone—wasn't a very cool thing to do while you were in the bathroom."

"No, it's fine. I was gone for a while."

"It's okay—"

"I think maybe I'm not ready." She takes a step toward me, like she might hug me again, and I can almost see the thought process pass over her face, how she started the date with a hug, and it went south so quickly, and she really doesn't want to do that again. Daisy stretches out her hand to shake.

"I'm here if you change your mind," I say, releasing her hand.

But as she turns to walk out of the restaurant, I know it's not really true.

I don't get up and leave right away. In part because I feel like I have to linger after she leaves in case she's sitting in her car freaking out, and in part because I'm actually super hungry and the chicken piccata sounded fucking awesome. In the end, I eat my dinner alone, ignoring the questioning glances from my fellow diners because there are two dinners in front of me. When I finish, I have them pack up Daisy's linguini to take home.

But when I get out to my car, I realize it's only nine; I don't want to go home yet. Any hopes about tonight being the answer to my Catherine/Millie conflict are totally deflated because Daisy was a terrible fit for me. I like having sex with Millie. I love being around her. Her loyalty, her wit, and the small ways she knows exactly when we need to be buoyed speak to the depth of her intelligence. But I can't stand how she lives in a Teflon bubble and doesn't trust any of us to carefully handle *her* more delicate truths. Or more depressingly: the thought that—emotionally—she doesn't actually go a whole lot deeper than what I've seen. I honestly just can't believe that about her.

I'm not sure why I drive straight there. I mean, before all the sex, it would have been natural to come over after work, or after a bad date. We'd kick off our shoes and put our feet up on her coffee table and watch a movie or have a couple of beers and play cards. I didn't need more than that from her; it was perfect.

But now it feels like there's something else to be had, which makes me not only want it, but feel like I'm starting to need it.

I wonder whether, after the first time we had sex, if one of us had said, "I'd really like to try having a relationship," that would have changed everything and I wouldn't be weighing the balance of her sexual availability against her emotional intimacy so much. What is it about talking to women online and evaluating interactions that makes a checklist appear in my head, giving equal weight to all these things, forgetting that we all have strengths and weaknesses, and that no one comes into a relationship fully grounded?

I don't have a plan in mind. I park, I walk up her steps,

I knock. I think maybe I'll turn tonight's Daisy Disaster into a comedy show or ask Millie to mull over these existential dating questions with me, but there's something about her face when she opens the door that throws me. It takes a couple of seconds to register that she's relieved that I'm here on her porch—that I didn't go home with Daisy.

Her cheeks go pink—I can tell she's a little tipsy—and she touches her ear and then tucks her hair there, and I scramble back in time, trying to remember when I first noticed all these little things about her, like the tiny dimple she has at the corner of her mouth, and that her left eye is a few shades darker than her right, and that she breathes through her mouth when she's nervous.

We're just standing there, staring at each other, and then she cracks and her smile breaks like the sun coming out, and it makes me laugh, too.

"So it was terrible?" she says. She's giddy.

"Awful."

Her hand comes up to my chest and curls, making a fist around my shirt, and it's like being in an old movie, being pulled in by the scruff, door slammed behind me.

"Seriously?"

I smile against her lips. "Does it make sense if I say that I felt like I looked at her and saw all of her, in a single glance?"

She pulls me down again, more eager now. The first time, we were sweet, tender, talking. The second time was heat and passion—full of a sense that we were working something out of our systems. But tonight, it's urgent and immediate: Her mouth comes over mine the same moment she starts to lift my shirt up. I probably have her shirt unbuttoned and her jeans on the floor before my car engine has even cooled outside.

We're naked, stumbling down the hall before giving up and leaning into the wall, where I lift her up, holding her, taking her in a breathless flurry of movement. I keep moving until she comes, until she's a boneless, soft weight in my shaking arms.

Carefully, I set her down, kissing the crescent-shaped scar on her shoulder.

"Did you come over here for that?" she asks with a sleepy drawl. Her fingers trace the side of my face and I can't seem to help myself, I lean into the touch.

"I came over here for you."

There's so much truth embedded in my words that I'm surprised when she laughs, a single, breathy chuckle. It's either disbelief or relief.

"What are we doing, Mills?"

She laughs again, pressing a kiss to my neck, sucking in the exact way that I like. That she's *learned* that I like.

We've done this three times now, it's no longer just an accident. "Having sex, Reid."

And it's that—the condescending words, yes, but also the tone, so lighthearted—that hits a dissonant gong in my head. Her response is the verbal equivalent of a marshmallow, a Peep, something with shape but no volume. I wanted her to say something better, maybe even "I don't know"—that at least would invite conversation, at least show that she's as confused and affected by all of this as I am.

I step back, surveying her flushed chest, her weak legs and sated smile. Turning, I head to the living room, gathering my clothes as I go.

"You can stay," she says behind me. Relief flushes warm through my bloodstream, until she adds, "I have to run to my office to grab a couple things, but you're totally welcome to hang."

At this, I actually laugh. "I mean, don't get all needy on me, Mills."

"Oh, no fear of that," she says, and it doesn't feel like a joke, it feels sincere. It's as if she really doesn't know why it would be weird for her to take off right after we have sex, without any emotional understanding, and expect me to just hang out here and wait for her to come home. In the past I would have gone with her, to keep her company in her office or do something at work myself, but she doesn't want that or even *expect* it.

I feel half-oblivious and half-chauvinistic for assuming that recurrent sex with Millie would eventually mean more than sex to her, but I'm not sure it ever will.

"It's cool, Mills. I'm gonna head home."

My car door closes heavily and I let my head fall back against the headrest. Postsex, I feel like a well-used glove, a warm blanket, a body pillow. Soft and warm and sated. But inside, somewhere deeper, I'm a knot of angst.

I *want* Millie. I think I'm falling in love with her. And she just does not see me that way at all.

I text Chris.

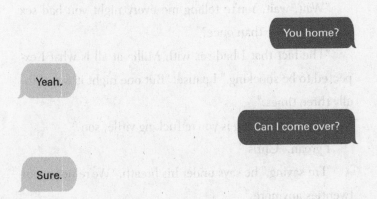

You home?

Yeah.

Can I come over?

Sure.

His front room is lit warmly, and from the street I can see him standing behind his couch, facing his television, fiddling with something. He looks up when he hears my footsteps on the stairs, moving to open the door.

I don't even let him get a word out: "I'm going to tell you some shit, and you cannot freak out on me."

He glances at me, dropping the remote on the couch. "Oh, boy."

"It's about Millie." I pause, and his eyes narrow. "And me," I say.

"Millie," he says, "and you. As in . . ." His brows go up. "Oh."

"Three times." I stop, wiping a hand over my face. "No, like six times. But three separate occasions—"

"Wait, wait. You're telling me every night you had sex you did it more than once?"

"The fact that I had sex with Millie at all is what I expected to be shocking." I pause. "But one night it was actually three times."

"What's shocking is you're fucking virile, son."

I groan. "Chris."

"I'm saying," he says under his breath. "We're not in our twenties anymore."

I push my hands into my hair, wishing I could reach into my head just as easily and shift everything around until it made sense. "But she doesn't like me that way."

"She . . ." He scrunches his nose and looks at me with suspicion. "What?"

"I mean, no, no, she liked the sex—that was both of us—but she doesn't want *more*."

"You know this?"

"I *sense* this."

He laughs again. "Oh, boy. I don't think this is the kind of thing you can assume, especially where Millie is concerned."

"How else would I figure anything out?" I walk deeper into his house, into his kitchen, fetching a beer from the fridge. "We have so much fun together, and the sex is . . . God, the sex is unreal, but when I try to imagine having an actual relationship? Where we talk about feelings and goals and fears?"

At this, Chris bursts out laughing, harder now.

"So you see what I mean."

He nods. "Yeah, man, I see what you mean."

"Then there's Catherine," I say, and Chris whistles long and low. "I've never met her, but online it's like . . . we just click. We talk about everything—about family and work, and life. It's *good*. I feel like we'd really vibe."

263

"So, ask her out." His tone says, *What's the problem?*

"Tonight with Daisy was a bust. So I went right over to Millie's."

"Aha. And let me guess—"

I nod. "Yeah . . ." I scratch my chin. "I want to be with Millie."

"So tell her that."

"But if she isn't on the same page, it will honestly make everything so awkward."

Chris shrugs. "As opposed to now?"

I groan.

"Maybe you'll want to be with Cat, too, once you meet her," he suggests hopefully.

"I can't really imagine wanting someone the way I want Millie. I just want Millie to be . . . more."

Chris pulls out a chair at the counter and stares at the floor for a few long beats. "I don't know, man. The Millie thing doesn't surprise me, because I sort of assumed you guys hit it a while ago and got it out of your systems. But if you're with that, and into it, I can't exactly tell you to walk away just because Millie isn't exactly the most emotionally deep person. I feel like maybe she could get there, with you."

"So you *do* think I should tell her how I feel?"

"Then again," he says, holding up a hand, "I've seen you after you've read a message from Cat. Why not explore that?"

"So you think I should ask Cat out?"

Chris looks up at me. "Do you need me to write out a flow chart? You can't calculate your way out of this. Shit, Reid."

I throw my hands up. "I just don't know what's the best decision!"

He stands and gets himself a beer, too. "What I think? Ask Cat out. See how it goes. If it bombs, either because there's no chemistry or because you know you want Millie, then at least you know. You'll have to tell her."

From: Reid C.
Sent: 1:28 am, April 7

I can't tell you how hard this last message from you made me grin—well, the end of it, at least. Not that the things you were talking about were funny, but the stream of consciousness is honestly refreshing.

I'm lonely, too. I know that feeling, and the energy threshold to do something about it sometimes feels insurmountable. Seriously, I get it so hard, even if I don't necessarily think I'm bad at asking for what I need—I'm just not finding it anywhere. But it sounds like you have a good group of friends, and as someone in a group of friends myself, I can say that being needed is a really important part of feeling connected to people. I'm sure if you asked more of them, they'd step up. They might even surprise you.

And I'm so sorry to hear about your dad. I don't know what I'd do if something happened to my parents. You've lost your mom, and now your dad is sick—of course you're feeling emotionally loose and filterless (even if I will never forgive you for the phrase "emotional diarrhea"). Ramble at me anytime.

All that said, your message threw my night into turmoil and I don't know what else to do but to tell you about it. You've always been honest with me, so I'm going to keep being honest with you.

I was on a date tonight with another woman. I'm sure you're talking to multiple people too, so I don't feel the need to explain that away, but I'm sure you can understand that it wasn't the right time to be reading a message from IRL (yours). This woman, we'll call her D.D. (endless jokes), went to the restroom and stayed there for a while. I got restless, started reading your message, and was absorbed in a second read when I realized she was standing there, waiting for me to look up so she could tell me she was leaving.

Suffice to say, it was awkward.

Afterwards, I went over to my friend's house—I've mentioned her to you before, she's one of my closest friends, and we've become a bit more than just friends in the past couple months. Again: going for honesty here. Well, we had sex again tonight but instead of feeling amazing afterward, I felt pretty terrible. I think my feelings for her are deeper than hers are for me, or maybe I'm hoping hers turn into something more, but we both know they won't. She's wonderful, and I feel like we know each other inside out, but then she'll say something and it registers that I hardly know her at all, deep down. When I tried to ask her tonight what was going on with us, she answered the way I most worried she would: we're just having sex.

I hope this isn't upsetting you. Or, maybe I hope it is a little, because then it will mean that you feel things for me the way I think I feel for you. Despite wanting things to happen with this friend, I've also held a piece of myself back because I haven't wanted to shut out the possibility that you're a better fit for me. But not knowing you in person, and knowing her, it's been easier to hope that things with her would start developing, start going somewhere. What if I meet you, and we have fun, but the connection we have by letters diffuses in person?

At the end of the day (and it is, the end of a very long day), I need to know. I'd love to meet, and have dinner and spend some time just talking together to see if it's worth pursuing something. This isn't an ultimatum, or a date meant to rule something out. It's just needing to know whether the reason things haven't slotted into place with my friend is because the right person for me is still out there.

Call me?
(805) 555-8213

—Reid.

chapter thirteen

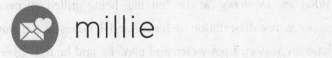 millie

I stare down at the phone until the screen goes dark with inactivity. My reflection gazes back: brow furrowed, lips turned down at the corners, expression a mixture of terrified, bewildered, and hurt. Reid's email is the equivalent of an emotional grenade going off in my face.

It's only six in the morning, I haven't had coffee yet, and my head is reeling. I'm not even sure where to start.

Reid felt terrible after we had sex? Is there a way to read that and not be devastated? I'll admit things were awkward between us, but I'd been home five minutes—back from spilling my guts to Ed and Alex—to find him at my door. I'd barely processed anything. I didn't even know if he'd read my letter.

All I knew was that he wasn't with *her*.

I wasn't thinking as I pulled him through the door and down the hall. All I could do was feel—feel how right we were together, and an overwhelming relief that he was here, and that I didn't want him to leave. Afterward, the question *What are we doing, Mills?* felt like being grilled all over again at my dissertation defense, and I honestly did not have an answer. I got weird and panicky, and he left. Even Emotional Mutant Millie is aware it's my fault.

"You're really terrible about sharing personal shit. You know that, right?"

"Why you gotta be such a secret?"

"Come on, Mills. We all know you keep your cards close."

They're not wrong; I've never been good at opening up.

I had just turned twelve when Mom sat Elly and me down over ice cream and told us she was sick. She went so fast after that. It felt like one day she was carefully explaining what the word *cancer* meant, and then she was plugged into every manner of tube and wire. The sharp smell of hospitals and antiseptic replaced the lingering scent of Elizabeth Arden Sunflowers that she would spray every morning.

Toward the end, Dad kept us carefully away. "Don't

worry your mother," he would tell us. "Let's not give her something else to think about."

So we didn't. We told her that everything was great at school. We told her we were happy, that we loved her, that we didn't need anything. And I kept the things I really wanted to tell her tucked away for when she was better. I didn't bother her with details of a fight with my friend Kiersten, or how Mr. Donohue was the meanest teacher at the entire school. I would tell her later.

But then she died, and I didn't have anyone to tell any of those things to. Beyond the ache of missing her, I found that life still went on. My quieter truths weren't bursting to get out of me; I was fine keeping them inside.

It became habit to sidestep and be the listener instead. I got very good at listening. In college, I read somewhere that if we let someone talk about themselves long enough, it sets off the same neurological signals of pleasure in the speaker's brain as do food or money. I'd been unintentionally exploiting that for years by then.

Anyone who needed something more from me gave up, and the ones who stayed have been fine with letting me hang in the metaphorical back when conversations get too deep. I'm an expert at knowing when to change the subject or crack a joke.

How convenient this must have been for Dustin. I was

an easy girlfriend because I never wanted to analyze anything. We rarely fought because neither of us was entirely invested. He was happy to keep the status quo, and he never asked me to move out of my comfort zone.

Reid, on the other hand, has always been onto me—and, just like my sister, he's about had it. It's a real testament to my emotional deformity that I am capable of exhausting even the best people.

I reread his message to Cat, and it hurts more than it should. To him, Catherine is another woman—not Millie. He's talking about all of this with someone else, not me. I have no claim to Reid, no right to be upset that he wonders if someone else is a better fit. So why does it feel like the rug has been pulled from under my feet? He told a total stranger that he doesn't think he knows me at all.

Can I blame him?

I think back on what has always been my favorite smile, the patient one that says he's exasperated but charmed—and loves me anyway. I compare that to his expression last night when he left. The tired eyes and disappointment that etched his features, the frown that got deeper and deeper until it resembled something hard and unfamiliar.

Now he wants to meet *her*, and I don't know how to be her with Reid.

I am so totally fucked.

Ed's neighborhood is composed of row after row of little brown condos, each a carbon copy of the one next to it. Community bike racks sit on each corner; the same shrubs are planted in each yard. I'm sure it was intended to be aesthetically pleasing, but it's a logistical nightmare. If I'm singing along to the radio, or not really paying attention, I find myself on a random street, wondering if I was supposed to turn at that tall, skinny tree, or the one before it.

Like now. I drive around the block twice before pulling up in front of his condo, where my engine ticks in the quiet. The drive from my place to his has done little to calm me. I sit in the car for a moment and wish I had a Time-Turner so I could tell Past Millie to not be a dumb-ass.

Glancing at my phone, I'm hit with another blow when I realize Reid hasn't called or texted once since last night. To be honest, I probably wouldn't answer; I'm not confident enough in my bullshitting skills at the moment to fake my way through any sort of normal conversation, even one done over text.

It's almost noon, but Ed answers the door in his bathrobe, holding a game controller. I would usually give him some shit about this, but alas, I'm also in pajama pants and didn't bother with a bra.

273

"You're not the pizza guy," he says around a bite of Pop-Tart.

I brush by him, heading deeper inside, where I can hear Alex shouting at the video game.

Instead of couches, Ed has a set of high-back reclining gamer chairs that sit opposite the largest, most expensive TV I have ever seen. Alex is sitting in one and pauses their *FIFA* match when he sees me. "Mills, you here to play?"

"I'm here to flail," I say. "I'm busted, you guys. Reid wants to meet Catherine."

"What, your message meltdown didn't scare him off?" Alex is mocking me, but I can't care.

"You guys were right. Emotions give him a total boner." I toss him my phone and drop like a lump into a flimsy beanbag in the corner.

Ed steps up behind him, and they silently scan the latest message from Reid. I try not to decode every one of Ed's brow lifts and Alex's muttered *yikes*. It's hard not to feel naked as they peer down at the screen where my shortcomings are laid out so plainly.

Alex is the first to look up. "He sent this today?"

I chew on my fingernail. "Last night. While I was sleeping."

"He wants to meet you—her," Alex says. "Holy shit."

Ed straightens, turning around to tug on his hair. "If I don't say much it's because I'm screaming inside."

"Okay, this doesn't have to be *that* big a deal." Alex looks up at Ed, confused. "We knew he'd ask to meet her eventually."

Sweet, breezy Alex.

But sweet, emotional Ed drops into a chair and wipes his palms on his robe-covered thighs. "It is a big deal, though, Alex, since *these are our best friends*, and one of them has been lying to another. Not to mention the tiny fact that both of us knew. We're aiders and abettors."

"Not helping." I whimper and sink deeper into the cushion. The beads in Ed's cheap beanbag choose this moment to shift underneath me, folding me in half and causing me to roll awkwardly to the floor. I land on my face with a groan. And remain there.

"Oh, that's just sad." Alex lasts about five seconds before bursting out laughing.

At least Ed takes pity on me. "Come on," he says, and offers me a hand. "Let's get you up."

"Leave me," I mumble from the floor. "This is where I belong."

"Don't you think you're being a little dramatic?" Ed bends one knee to kneel near me, and I squeeze my eyes closed when I get an eyeful of vague dickness up his robe.

"You mean, I'm being too dramatic about Reid having feelings for a version of me who doesn't exist? Or am I being too dramatic about the reality that he thinks I'm emotionally barren? I mean, let's not forget I basically catfished my best friend." I push to sit up. "Who does that? I didn't even really know what that was a few months ago. I thought it was just a show on MTV."

Ed, thankfully, moves to drag a milk crate across the floor to use as a seat. "Please take this the way it's intended, because you know that I love you, but what did you expect to happen?"

When I whimper again instead of answering, Alex has no problem hopping in: "This. This is what happens. Secrets are cancerous."

"Thanks, Alex."

He shrugs. "Someone's got to be straight with you, and who else would do it? We're your only friends."

"I have other friends," I say, indignant.

"Who?" Ed asks, quickly adding, "Baristas don't count."

"What, you want names?" I try to laugh but it comes out wheezy. "I have lots of names. Like, all my friends at work. And my sister."

"A sister we've never met, and who you never talk about," Ed reminds me.

I open my mouth to argue, but there's nothing but dead air.

"And *all* these friends at work," Alex says, "why not introduce us to some of them for dating purposes?"

Again, I want to argue, but can't. I have *acquaintances* at work, people I talk to on the way to faculty meetings, or at lunch. I have casual friends like Avery—okay, maybe she's more frenemy, but *others*—who I see at the gym, or might run into somewhere, but I've never been great with girlfriends. At some point, every female friendship I've had has turned south somewhere, and I never knew how to fix it because I'd never learned how to fight. I always thought a fight meant the end. I may be older and wiser now about these things, but I'm still terrible at confrontation.

"I've never had, like, deep friendships," I say, and hate how I feel myself shrug defensively. "After my mom died, we just sort of . . . rallied. Dad's motto was 'Don't sweat the small stuff. And it's all small stuff.' I guess to him, after Mom died, that saying was pretty accurate. Nothing felt big in comparison." Realization unfolds as I let this all out. "If I made it through that, I can make it through anything, right? No sense making something bigger by dwelling on it."

Ed struggles to hide his exasperation. "Sharing things doesn't mean you're *dwelling*."

"I know, but—"

"It's about us knowing who you are." He holds up a hand to keep me from arguing. "Tell me five important things about Reid."

This I can do. I give them both a knowing smile and Alex adds quickly, "Above the belt."

"Okay," I say. "One, he loves his work—like, genuinely *loves* doing research on optic neuritis in multiple sclerosis. See? I don't know what any of that means, but I know that's what Reid studies because he's always so excited about it."

Ed leans in like he's going to start explaining all the science to me, but I hold up a hand to stop him.

"Two, he loves his parents to death, and even when he complains about his mom being crazy, he still loves being home second only to being in the lab." I sit up, adjusting the beanbag beneath me. "He's so proud of Rayme because she's smart and beautiful and confident, but more than anything he's secretly relieved that she's taking on the family business so he doesn't have to."

"Good one," Alex says.

"He wants to travel more," I say. "And, um, he's claustrophobic."

"See?" Ed says. "Now if you asked me what five things I know about you, they'd mostly have to do with murder, belching, and Monopoly."

I laugh, but it sounds like it's coming from someone else's body, because suddenly my brain is full of Reid.

He likes when I bite his neck, I think, and heat builds in my belly. *He likes when I'm on top. He likes quiet afternoons watching tennis in the summer, likes his coffee extra hot. He doesn't like strawberry pie, but loves cherry. His favorite band is the Pixies, although seeing Pink Floyd live is at the top of his bucket list. He didn't think he liked brussels sprouts until I cooked them for him. He runs a six-minute mile, sleeps on his left side, usually forgets to eat breakfast. He loves my laugh, likes holding hands, hates when someone is looking at their phone while he's talking.*

I blink when Alex snaps in front of me. "Hello?"

"Sorry, what?"

"I asked what you want," he says.

"Other than a Time-Turner or to be blackout drunk so that I don't have to think about this anymore?"

He doesn't even crack a smile.

Embarrassment feels like a tight band around my throat. "Okay, I don't know what you're asking."

"With Reid," Ed clarifies. "What do you want with Reid?"

The answer has been forming since I woke up this morning. I knew days ago that I didn't want anyone else to have him, but that's not exactly the same as wanting him for myself, is it?

Except in this case, it is.

But the idea of admitting this to Ed and Alex before I've said it to Reid feels . . . cowardly. "I'm figuring it out," I tell them. "I just want to talk to him."

Alex stands, tugging me up, and we make our way to Ed's disaster of a kitchen. There are about six cereal bowls in the sink, brown bananas hanging from a banana hook and hovering above some wrinkly apples. The recycling is overflowing, and when Alex opens the fridge, the only things visible are a few six-packs of beer.

Before I can say anything, Ed is standing in front of me, frowning. "Don't judge. I order takeout most nights."

"I mean, if you ever manage to get a woman in here," I begin, and then sweep my arm around the room, "she'll be horrified."

"My mom is coming to help me clean this week," he says.

Alex smirks. "I don't think that's what she meant by 'woman.'"

"Do you ever hear the words you're saying?" I ask Ed, taking a beer when Alex hands it to me.

He sits at a barstool and takes down about a quarter of his beer. "Selma still hasn't replied."

Ugh, poor Ed. "Wait. You mean after like two weeks of amazing conversation, you asked her to meet, and she vanished?"

Ed nods, clearly bummed. "I'm getting some other matches, but . . ." He shrugs and lets out a long, rumbling burp. "Can we get back to fixing this mess you've created with Reid?"

"I'm definitely not helping you clean this kitchen," I tell him, "so why not."

"Maybe *you* should disappear like that," Alex says. "Catherine, that is."

I frown at him. "What? Just not reply?"

Ed stares at me and then shrugs again. "I mean, it's effective. It's not like I can go out and find her." Pausing, he seems to hear the stalkery vibe to his words and adds, "Okay, not that I would try."

My beer sits untouched in front of me, and I watch as tiny beads of condensation run down the sides of the bottle and form a puddle on the countertop. The idea of someone just disappearing on Reid—even if it's me, and I'm still going to be here—makes me feel all twisty and protective. "I'd feel so bad, just pretending I don't know everything. And what if someday we are together—"

"I *knew* it!" Ed interrupts, pointing at me and sloshing his beer. "I knew you wanted Reid!"

"Good sleuthing," I tell him, dryly. "I mean, if we do manage to make a go of this, I can't spend my whole life knowing this secret and keeping him in the dark."

"She said 'whole life,'" Alex says to Ed, with this soft, fond expression I've honestly never seen him make. "Like, marriage."

"Slow down." I hold up a hand, laughing. "Reid may never forgive me, but I don't think I could keep this from him."

"Normally I'd say yes," Ed says, "own up and come clean. But you've learned your lesson here, Mills. What is telling him going to solve? He'll be hurt and upset and . . ." He hesitates and my stomach drops to my kneecaps. "I mean, I'm not saying he'd never talk to you again, because this is Reid and he's a good fucking guy, but . . ."

But?

But?

Ed trails off and my brain frantically tries to finish the sentence for him.

He's a good fucking guy, but . . . this may be too much to forgive.

He's a good fucking guy, but . . . you're too much work for him to bother trying to be romantically involved.

My heart follows possible Future Reid in each of these scenarios, and I want to scream. How many of the women

I write about thought they were good people? How many mistakes does it take before you're bad? Does it start with a little white lie, and slowly progress to fraud . . . and worse? Does it matter if you do the wrong thing for the right reason? Okay, obviously at first I was just being competitive, but then being Cat was almost more fun than being Millie, because I got to have something with Reid that I've never had with anyone before, and I fell in love with him.

The wind is knocked from my lungs as the word bounces around inside my head. Because now that it's there, I don't want to let it go.

Love.

Did I know this an hour ago? Yesterday? How long have I felt this and just left it totally unlabeled?

My existential crisis can't be bothered with the fact that Ed and Alex are still in the room, and so it takes Ed shaking my shoulder to bring me out of it.

"Are you listening?" he says, hand waving in front of me but eyes lit like he's just figured something out.

"Yeah," I say, and attempt to blink myself back into focus. "You were saying . . ."

Ed frowns in a way that makes him look just like his mother did when she found a Fleshlight in his kitchen drawer and thought it was an actual flashlight. She spent five minutes trying to put batteries in before I realized what she was doing.

"We need to get rid of Catherine," he says. "So, tell Reid she met someone, she's moving. Anything. Alex agrees."

I glance to Alex, who gives me a noncommittal shrug.

"But then I'll be lying to cover up a lie," I tell them both.

"Yes," Ed says, pausing dramatically. "But you can still make this right. Get Catherine out of the picture and *talk to him*. Tell him how you feel and let him really see you. That's what he wants, Millie. You read it yourself, he *wants* something to happen with you. Catherine is what's making him second-guess that, and that's you! Give him what he wants."

I reach up to rub my temples. Can I give Reid what he wants? I don't even have to think about it: I certainly don't want to lose him.

"How would I do this?" I ask, almost *wincing* like I'm afraid to admit to myself that I'm considering it. "What would I say?"

Ed and Alex both lean forward; the three of us huddle together around the kitchen island.

"Tell him your grandfather died and he left you some giant house, and it says in the will that you have to live there and—"

"This isn't *Scooby-Doo*, Ed," Alex says, shaking his head. "Let's keep it simple."

"Right. Simple is better." Straightening, Ed looks around the room, his eyes brightening when they land on his laptop bag. Once his computer is powered up in front of us, he turns it to face me.

Still unsure, I log into the site, and then Catherine's account. The REPLY button practically pulses on the screen.

"Okay," Ed says, and swallows nervously. "Here's what we're going to do."

chapter fourteen

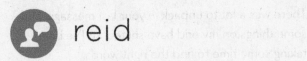 reid

There are few things that settle me more when I'm stressed or preoccupied than going into the lab, grabbing a set of slides from one of my graduate students' cabinets, and heading into the dark calm of the scope room.

My newest student, Gabriel, is measuring dendritic spines in the visual cortex, and he's really starting to get the hang of the staining protocol. The fluorophores are brilliant green, sharp, low-background. As I go through his latest experiments, a thrum of pride begins to take over that space where the anxious gnawing resided only twenty minutes ago.

In the darkness, my phone lights up with a notification

from IRL: a new message from Cat. Within seconds, my stomach is tight again. This is it: after all of our messages, we are going to meet.

From: Catherine M.
Sent: 5:54 pm, April 7

Hi Reid,

There was a lot to unpack in your last message, and some things on my end have shifted, so I've been taking some time to find the right words.

First up, I just want to say thank you for being so honest with me, and for being willing to just put it all out there. The information about your friend wasn't upsetting to me, I know how this works. I really admire how you cut right to the chase and shared what you need and want. It's something I need to learn how to do better myself.

So, because we're talking about it openly now, of course we're both communicating with multiple people online. I had a date last night with another man. He's someone from my past, and it went really well. So well, in fact, that I'd like to see where it goes. Given the situation with your friend, and this man, it seems like it might be good for both of us if we put our correspondence on hiatus.

I'm sure if I were you I'd be reading this thinking,
Ok I've definitely been messaging with a dude who
lives in rural England somewhere and is having a
laugh, but I promise. I am a woman, who came into
this with good intentions.

All this to say, I really do hope that things work out
with your friend.

Sometimes, the thing we want is right in front of us,
and we're the last ones to see it.

Take care, Reid,
C.

I read it again, because it doesn't feel like it sinks in
the first time. After all of that—every letter, every bit of
honesty—we're never going to meet?

The feeling of bewilderment that slams through me is
almost impossible to describe. On the one hand, realisti-
cally, I'm no worse off than I was a month ago when this
entire adventure started: things with Millie are murky, and
I've got no other relationship prospects in sight. Sure, the
romantic life has no momentum, but in all other respects,
I'm fine.

On the other hand, I feel like I've just been dumped
twice.

I'm halfway into my third read of Cat's message when Millie's photo—one she took and entered into my contacts, and is of her with a huge cheesy grin while wearing my Cal baseball hat and Chris's sunglasses—pops up on the screen.

I want to laugh. Cat just blew me off. I haven't talked to Millie since last night, so of course now she's calling.

"Hey, Mills."

"Hey, Reidy." On the other end of the line, she sounds either sad or nervous. In any case, she's subdued enough to make me wonder whether she realizes that her postsex routine wasn't great.

In her beat of silence, I pull the slide off the microscope tray and file it back in the slide box. "What's up?"

"Would you come over?" she asks. "For dinner? Or I can come to you?" Another unsure pause, and then, "To talk."

"Talk?" I ask. Millie doesn't ever ask to *talk*.

"About us," she says, clearing her throat. "The other night. I mean, the first night, the night at your parents', last night. All of it."

Wow. I feel thunderstruck. "Sure. I'll be there in twenty."

She lets out a shaky laugh. "Take your time. I have to get a little drunk first."

I pause, quietly annoyed, and in the silence she goes still, too, and then she groans.

"I'm kidding," she says. "God, I am so terrible at this. Reid, just come over, okay?"

Spring is creeping into Santa Barbara with warm fingers; the heat from the day lingers after sundown, and even inside my car, the scent of the blooming vines outside Millie's town house makes my head feel full and claustrophobic.

At the curb, I pull out my phone and look at Catherine's profile. Honestly, I'm bummed that she's found someone else, and is interested enough in seeing where it goes that she wants to put our communication on hold. I wanted that level of connection with someone. I thought maybe Millie and I could go back to being just friends. Maybe Catherine was it for me somehow. But even in the past hour, her profile has gone inactive—I can't click through to her pages anymore. There's only the photo she's always had: that turned-away jawline, the bare shoulder, the tiny scar. Over time, I actually liked that she didn't give everything of herself up front but seemed to share much more than I'd expected in her messages.

"Well," I say into the quiet car, "I guess that's it."

With my thumb pressed to the IRL icon on the screen, I wait until the app goes wobbly, and then delete it.

Looking up, I see Millie is waiting for me on the porch, her hands clasped together tightly. Everything about this scene feels strange: she's out here waiting for me, she wants to talk, she looks anxious, she breaks into a huge grin when she sees me.

"You're being weird," I say when I hit the first step up to her porch.

"I know. I know." She wipes her hands on her jeans, and my attention is drawn to her bare arms, her long, smooth neck. "Just go with it. I'm super nervous right now."

And as soon as she walks toward me, it's like I'm deflating in relief. I'm bummed about Cat. I'm worried about me and Millie. I'm disappointed that Daisy was such a bust. And the reality that I'm about to get a hug right now makes me want to melt in front of Millie's door.

She steps into my arms, wrapping hers around my neck, pulling me close. I have the sense of homecoming, some weird trip of déjà vu in my blood that makes me squeeze her tighter. It's the kind of hug that comes after a fight, or a long time apart. There's relief there, a giant exhale into the soft skin of her neck, her shoulder, where I press my lips once, and again, against her faint scar.

Her scar.

292

My heart shoves against my breastbone in warning, and then lurches: a heavy, meaningful pulse. I mentally file back to one of Cat's messages:

managed to make tit halfway through the attraction without peeing my pants or otherwise embarrassing myself

The same stupid *tit* typo that Millie always makes.

The same scar.

I step back, pressing the heels of my hands to my eyes. No way can this be right.

"Reid?"

I try to be objective, to take the data in front of me at face value.

Millie's mom died when she was young.

That friend of hers, Avery, mentioned that Millie's dad was sick.

And now, Millie's scar. Millie's typo. The Monopoly joke. *Girls Trip*. And Cat is pursuing a relationship with someone else just when I tell her I want to meet.

The last line echoes in my memory: *Sometimes, the thing we want is right in front of us, and we're the last ones to see it.*

What the fuck?

"Reid?" Millie's hand comes over my forearm, gently squeezing.

"Sorry, just—light-headed."

I stare at her, into her mossy green eyes, and try to puzzle this out. I want to turn her jaw just so, ask her, *Look down a bit, to the side, just like that. I need to see if you're her.*

Am I crazy? Is this connection absurd? But I know it's not. I know in an instant that Catherine is Millie. I know it in the way that Dad knows when it's going to rain, and the way that Mom knows exactly when her bread is baked without setting a timer.

And I know it because it's been there in front of me this whole time.

The information is almost too new for me to know what to do with it. I'm standing with her on her porch—with Millie, with Catherine—realizing that she's not only my best friend and the woman I've been having sex with, she's also the woman I've been spilling my heart to online.

Amid the chaos of my reaction—embarrassment, relief, hope, thrill, confusion—I can't find my grounding.

Is this why she asked me to come here?

I blink tightly to clear my thoughts, and then look down at her.

She's worried; the little line on her forehead has deepened, her lips arc downward. "You okay?"

"Yeah," I say, taking a deep breath and then letting it out slowly. I've been falling for two women, and they're both her. "Just got dizzy for a second."

"Come inside," she says, "get some water."

Through this fresh lens, everything in here feels new. The couch is where she probably wrote to me as Cat. The kitchen where we first kissed—I was kissing Cat, too. Down the hall, there's her bedroom, and about half as far is the wall against which we had sex only last night. I left her, and immediately wrote another woman—also her—and told her everything.

Oh my God, I want to remember verbatim what I said in that last message. How much did I tell Cat about my feelings? I said Millie made me feel terrible! And Millie responded as Catherine by telling me she was moving on with someone else.

My stomach drops.

"Reid, you look sort of . . . green."

"No, I'm good." I take the water she offers, and down half of it before coming up for air. "What did you want to talk about?"

She laughs shakily and motions that we should go sit on the couch. Slapping her hands on her thighs, she says, "Right. That. Okay, so last night, after we"—she waves her hand vaguely in the direction of the hallway—"over *there* . . . and you left . . . I thought maybe I did something wrong."

"You mean like shutting me down when I tried to talk

about what the sex means to us and then suggesting I could make myself at home while you went back to work?" The words surprise even me a little bit.

Millie laughs uncomfortably again and runs shaking fingers through her hair. "Yes. That. I guess . . . I guess I was freaking out a little. I mean, I *did* have to run in for a few minutes, and I thought maybe it'd be nice to have you here when I got home, but I realize the way I said it just sounded really . . . wrong."

I lean back against the couch, closing my eyes. There are two ways this is going: Millie realizes I'm falling for her and is ending all aspects of our romantic relationship, including as Catherine. Or, Millie realizes I'm falling for her and wants to get Cat out in the open so we can be together for real. It worries me that I don't have the faintest idea which route she's taking.

It all makes me feel really tired. "It's okay, Mills."

"It isn't okay," she says quietly. "I want to be better about those things. Talking, I mean. I think . . ." She pauses, glancing at me and then rolling her eyes at herself. "I think—I mean I know—that I want to . . ."

"Spit it out." I laugh a little, trying to be gentle about her fumbling.

"I want to try to be with you. Like . . . that."

"Like *that*?" I tease.

She reaches over and tries to tweak my nipple. "Romantically, okay?"

I weasel out of her reach. "What's more romantic than a nipple twist?"

"Right?" She breaks out into an enormous smile. Flowers push up through the dirt to see that smile. Relief is like light hitting my retina, illuminating everything. "So, is that a yes?"

She leans forward, I lean a little, too, and her mouth meets mine for a single, sweet kiss.

And the moment turns a little shadowed.

That's it, I realize. She hasn't said a word about who else she's been. She hasn't admitted to being Catherine.

Am I okay just letting that go? Regardless, if we're going to be together for the long run, she's going to have to learn how to talk to me. She's going to have to *not lie* to me. As it stands, Millie and I have no history going anyplace deeper than where we are right now.

"I want to try this, too, I think. But I want to be honest with you." I meet her eyes, looking for some fault line there. She's calm, but there's anxiety beneath her expression. "There was someone else," I say, and notice the way her cheeks pink just slightly. "Cat, remember?"

"Right, I know." She shrugs. "It's okay. I was writing someone, too."

No, Millie. Don't.

I watch her carefully, and she blinks away.

"She was . . ." I trail off. How do I describe Millie's vulnerable side to her tough one? "She was really great, and I thought maybe we had something. She *talked* to me about things. It felt like we were really becoming friends. And," I say, wiping a hand down my face, "I'll admit—I maybe wanted more." I pause, waiting. "But she went out with another guy and wants to pursue it. She backed off with me, and it's sort of a bummer that it looks like now I'm not going to meet her."

There. Take it, Mills. Take the opportunity. Own this. Tell me.

She searches my eyes, back and forth, back and forth, and then smiles with effort. "That is a bummer."

My heart drops. I give her another few beats.

"Do you think your feelings for her will affect . . . ?" she starts, and then motions between us. Cat would have just said it outright: *Will your feelings for her get in the way of starting something with me?*

So why can't Millie do it?

"I'm not sure," I tell her, honestly. "I liked our dynamic of straightforward honesty. I want that in a partner. I'll be frank, Mills, I am intensely attracted to you—to the point of distraction—and I love spending time with you, but I need to know you can talk to me about things. Things that really matter to you."

"I can," she says immediately.

Like this, I think.

"I need to know you'll be *honest*."

She nods. "I can be. I will. I know I'm not the best at being open, but it matters to me that I get better." She lifts my hand, kisses it. "I want to be better for you."

Then, as if a switch is flipped, she stands quickly, using my hand to tug me up. "Hungry?"

And I see now that she's going to let Catherine go. She's going to send her alter ego away and pretend that it never happened—hilarious, given we're having this conversation about her ability to be open and honest.

I shove my shaking hands deep into my pockets. "Do you mind if I take a rain check on dinner?"

"You want to *go*?" she asks, realization settling into a small V on her forehead.

"I want to think about all of this before we move forward. You're my best friend, you know. Seems like we should make absolutely sure we're ready to do this."

Millie tries to hide a deeper reaction, but I get a small glimpse of it when her face falls for only a breath.

"Sure," she says. "Of course. I'm just springing this on you out of the blue." She runs a fingernail over the fabric along the back of the couch. "I get it."

I lean forward, kissing her cheek, and then robotically

make my way out of her house, down her steps, and to my car at the curb.

"Reid!" she calls out.

I turn. My stomach has dissolved away. "Yeah."

She stares at me for a few lingering seconds. "You sure you're okay?"

She *knows*.

She knows I know.

I hold her gaze.

"I'm not sure," I tell her honestly, before climbing into my car.

After all of that, the strongest sense I have is mortification that I've been played. That Millie has been sleeping with me, and writing me as another woman this entire time, and probably never planned to say anything. That she thinks I wouldn't eventually figure it out. What is she getting out of being Catherine? And if she wants to be with me—*really* be with me—why does she think we can start with a lie?

I lean back, turn on my car, and take a long, slow inhale, trying not to get back out and confront her. Trying not to jump to conclusions. Pulling away from the curb, I keep my hands steady on the steering wheel and try not to think about anything except the road in front of me. I certainly try not to think that I may have just lost my best friend.

Reid Campbell

Arranged marriage is looking pretty tempting.

Christopher Hill

Man, it's just a dinner.

Stephen (Ed) D'Onofrio

Who's getting married?

El Cabrón

Reid is being rhetorical dumbass

Stephen (Ed) D'Onofrio

Wait. Who is that? Alex?

El Cabrón

Yeah.

Stephen (Ed) D'Onofrio

What the fuck with your name?

El Cabrón

I took out a chick from the UC tech department and it didn't go well.

Christopher Hill

So all your outgoing information is from 'the asshole'?

El Cabrón

Pretty much.

Reid Campbell

Emails?

El Cabrón

Everything. Emails, IMs, my name in the grading portal, on the department website.

Christopher Hill

Holy shit that is hilarious

El Cabrón

My admin doesn't think so. But he can go fucking fix it, I'm not going down there.

MY FAVOURITE HALF-NIGHT STAND

Christopher Hill
I want to meet this woman.

Reid Campbell
Ditto

El Cabrón
Trust me, you don't.

Reid Campbell
At least she wanted to meet in person

Stephen (Ed) D'Onofrio
Uh oh. Are things not going well with
Catherine?

Reid Campbell
Dating in my early twenties was amazing.
Dating in my early thirties is a drag.

El Cabrón
You know, the thing you all are failing to
remember is that WE DON'T ACTUALLY HAVE
TO BRING A PLUS ONE TO THIS EVENT

Reid Campbell
I know.

Reid Campbell
I realize we all got wrapped up in the date thing, but I think it was time we all got out there anyway.

El Cabrón
Um, hello, I've BEEN out there

Christopher Hill
And it's clearly going well for you, El Cabrón

Reid Campbell
Yeah, plenty of action to be found in the darkroom

Christopher Hill
What?

El Cabrón
Ed's running his mouth, apparently.

Stephen (Ed) D'Onofrio
Oh, my bad, was it a secret?

El Cabrón
lol

Reid Campbell
Can I sit down with you guys later today?
Under the cloak of confidentiality?

El Cabrón
I mean, if there's a cloak, sure

Christopher Hill
You want to meet up at lunch?

Reid Campbell
I'd rather do it over drinks. Tonight at the
Red Piano, 8 pm?

Stephen (Ed) D'Onofrio
I just realized Mills isn't on this thread. Is this a
guys-only thing?

Reid Campbell
Oh yes.

The bar has the same calming darkness as the microscope room, but it has the added benefit of booze. I'm two beers in before Chris shows up, followed closely by Alex and, ten minutes later, a harried Ed, who must not realize he's still got a pair of lab goggles atop his head.

"Sorry I'm late," he says, and startles when Alex carefully plucks the goggles from his mess of curls.

"Everything okay?" I know he was helping Gabriel with an experiment today that they'd been planning for a few weeks. One look at Ed and I'm guessing I don't want to know how it went just yet. "Never mind. I'll ask you later."

He rakes a hand through his hair before reaching for the beer menu. "Probably a good idea."

"Okay, so," I start, staring at the remaining foam in my half-full pint glass. "I feel like a bit of a dick doing this—talking about this here—but I need some advice and I think I need all of your input because I suspect you'll each tell me something different."

Alex shifts in his chair, glancing at Ed.

Chris is the only one looking directly at me. "Sure."

"Chris knows this," I say, "but about a month or two ago, Millie and I slept together."

There is no reaction to this. No gasps, no outburst. Just even expressions and expectant silence. So apparently Chris wasn't the only one who assumed Millie and I had already gone there.

"It happened again at my parents' place," I continue, "and again a couple nights ago."

Alex nods slowly. "Okay?"

"But during all this, I've also been talking to Daisy online—which by the way, didn't work out in person—and Catherine." I take a quick sip, and focus my attention on the table. "After leaving Millie's the other night, I was a little messed up about what we were doing, and I messaged Cat and sort of laid out what was going on."

Ed coughs into his fist.

"I told her that I have feelings for this friend of mine—Millie—but that I also wanted to meet Cat as well. Long story short, Cat wrote back and told me she'd gone out with someone from her past and was going to try to make it work with him."

"Dude, seriously?" Chris asks. "That's . . . that's weird."

I don't miss the way Alex bends and cups his forehead.

Watching him, I say carefully, "If what you're thinking is that Millie is Catherine, you'd be right."

All three of their heads shoot up and they stare at me.

"Wait, *what*?" Chris says, pulling back.

"I figured it out at her place last night," I tell them. "She was telling me she wanted us to try to be together, and when I bent to hug her I realized she's got the same scar on her shoulder as Cat did in the profile picture. And Cat made that same typo, the 'tit' typo, that Millie makes." I look up at them, making sure they're not looking at me like I'm insane. "A few other things, too—her dad being sick and her mom dying when she was younger. Her little sister she's not so close to. I figured it out and gave her the chance to tell me about Cat . . . and she *didn't*. I'm, like, ninety-nine percent sure she's Catherine, and I gave her so many openings to tell me, and she didn't. She just continued the lie."

No one says anything. They just absorb all this in shock.

"And on the one hand, I get it," I say. "Something happened between us in person and she doesn't want this other persona in the way. But on the other hand, why the fuck did she do it in the first place, and why would she keep it from me?"

"Man," Chris says quietly. "If this is true, this is fucked up."

It takes me a few seconds, but then it registers that Ed—who has something to say about *everything*—is dead silent. His expression is tight, like he's waiting any second to be yelled at . . . the way he looks when I catch him staring at grad students' asses.

"What's with you?" I ask.

He doesn't look up from the napkin he's methodically shredding. "Nothing."

"Bullshit." I'm reminded of that morning on the patio at my parents' place, when he was acting like a lunatic. "Seriously, Ed."

"I just . . ." He glances over to Alex. "I *told* her she should tell you."

This honestly doesn't penetrate at first. I know what he's said, but at the same time, the meaning doesn't fully hit me until he glances at Alex again, and Alex lifts his beer to his lips, shaking his head.

"Dude, you were the one who helped her write that last message," Alex says under his breath.

"I'd told her a million times to tell him!" Ed protests to Alex.

"Wait." I put my glass down, hold up a hand. "Wait.

Wait. What is happening?" I am so flustered I don't have any more words. I just stare at Ed, and then Alex, and then back at Ed again.

Ed drops his hands to the table. "This kind of shit never works out!"

A hush falls across the table, and Chris lets out a low whistle.

"You *knew*?" I ask, hearing the angry lean to my words. "Since when?" I stop, shaking my head. "Wait, you knew that morning at my parents' place, didn't you?"

Ed seems to shrink into himself. "I heard you guys."

"You heard them having sex?" Chris asks, laughing. "That is unfortunate."

Alex signals to the waitress that he wants another beer. "I'm *still* laughing that they had sex at his parents' place when we were all there."

I turn to Alex. "When did you find out?"

"I only found out like two days ago."

"'Only' two days ago?"

My blood is rioting.

Anxiety builds in Ed's expression. "I've only known about it for a week. You should know she's been a total stress case about this."

Chris shakes his head, staring at Ed like he's unbelievable. "She should be, though."

"She came over and wanted advice on what to do. She read your last message and—"

"Did *you* read my message?" I ask.

Ed looks to Alex and then back to me. "We both did, yeah."

"Holy shit." I press the heels of my hands to my eyes. "You guys. This is so fucked up."

"It just only recently got out of hand," Alex says, trying to smooth things over. "Seriously. All of this happened really fast. She's been a mess, man."

"Regardless, I gave her a dozen openings today, and she sat and lied to me. *Again*," I say.

"Okay," Alex says, "to be fair, though, she wanted to tell you, but we thought it would be easier if Cat just vanished. She didn't ever mean to be malicious."

"If she wanted to tell me, then why didn't she? How am I supposed to feel about this? She wants to start a relationship with me but she can't even be honest on day one?"

"I mean," Alex says, "you sort of played her, too, because the whole time today you knew that she was Catherine but she didn't know you knew."

"Oh, I think she knows I know," I tell them. "And it's not the same."

Chris drops his head into his hands, groaning. "This is making my head hurt."

"Why did she even start a separate account?" I ask, feeling my patience fraying. "Why did she let me view her full profile?"

"Honestly?" Ed spreads his hands, shrugging. "I think she assumed you'd figure it out. It sounds like it started as a way to not get so many dick pics, and to be able to be more 'herself,'" he says, using air quotes, "then she matched with you and thought it was funny, and it just . . . grew."

"That's pretty reassuring, though," Alex says, nodding. "Isn't it? That it turned into something real for her, too?"

"Are you *really* fucking defending this right now?" I ask him.

"I'm just saying, I think shit can snowball, that's all. You can start off with good intentions and . . . things can get out of hand."

I gape at him. "That's a decent excuse when it's a total stranger, not your best friend who you are concurrently *fucking*."

Everyone goes quiet, and I get it: I don't often yell. But I am on fire right now. Alex and Ed knew that Millie was lying to me, and then encouraged her to keep doing it. And she's so goddamn out of touch with herself that she couldn't just do the right thing.

I feel like an idiot.

I feel like I'm on the outside.

I feel totally humiliated.

I stand and toss a couple of twenties down onto the table. My heart feels like a boxer, beating and beating at my ribs. "Fuck you guys."

chapter fifteen

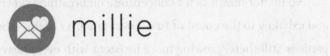 millie

I shut off the TV and the house falls into silence. I couldn't even tell you what I've been watching. A car goes by on the street outside, and for the first time since Reid left last night, I don't bother to look out the window to see whether it's him.

He said he was going to think about things, but I worked from home today, and kept my phone and laptop right next to me the entire time and looked for him every time I heard anything outside . . .

I'm pretty sure he isn't coming back.

My legs are stiff by the time I straighten them to stand and walk to the kitchen. I scan the contents of my fridge unseeing, trying to convince myself that the niggling voice in the back of my head is wrong, and Reid wasn't totally freaking out.

I think he *knows*.

I don't know how, but I felt it. I saw it on his face, some dawning awareness and then: the struggle to hide his anger.

No matter how much I concentrate on breathing slowly and exhaling to the count of five—over and over again—the panic is still there, growing more insistent with every heavy slam of my heart. Reid has never been *mad* at me before. I'm pulling apart at the seams. The room is too hot. The scent of Reid's soap hangs in the air and when I turn my head, I can smell him in the fabric of my shirt, too.

I push away on unsteady legs and search for my keys, and then I just drive.

The sun is barely hanging on by the time I make it to Hendry's Beach. I hadn't planned to come here; I got in my car with no real destination in mind, but when the little blue pickup in front of me with the surfboard in the back turned, I followed.

Even with the windows up I can smell the salt in the

air. It feels heavy and humid, and chilly enough here in the parking lot that I know it will be even colder down by the water.

I climb out and reach for the sweater in my trunk. It's hideous but warm, a ratty old thing I keep ready for over-air-conditioned stops at Cajé and spontaneous beach moments just like this. I've had it for years, but no matter how many times I wash it, it still smells faintly of coffee.

With my keys and phone in the oversize pockets, I cut through the lot and down past the dog-washing station and the restaurant with blue and yellow umbrellas. Clumps of grass stake their claim near rocks in the sand, and I cross the sidewalk to the small set of steps down to the beach.

On the left side of the lifeguard tower, where dogs are allowed to run off leash, a particularly hyper golden retriever races into the surf, pouncing on waves as they break the surface and chasing them as they roll out to sea again. I take a seat in the sand: close enough to watch the waves but far enough away to stay dry. At least for a while.

A look around reminds me that I was here with Reid once, shortly after Dad was diagnosed. The trip home had been rough—so bad that I'd made up an excuse about work and flown back to Santa Barbara a day early. It was like the cancer talk with Mom all over again, and I'd literally panicked, heart racing and unable to breathe as I sat on the twin bed in Elly's tiny little guest room. I had to go. Reid didn't know what was happening, but he could see something was wrong as soon as I knocked at his door. I told him I'd had a bad day, and he drove us here. *To watch the dogs*, he'd said, because who can have a bad day while watching puppies run free and frolic in the ocean?

He was right. We'd rolled up our pants and found a spot on the beach and spent the next two hours just sitting in silence. Eventually, we talked about work and life. He told me about a date he'd been on while I was away, and how they made out in his car for an hour after he dropped her off, too wound up to say goodbye, but not wound up enough to have sex on the first date. There was an imperceptible ringing in my ears, a low-level hum of annoyance that seemed to grow with every detail that he shared. I watched his lips as he talked, imagined him doing the things he was explaining, and sort of . . . hated it.

When I look back on moments like that, it's hard to convince myself that things between us have ever been one hundred percent platonic. The glances, the casual touches in the car, the subtle flirting—I wrote it off as us being comfortable with each other, but, holy shit, I am an idiot. I'd spent that afternoon stretched out in the sand with my head on his stomach, eyes closed while I matched my breaths to his and listened to the ocean. Would I do that with Ed? With Chris? Alex?

Not a chance.

I glance out over the horizon to where the sun is melting into the sea. The tide has come in, breaking against the shore and leaving clumps of seaweed behind as it recedes. I scrunch my toes, just out of reach of the foamy water as it inches closer and closer. I think I've always been jealous where Reid is concerned. Even then, I didn't necessarily want to kiss him, but I didn't really want him kissing someone else, either.

This makes me a really shitty person . . . a reoccurring theme as of late.

My friendship with Reid has been the easiest of my life. I'd never had a best friend before—never mind four of them—because I think I honestly don't know how to do it. A summary of my last ten years would show a boring list of acquaintances and mild romantic serial monogamy. Nothing dramatic ever happens to me.

By design, I guess.

I didn't even tell my sister when I moved in with Dustin. I wasn't hiding it, exactly, but it didn't seem like that big a change in our status. We were still together, not getting married. Living together sounds like such a huge leap, but it was still us, day to day. He still irritated me when he sucked his teeth after eating. I still irritated him by leaving my laundry on the floor. We weren't ready to say *forever*; we were just being frugal and splitting rent.

I explained that to Reid once and he laughed for about fifteen minutes before kissing me on top of the head.

"What?" I said.

"You crack me up."

"Because I'm smart about money?"

He shook his head. "Because you're dumb about love."

It didn't even land in any aware spot in my brain. Like most of Reid's teasing jabs, it just sort of rolled over me. I probably laughed and said, "I know, right?"

But I imagine living with Reid, and a small burst detonates in my belly. It would change everything, every first inhale and every last exhausted exhale of my day. It would influence every mood in between. I imagine shuffling sleepily around each other at the kitchen counter, waiting for the coffee maker to finish brewing. He's wearing his soft, worn gray shirt and I can slide my hands up under it, warming them on his stomach. I imagine complaining about his morning breath, and him chasing me for a stinky kiss. I imagine grading papers on the couch together, my feet in his lap, him grumbling that I'm making it hard for him to work. I imagine the relief of sliding under the blankets with him—not just a warm body, but *his* warm body—every night.

I want every single one of these things flashing through my head.

I close my eyes, breathing in the salty air. I know people are more complicated than just *good* and *bad*, and that I can do something wrong and still be a good person—but it doesn't feel that way right now. Shame claws its way up my throat when I think of how careless I've been with Reid's feelings, and how I rationalized my way into hurting him. I think of how terrible I've been to my dad, and how I always assume Elly will be there to do the right thing when I inevitably drop the ball.

I love Reid but lied to him, and he knows it.

I love my sister and my dad, and haven't been fair to either of them.

It's time to grow up.

My hands are shaking by the time I ease to a stop in front of Reid's house.

It's after ten, but the TV is on in the living room, so I know he's home. I sit in the dark, watching the shadows flicker across his front window until a man walking a dog stops and peers at me from the other side of the street.

I give him what I hope looks like an *I'm a friend, not a*

crazy stalker! wave before pulling the keys from the ignition and climbing out.

I haven't even stepped onto the porch when the light flips on and the front door slowly opens. He must have seen me pull up.

My heart jumps inside my chest when I get a look at him. His dark hair is messy, falling over his forehead. He looks tired, is barefoot and dressed in a worn pair of jeans and a blue T-shirt. When he steps into the pool of light on the porch, my body reacts almost on instinct. I start to move forward to hug him and have to force myself to stay still.

I give him an awkward wave instead. "Hi."

Crickets chirp from a pair of bushes on either side of the porch, the sound amplified in the duration of his answering silence.

He shifts on his feet, sliding his hands into his pockets. "It's late, Millie."

I take a breath. "I know. I was wondering if we could talk."

That's not something I'd have needed to ask before. On a normal night, I would have just barged in and dropped my things by the door before collapsing in a heap on his fancy leather couch. Nothing's been normal between us for weeks now.

Surprising me, Reid takes a step back and holds the door open enough so I can pass. The small light over the kitchen window is on, and I can see that the counters are clean, the sink empty. I follow when Reid crosses to the TV, muting the volume before tossing the remote on the couch.

His mood is unfamiliar and solemn. Things were clearly strained when he left my house yesterday, but there's something else in the closed-off look of his eyes, the way he holds his body, stiff, like there's a wall around him and he's being careful to keep everything tucked safely behind it.

He motions to the couch and I sit, relieved when he takes the spot next to me.

"I know I'm supposed to be letting you think," I say.

I've never been scared in front of Reid, but the half inch of space that separates where our hands rest on the couch is terrifying. The act of simply *not touching* is intentional. I want to cling to his hand and feel its solid, reassuring weight. I want to hear that his love for me is unconditional, even though I know I don't deserve it.

Reid clears his throat and I know I've been quiet too long. I'm sweating, hyperaware of how warm the night is and that I'm still wrapped in my giant sweater. When I look down at our hands again, I see tiny grains of sand that still cling to the sleeve.

"I should tell you something," I say, wincing because *of course* I wanted to tell him something. That's why I'm here, and we both know it. "Something I should have told you a long time ago."

Reid's finger twitches where it rests against the cushion. His hands are large, skin tan, tendons visible. I've seen those hands in the lab, calibrating the most sensitive pieces of equipment, and then in bed, holding me down, inside of me. He can tell I'm nervous—that I'm stalling—but for once he doesn't reach out, doesn't offer comfort.

"Go on."

I tug on my sleeves, pulling them down over my fingers despite the heat. I feel like I need a force field around me, some mental armor. "I lied to you—have been lying to you. For a few weeks now."

Reid leans forward, away from me, to rest his elbows on his knees. "Okay."

I'm not sure how to say it, so I blurt it out to get us both out of this miserable tension. "I'm Cat. I wrote the letters." A heavy silence rolls through the room. He's staring straight ahead to where Jimmy Kimmel is giving a monologue on the muted TV. "I never meant for it to get this far, and I don't even know why I did it. Actually, I do, I guess. But those are excuses and—"

"I know."

His voice is quiet. So why does it feel like a lead weight has just swung from a crane into my torso?

Reid straightens, rubs his palms on the front of his pants, and then stands to face me. He stares down at me, and he doesn't have to say anything else for our entire conversation to echo in my memory.

"*She was really great, and I thought maybe we had something. She talked to me about things. It felt like we were really becoming friends. And—I'll admit—I maybe wanted more. She's moving and it's sort of a bummer that I'm not going to meet her.*"

"*That is a bummer. Do you think your feelings for her will affect . . . ?*"

"*I'm not sure. I liked our dynamic of straightforward honesty. I want that in a partner.*"

Straightforward honesty.

He prompted me, gave me chance after chance to come clean, and I lied, right to his face.

I can feel the pressure of his attention, but I keep my eyes on the carpet, too humiliated to look anywhere else. "I think I realized when you figured it out."

I hear his exhale. "I noticed your scar. Plus Monopoly, *Girls Trip*, the mentions of your dad, of a sister. Then I think it really clicked when the typo in one of your messages suddenly jumped out at me."

"I'm *so* sorry, Reid."

His silence seems to morph in front of me, and it's in this moment I realize I've never *really* seen him angry before. I've seen him yell at someone on the freeway, watched him rebuke a careless intern for doing something unsafe in the lab. But I've never seen this. A frown pulls at the corners of his mouth and contorts it into an expression that seems almost perverse on his perpetually patient face. It's disappointment, *anger*. The house is so quiet around us I can practically hear it rolling off him in waves.

He turns away, reaching for an empty beer bottle to take to the kitchen, but he stops halfway there. "What the hell were you thinking, Millie? Was it a joke?"

I choke on the words. "No! Of course not. I didn't really think it through. I just— You guys were right about my profile, and so I changed it without telling anyone."

"Why the name Catherine?"

"It's my middle name. It made it feel less—"

"Deceitful?" He spits out a sharp laugh, and I wince.

Of course he didn't know my middle name.

"I never set out to be dishonest. I was as surprised as you were when I got the message saying we'd matched."

"So, you couldn't have said, 'Oh, funny thing, *best friend*. Even a computer program figured out that we're sort of perfect for each other. Maybe we should give it a shot?'"

He stares at me as I stand and walk toward him, his gaze cold and unyielding. "I swear I thought you'd figure it out," I say. "The Monopoly thing was meant to clue you in. But then it didn't, and—"

"And you decided just to roll with it, have some fun?"

"No! I was going to tell you! But then you guys were making cracks about how the girl in the photograph must have been ugly, and how hot Daisy was . . ." I stop, swiping away hot tears with the sleeve of my sweater. "I got a little competitive and—"

"Jealous?" he finishes.

I look up at him. Something in me gets a little angry, too, at this being acknowledged out loud. But I really can't justify that feeling, so I just nod. "Yeah. I was super jealous, Reid. I didn't want you with her, even if I didn't exactly know why yet. But it changed after that." I move another step toward him and take a chance, reaching out to grip his arm. "Everything I wrote was true, every word of it. I said those things, that was *me*."

He pulls away, and I crumble.

"But it *wasn't* you. I love being with you, Millie. You're smart and funny and I want you more than anyone I've ever known . . . but you never tell me *anything*. What's missing— what's always been missing between us—is the honesty I got in those letters. And you expect me to give you credit for being honest, in disguise, on some stupid dating app—*after the fact?*"

"I know, and you're right. It's hard for me to be like that in person, to talk about feelings and emotion. I'm just . . . I'm not good at it."

"Maybe you're just not good at being honest."

It lands like a physical blow. I imagine a missile launched with pinpoint precision, crashing through my ribs to obliterate the hidden places I rarely examine myself, never mind share with anyone else.

"Is there—is there *anyone* you're totally honest with?" he adds, and I wouldn't have thought it was possible, but somehow, this is worse. Because it's not just anger or hurt in his voice anymore, it's pity.

I shake my head, because what else can I say? Reid was that person for me—my first, true best friend—and it's hard to hear how much I've hurt him. Disappointed him. I blink around the room; my eyes are hot and burning with tears, and it really hits me what a mess I've made of things.

"I think—" Reid says, scrubbing a hand over his face. "I think you should probably go. It's clear we both have some things to work out, and I don't think we can do it with the other around. I get why you did what you did, Millie. And maybe if it hadn't gone on so long, maybe I'd be able to overlook it. But—"

I step forward, reaching for him. "Reid, the only way I was able to be that open was because I knew it was *you*. I can do this. I promise."

He takes my hands and cradles them in his. "Listen to me, okay? I love you, Millie. I do. But I think you're worth more than just the easy parts." He lets my hands fall to my sides. "And I need someone who thinks I'm worth it, too."

The tires scrape as I turn into my driveway and shut off the car. Most of the houses on the block are dark, so I climb out, careful not to slam the door. A weird numbness has taken over. My head is full of static; my limbs are stiff and heavy with exhaustion. My head hurts. But I'm not tired, not really.

The chair out back is still where I left it, pulled away from the table at sort of a haphazard angle, and I sit, staring at the tree in the yard. My computer is nearby, but I don't need to reach for it, knowing what I'd find there wouldn't matter anyway. I know what I need to do and that calendars and schedules are the last thing I care about right now.

My fingers slip into the pocket of my sweater and wrap

around my phone. It's too late to be calling, but I know it can't wait. I search for the name and open a new window.

> Hey. I know it's late so call me when you're up. I'll make all the arrangements as soon as I hear from you, but I wanted you to know that I'll be home this summer to help. Tell Dad that I love him, and I can't wait to spend some time at home. Hug each other for me. I love you both. I miss you.

chapter sixteen

 reid

C hris peeks his head in my office door. "You coming?"

I push away from my keyboard and rub my eyes. They're burning, like they do when I haven't looked up from my computer monitor in hours. I should have expected him: he comes at the same time every Monday.

"No," I say. "I'm going to grab something later and eat in my office."

This time he steps in, resting his hands on the back of a chair, and levels me with a disappointed look. "You know it's been three weeks?"

I give him a flat *I'm not talking about this now* look, and reach for my coffee. I'm acutely aware of every *hour* that passes.

It's killing me. I don't know if she's still joining them at lunch twice a week—I don't ask, and Chris has never offered.

Until now: "She's never there, man. Not since everything went down. It's just us. The guys. In all our glory."

I'm not sure what to do with the reaction I have—sadness—and how he seems to be telling me this not as a guilt trip, but as reassurance that I don't have to see her. But I don't like the idea that she's alone, suffering, either.

"I'm serious." Now he sits down. "Don't even pretend like that isn't the reason you're avoiding all of us."

"I'm not pretending," I tell him. "That is exactly the reason I'm avoiding you guys. I'm also pissed that everyone *knew*—"

"I didn't," he reminds me, hands held up in defense.

"It feels like it became a game, and I think that's the part that feels the most fucked up."

Chris shakes his head. "It wasn't a game, at least from what I can tell. Ed did not like having the secret. Alex . . . I mean, who knows. I'm sure he just didn't want to get involved. But it sounds like everyone's advice to her was, 'Talk to Reid.'"

"Well, except when they helped her write the last letter. And anyway, she didn't talk to me."

He pauses, looking at my shelves. Finally, he agrees, "She didn't. Until she knew she had to."

"So how fucked up is it that I miss her?" I ask, and the admission pushes a sharp blade of discomfort through my sternum. I've turned this over a thousand times in my head. If it were Chris in this situation, not me, wouldn't I be telling him to write the woman off for the rest of his life?

Chris turns back and looks at me evenly, and then nods. "I know, man. I miss her, too."

Because it isn't *the woman*. It's Mills.

"Like, *really* fucking miss her. And I'm not sure how to stop. There's no one like her. No one makes me feel the way Millie does. And I know that she's out there, waiting for me to figure out whether I'm going to forgive her. But how can we start something meaningful on that kind of betrayal?"

"Reid," he says gently, "you know I'm on your side in all of this, but at some point, we all have to admit that Millie is just really bottled up. It's part of the deal of being her friend, and if you're going to be with her in a more serious way, and can't deal with that aspect of her personality, you're going to have to figure out how to get her to be more open."

"This is what I'm struggling with, honestly."

"We all knew there were secrets. I mean, come on, this is Millie we're talking about. She likes to pretend she doesn't *have* a past."

"Yeah." I pick up a paper clip, slowly straightening it. "And truthfully, I know with the Cat thing that her intentions weren't malicious. I know that she was able to open up because it was me. I know all of this, but it is still so hard to reconcile that with how it felt to be in the dark and find out that everything I was telling Cat about my life, I was telling Millie. Even things about being messed up with Millie." I pause. "And the guys knew. That's fucked up, okay? They knew, and were loyal to her—not me—to the point of supporting her lie."

We fall into silence, because there's nothing else to say about this. I've gone around and around about it, nearly constantly: My life doesn't feel complete without her in it; these past few weeks have felt like there was a death in my family. But every time I'm about to call her, embarrassment rises like smoke in my lungs and I put my phone back down. She had so many chances to tell me, and didn't.

"All right," Chris says, and his hands land on his thighs in a gentle slap before he stands. "I'm off to meet the guys for lunch. It's weird, man. You two are the glue, you know?"

I think he's going to say something more than that, but when I look back up, he's on his way out of my office.

Work.

Focus on work. It's the best way to cope, the most productive way to handle stress.

I blink over to my inbox before returning to the journal article I'm working on and see an email notification that I have a new contact request on IRL. The appearance of the site name in my inbox is jarring; I haven't been on the app since the day Cat—Millie—told me she was moving.

I open the notification and my eyes instinctively drop past the logo to where I know I'll find the information about who's contacted me.

My pulse rockets. I have a new contact request from Millie M.

From: Millie M.
Sent: 12:45 pm, April 30

I've given you almost a month to process everything, and it's killed me, but I know you needed space. Ignore these if you want or deny my contact request. But I miss you like crazy, Reid.

I'm giving you access to my full profile, which I updated just for you. I'm not trying to meet anyone else. I've already found the love of my life and I didn't even need this website to do it. But I thought maybe this would be a good way to start getting to know each other again, if you'll let me.

Love,
Mills

I stare at the green and red button options at the bottom. Allow or deny?

With my hand on the mouse, I slide to the left, clicking ALLOW.

Her new profile opens in front of me. There's a photo I took of her standing in Chris's yard, wearing a lobster oven mitt on one hand, holding a tray of salmon aloft with the other, and grinning like an idiot. She once told me it's the only photo taken of her that she absolutely adores. "Most of the time I look like either a bitch or a stoner," she said.

I remember that day like it happened a week ago. Ed thought he would make us all dinner, and decided to grill duck, which resulted in Chris's grill catching fire and Ed nearly losing his eyebrows. Millie saved the day by running to the store and grabbing some salmon, which she barbecued to perfection. I snapped the photo just as she turned to present it to us, proudly.

Beneath the photo are a few new paragraphs where her old profile used to be.

> Hi. We both know the generals: Born in Bellingham, always a quirky kid. Mother died too young, sister needed too much, dad was a quiet mess. The sad specifics aren't a secret—they're just sad. It's the quiet specifics that are hard to explain, the years and years where it feels like nothing of interest happened to me.
>
> I realize I'm a late bloomer, socially. If I went home, I'd run into people who would be perfectly pleasant to me, but would never say, "Oh, Millie and I were super close in high school." I was easygoing, upbeat, nice to everyone. Maybe I got sick of being nice. Maybe that's why I'm so mean to Ed.
>
> That's my only joke, I promise.
>
> Did I become fascinated with murder because, in comparison, female psychopaths make me look well-adjusted? Maybe. I don't know if it's because of my mother dying, or just the way my life would have unfolded regardless, but I think I managed to roam through life until my late twenties not really knowing how to take care of people. I want to do better.

That's it. That's all there is, and I'm not sure what to do with it. I sit back and stare at my screen. Millie's new profile feels like a beginning, a warning maybe, that what comes next might be messy, but at least it'll be intentional.

There's a brightness in me, something blooming warm and tight. I worry that it's hope.

Putting my phone facedown, I turn back to my computer and find where I've left off in my article.

From: Millie M.
Sent: 1:39 am, May 1

You haven't written me back, but you did let me write you, so I'm going to limit myself to one a day. If I'm bugging you, at least you can be comforted knowing that the Block button is really simple. Trust me, I used it a few times in the early days with Mr. Dick Profile Pic and Mr. Show Me Your Rack.

Anyway, here's something I don't think you knew: I lost my virginity to a guy named Phil. PHIL! I know, right! It's the least sexy name I can imagine. Sometimes when I'm alone and feeling glum, I think of the name and say it in sort of a breathless sexy voice, and I can't stop laughing. Maybe it's slightly sexier than Ernest or Norman. But only slightly. Philip? Now that's sexy. But Philllll.

Bottom line, I was fifteen, he was seventeen, and we had no idea what we were doing. I remember it being messy and being more embarrassed about that than anything. I ruined my sheets, and Dad found me trying to shove them in the washer, and I'm sure he was furious but per usual, he didn't say anything and so I didn't either.

It's always sort of been that way, but I'm sure you've figured that out by now.

Love,
Mills

From: Millie M.
Sent: 3:14 pm, May 2

I'm afraid of the following things: vans with no windows, confined spaces, moths on my front porch, crows, dust bunnies, and giant boats like cruise ships.

Love,
Mills

From: Millie M.
Sent: 9:23 am, May 3

I never said "I love you" to Dustin. Actually, I don't
think I've ever said it to anyone except you, and my
mom. Looking back, I realize I probably should have
said it to Elly every day. For someone who grew up
the way she did—with two people mourning a ghost,
and who never figured out how to say the right
words—she's pretty amazing. You should meet her
sometime.

Love,
Mills

From: Millie M.
Sent: 11:59 am, May 4

We had a faculty meeting today and I so badly
wanted to tell every man in there to shut the hell
up for fifteen minutes and let the TWO WOMEN
OUT OF THE SIXTEEN FACULTY speak.

I wish that I'd had lunch with you afterwards, but
I'm sure you're relieved you didn't have to listen
to me rail about the patriarchy for an hour over a
shitty Cobb salad. (It's Friday, and Fridays always
feel like Reid days—Mondays/Wednesdays too—but

we always seemed to make Friday nights happen.
It's probably why I'm a little blue.) Anyway, late in
the meeting, Dustin said something too asinine for
me to let slide, and I just blew up at him in front
of everyone. He approached me afterward and
suggested that I was bringing our past into the
faculty meetings.

I actually laughed. I mean, I laughed for like ten
solid minutes in his office, and once I got myself
together I reminded him that he and I broke
up over two years ago, that I'm in love with you
(though it's most likely unreciprocated), and that
my frustration was primarily about his inability to
hire women and people of color. Of course, being
Dustin, he focused on the thing I'd said about you.

So, apologies in advance if it's awkward the next
time you see him on campus.

Love,
Mills

From: Millie M.
Sent: 4:34 pm, May 5

I watched *Rudy* today and fuck that movie! I'm not
even that invested in college football but was still
crying like a baby at the end. Then I ate that pint

of Cherry Garcia I found in my freezer that you left here probably a decade ago, and felt gross. Why do you like that stuff? Chunky Monkey 4 lyfe.

Love,
Mills

_____

From: Millie M.
Sent: 11:11 am, May 6

It's 11:11, Reid. Make a wish.

I miss you.

Mills.

_____

From: Millie M.
Sent: 10:41 am, May 7

I swear to god, Reid, I'm trying to make these interesting but today was probably the most uneventful day on record. I worked all day, went to Cajé about seventeen times because I kept nodding off at my desk, and then left early and got measured for all new bras. Turns out I'm a 34C, and I don't know why that makes me so proud but my whole life I thought I was a B cup and I'm not!

I wanted to gloat to someone, but Elly and I don't really have that relationship and turns out, I don't have that relationship with anyone else who has boobs! So, working on that. But for now, I'm gloating to you, Reid. My boobs are bigger than yours! And they're in a nice, new, silky red bra.

Love,
Millie

From: Millie M.
Sent: 7:57 pm, May 8

I barely slept last night. I've been working on the book, and it's going really well, but I miss you, and you know how things always feel worse at night? Last night was one of those where I just lay in bed, thinking over every shitty thing I've done, and feeling terrible. I'm so sorry about Catherine, and not telling you. I wish I'd been strong enough to do the right thing from the very beginning, but I wasn't. I feel like such a cliché even saying this, but the reason I lied wasn't at all about you or anything you did. The secrecy was about me, and how terrifying and exhilarating it was to be so open with you in a way that felt safe. Unfortunately, that safety came from the fact that you weren't aware it was me, and that's shitty. You're honestly too good for me, but it doesn't mean that I don't want you anyway.

I've seen so many movies where one person in a
couple says, "I was fine before you came along!"
and is that supposed to mean that they were fine
before and will be fine again, but don't want to be
fine alone?

I'm not sure. Because I don't think I was "fine"
before I met you. I was lame. I was limited. I want to
be better for you.

Oh, my God, I'm becoming Jack Nicholson in *As
Good As It Gets*.

(Can we agree by the way that Helen Hunt was way
too hot for him? My god. Ew!)

Love,
Mills

From: Millie M.
Sent: 9:14 pm, May 9

I ran into Alex today while getting lunch, and I
swear we both had the guiltiest looks on our faces
after we hugged, like I'm not supposed to get the
guy friends in this divorce—and we both know it. So,
I wanted to tell you that I saw Alex, but I promise
not to make plans with any of them without your
permission.

It was so good to see him, though. I miss you, of course, but I miss them, too. I've never had friends like this, and I swear I am this close to getting a cat because I am so fucking lonely.

I want you to know that Ed and Alex really wanted no part of the secret Catherine situation. Ed was a basket case, and Alex seemed mostly perplexed by the whole thing. If you're mad at anyone, of course, be mad at me. Those guys are good, and you deserve good.

I'm sorry I ever let you believe otherwise.

Love,
Mills

Usually she writes at night. I've come to expect it, and I wonder what will happen if, one day, I check the IRL app when I head to bed, or when I first wake up in the morning, and there isn't a note there.

I look forward to them, even if I'm not sure how I want to reply yet. I find that by around four in the afternoon, my stomach feels like it's risen to my chest, my hands are restless, and I feel the same way I used to feel before starting a race: excited, but also a little queasy.

Millie's honesty is refreshing, but it's also disorienting. It makes me feel famished—I want more—and it's also frustrating to continue to read it, knowing that it's so much harder for her to do it in person.

But she is trying. Maybe it's a start.

I read last night's message again, and then get to work early to help Shaylene practice a presentation she's giving to the department at eleven. Since she's finishing up her first year of graduate studies, she has to present the work she's done so far. It's a big milestone for the first-year students, and Shaylene—who is much like my father, which is to say not a natural orator—has been dreading this for weeks.

So it is both nice and surprising to find Ed already there, going through it with her. It looks like they've been here for some time already: notes are scattered across the conference room table, the slide projector is on, and Shaylene is bent over her laptop, editing a slide.

Perhaps not surprisingly, things are still weird with Ed. Mostly what's weird is treating him like any other employee in the lab, rather than my right hand and one of my best friends. He's been nothing but professional since all the crap with Millie and Cat went down, but it stings a little when we both go to make an old inside joke then abruptly stop. Or when I see him leaving to go meet Chris and Alex for lunch and he no longer asks if I want to come.

Ed looks up when I come into the conference room, and with a quiet "Hey, Reid," he bends to collect his notebook and pen, like he's going to gather his things and leave me to help Shaylene prep solo.

"Stay, Ed," I say. "I was just coming to make sure everything was going okay."

We've spoken; it's not like there's a complete silent treatment happening in the lab, but I'm sure everyone notices that something has changed. Shaylene looks back and forth between the two of us, concerned.

"She's good," Ed says. "I pretended to be Scott and grilled her about all the experimental minutiae, and she seems pretty firm on everything."

Shaylene confirms this with a nod. "He was really helpful." She glances at Ed and gives him a shy flash of a smile. "Thanks, Ed."

"Good; good job." I hesitate, unsure whether either of them needs me there. I am increasingly aware of having become The Boss in the past year or so—especially after procuring tenure. With that awareness comes the next one—that I am somewhat scary, and therefore not always a grad student's first choice to work out practice talks. "Okay, I'll be down in my office if anyone needs me."

I turn to leave, but Shaylene stops me. "Dr. Campbell? Would you like to go get coffee with us?"

She looks at Ed and nods, like she's prompting him. He wordlessly scrutinizes her for a few beats before quickly nodding, too.

"Yes. *Coffee*," he says. "Right."

I check my watch. I've generally avoided spending much time with Ed if I don't need to, but right now I don't have any good reason to decline. "Sure."

But as soon as we get out in the hall, Shaylene pulls up short. "You know what? I think I want to go tinker with my transition slides a little. You guys go on ahead. I'll catch you in a bit."

Ed and I stand there, aware that we've been set up by a wily twenty-two-year-old. We watch her walk down the hall toward the stairwell leading to our lab.

Ed growls, and then silence descends. I feel him turn to look at me. "We don't have to go grab coffee, you know."

"Did Shaylene really just set us up?" I ask.

"Yup." He reaches up, and his fingers disappear in his mop of hair as he scratches his scalp. "The joke in the lab is that Mom and Dad are fighting."

I stare at him, somewhat speechless.

"I think I'm the mom," he clarifies. "Which is pretty rad."

And I don't know what it is about this in particular, but

I just burst out laughing. At first unsure, Ed finally grins. And then he throws his arms around me, pressing his face to my shoulder. "I missed you so much. I've felt like complete shit. I'm so, so sorry, man."

I reach up and pat his back. Forgiveness is so fucking freeing. I feel immediately like I can relax my shoulders for the first time in weeks. I feel the tiniest bit closer to not only the freedom of forgiving Millie, but the relief of being near her again, too.

From: Millie M.
Sent: 1:11 am, May 10

I guess you need an update on the Elly/Dad situation if you're going to understand the rest of this ramble, so here goes.

Dad was diagnosed with Parkinson's disease about a year and a half ago. I should have told you, I know. We hadn't known each other long, and diseased parents turn conversations serious, real fast. I'm shitty at talking about personal stuff not only because I feel awkward talking about myself, but also because I don't like turning a conversation into a downer.

Anyway. From the start, they started Dad on a medication called Sinemet, which I'm sure you know all about. So, for a while it was okay—it helped.

But as the dopamine cells in his brain continue to die, the Sinemet is less effective, right? Because it relies on the remaining healthy cells in order to work? I'm trying to understand the science behind all of it. Anyway, his neurologist is recommending deep brain stimulation, and he's resisting, even though Elly really wants him to try it.

Elly has been managing whatever he needs help with, but with the twins she's exhausted. She's asked me to come home a few times, and I have—for a weekend here and there—but she wants me home for a good month so that she and Jared can take a vacation, and probably also just so that Dad has some time with me.

I'd been resisting because I hate being home. Do you remember that time we went to Hendry's Beach to watch the dogs in the water? You knew something was off, and you didn't push me to tell you what was going on, but I'd just found out about the diagnosis. I lasted maybe four hours after I found out, and then flew back here. I felt so guilty, but I hate being there, and hearing that Dad was sick was like getting Mom's diagnosis all over again.

So, there are two things I'm telling you. One, I started therapy two weeks ago. I'm going twice a week and so far it's been really great. I'm actually talking. Her name is Anna, and she's funny and seems to get me, and is helping me fix my stupid emotional brain.

Two, I'm going home for three and a half weeks in July. Dad's having the surgery on June 22, and I'll be there when he gets out of the physical rehabilitation facility on July 2 until the 25th.

I don't even know what else to say. I'm dreading the trip, but I feel relieved, too, like I'm finally doing the things I should have been doing all along. It feels really good to tell you this.

I love you,
Millie

For eleven days I've read her messages and let them sink in, let them carefully smooth over the jagged damage her betrayal caused, but I can't stay away anymore. I slam my laptop shut and grab my keys as I jog past the counter. If I was asked to recount the drive from my place to hers, I would describe only a blur of scenery punctuated at the end by the high-pitched squeal of my tires coming to a stop in her driveway.

I can barely pull in a deep breath, and when she opens the door in her pajamas, with her hair messy, and eyes red from crying, I think I stop breathing entirely.

She doesn't say anything before she bursts into tears, and melts into me when I wrap my arms around her.

chapter seventeen

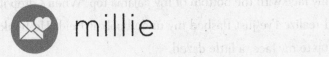 millie

It's about twenty minutes before I can pull myself together and stop crying, but throughout all the sobbing, and hiccupping, and senseless babble, Reid guides me inside, pulls us down onto the couch, and holds me. When he presses a kiss to the top of my head, it just makes me cry harder.

He's here, at two in the morning, which means that he read my last message and came right over. It means he's probably been reading all of my messages—just like I hoped—and that I wasn't just throwing my words into the vast internet void.

It also means that he doesn't want me to be alone after everything I told him in my last note. He read what I said about Anna, and my dad, and heading home this summer.

He made me wait over a month, but isn't going to make me wait anymore before telling me what he's decided. Relief is in the distance—even if he tells me he needs to move on, at least I'll know.

I sit up, reluctantly pulling out of his arms, and wipe at my face with the bottom of my pajama top. When I drop it, I realize I've just flashed my underboob at Reid. He blinks up to my face, a little dazed.

"Oops. Sorry."

He gives a wicked half smile that makes a flurry of bombs go off in my belly. "No red silk."

"I hoped you'd remember that detail."

The smile slowly straightens into something more pensive—but thankfully still fond—and he reaches out to tuck my insane hair behind my ear. "There's a lot to respond to in those messages, but after the one you sent tonight, I had to come over."

An opening. He's just given it to me, and I don't want to mess this up. Sure, it's easier to write all this to the computer and hit SEND, but the important piece happens when he's this close to me, his hand resting on my knee.

Anna's voice rings in my ears: *If Reid were here right now, what would you want him to know?*

Well, Reid *is* right here.

"I really missed you," I say simply.

An easy start. Baby steps.

I watch his mouth, mesmerized, as his tongue slips out and is drawn across his lower lip. "I missed you, too."

Needing air, I pull my attention away and study the rest of his face. He's stubbly, and his eyes are a little hollow, like he's gone for a long run without drinking enough water. On instinct, I lift my hand and press it to his cheek. "You did?"

He nods. "I almost called about five hundred times."

"I guess it's okay that you didn't. I had—have—some work to do."

"Yeah." He shifts his gaze back and forth between my eyes, trying to read me. His brow furrows. "You okay, Mills?"

I shake my head, and my chin wobbles. "Not really."

At his worried frown, I start crying again. What is with me? Seriously, it's like a dam has burst and I'm an unending, sobbing mess. I fight the mortification rising inside, and trying to focus on Reid's reaction helps: he seems completely unfazed by the tears and snot and hiccups.

"But I'm really glad you're here," I say through a sob. "Like, really, *really* glad you're here. I can't tell you how much I missed you. I have been—"

"Millie. Honey." He tries to calm me, pressing his hand to the side of my neck. "I'm here."

When I choke again, he leans in, cupping my face and covering my lips with his.

I don't know how he's interested in kissing my red, swollen mouth right now, but he clearly is, and he's doing it with such devotion and relief that I feel immediately light-headed. My arms find their way around his neck and my legs slide over onto his lap and all he has to do is let out a quiet, encouraging groan into my mouth and I'm rocking over him, and he's moving with me, and his shirt is gone, then mine—

But I pull back, pressing a hand to his chest just as he starts making his way down my bare neck to my collarbone.

"Wait." I swallow, struggling to catch my breath. His eyes move up from my bare torso to my face, and he looks as drugged as I feel. "I need to know you heard me."

He remains still, listening intently. "Okay."

"I'm sorry about what I did," I say, and I wait for him to acknowledge this with a tilt of his head. "And I'm working on being more forthcoming."

Nodding again, he whispers, "I heard you. Promise you'll tell me how I can help?"

I feel like a limp rag dragged through warm water; I am so relieved. "I will."

Reid leans forward, intent on resuming where we left off, but one last bit of Anna's instructions rises in my thoughts. "And I can't do this"—I gesture to where we are pressed distractingly together—"without some sort of understanding . . ."

With a smile, he stretches, pressing a sweet, lingering kiss to my mouth. "*This* is your condition? Commitment?"

I nod, fighting the instinct to make a joke about signing a waiver and my vagina no longer having hourly rates. "I love you. And I'm trying to be better about being clear about what I want and need."

He nods solemnly, with a playful gleam to his eyes, but catches my expression as I fight a scowl.

"I'm not trying to tease you," he says, and kisses me again. "It's just very sweet, seeing you like this."

I close my eyes, growling, "It's embarrassing."

"I'm in, Mills. I'm committed." He licks his lips, and I swear my pulse is racing a thousand beats a minute. "I want this, too."

"Okay." I exhale. "That's a relief."

I feel his breath on my neck just before he kisses me there. "I love you, too." He punctuates each small phrase with a kiss lower on my throat. "All of you. The silly, the quiet, the argumentative, the sarcastic, and even this side." He kisses my shoulder. "The softer side." His hands come up over my waist. "I like feeling that I'm getting all of you."

With a grin, I ask, "Well, do you want to get all of me on the couch? Or would you rather have all of me in the bed?"

Reid laughs, and the sound seems to gather up all the tiny broken bits I've left around my living room this past month without him. He stands, with me in his arms, and kisses my nose. "There she is."

epilogue

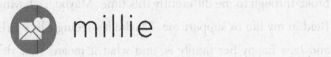 millie

Dad's dinner sits half-eaten on the TV tray in front of his lounger. He's already asleep, but I'm not going to bother trying to move him. One, because I couldn't lift him by myself even if I wanted to (I tried that one night when he fell, and my back still aches even two weeks later), and two, because he seems to sleep better sitting up. At least for now.

It's not been an easy recovery after the implantation of his deep brain stimulators. He also had to have two spinal fusions, which is the source of much of his discomfort. We hate to hope too much, Elly and I—because we really aren't that far out of his surgery, and he's on a lot of medications—but so far it seems like the stimulators are working. His symptoms are a good deal better than they were even the last time I visited.

My book advance has been able to pay for a nurse to stay here with Dad at night, which means that I can go back to the house I've rented for the month and decompress after a day of fussing, worrying, and daughtering in a way I'd never really mastered until now. Dad's vulnerability broke through to me differently this time. Maybe it's having Reid in my life to support me. Maybe it's seeing Elly's girls and how happy her family is, and what it means that she can lean on me a little, too. But being home hasn't been claustrophobic or scary. It's been stressful, sure, but it's also been pretty fucking great to feel like I'm doing exactly what my family needs me to do.

At around eleven thirty, I pass off the information to nurse Deborah—how much Dad ate, what meds he's had, how much he walked today, and any other relevant information—before heading out. It's not even that physically demanding to be with him all day, but it is emotionally draining, and my feet feel like they're blocked in concrete.

I've become acutely aware that we don't have decades left with Dad; I can't believe I almost let that time just slide away from me.

After a short drive, I step into the rental house and am overwhelmed by the scent of garlic, salmon, and . . . sulfur?

Dropping my bag in the living room, I round into the small dining room to find Monopoly already spread out on the table.

My smile wilts.

"Are you kidding me?" I ask.

Three sets of eyes swing up to me, and three grins spread wide.

"Come on," Alex needles, "we've been up here with you guys for almost a week and haven't played once. We're all getting sick of Pegs and Jokers."

Reid reaches his arms wide, invitingly, and I shuffle over, settling onto his lap before kicking my shoes off. "Okay, but let's at least play with the weapons from Clue. I get to be the rope."

Ed catches this just as he walks in from the back porch where, I can only assume, he was having his nightly phone call with his new—and adorable—girlfriend, Shaylene. "You're sure you don't have a murder kink?" he asks.

". . . . It's possible."

Reid goes still beneath me, and I turn around to boop his nose. "Just kidding."

Chris pushes back from the table to stand. "Your girlfriend is weird, Reid."

"So is yours," I fire back.

Alex stifles a whimper. He swears he doesn't want to set-

tle down with one woman, but I'm not so sure. Someday—
someday—he will no longer be emotionally eviscerated by
the ball of adorable that is Chris and Rayme in a room together.

"Weird," Reid agrees, "but awesome."

He kisses the back of my neck, and for the millionth
time I think: *This man is a saint.* Not only for being here for
a month, but for sharing me during the day with Dad, and
in the evenings with a revolving door of friends and family
who want a place to stay in Seattle. His parents came to
visit a couple of weeks back for a spontaneous getaway
weekend, and thankfully we were spared any extramarital
angst (Marla, as it turns out, is a lesbian and Reid's father's
interest in her extended only to the extent that he could
sample her soil—not a euphemism—for regional comparison purposes). Elly's twins have done a few sleepovers. And
I even let Avery stay in a spare bedroom for a few nights
when she came up to visit Elly.

I can report that I don't like her any more than I used to.

So I'm sure it's nice for Reid to have the guys up for the
week to do more exciting things than local vineyard recon-
naissance, gossiping, or "This Little Piggy."

I lift Reid's beer and take a long drink. "What'd you
guys do today?"

"Chris had to work on his grant," Reid says, "so after

you left we weren't allowed back in the house until three. We went for a hike, and then were all so dead, we found a new brewery and got pretty hammered."

"You do smell a little beery." I lift his wrist, looking at his watch. "And you're all still awake and drinking at midnight? My heroes."

These adorable men, taking vacation to be in Seattle with their hopeless, emotionally stunted friend, Millie. Of all the things that we've done as a team—cornhole tournaments, online dating, renting a limo and going together to listen to and share the same air as Barack Obama—this week of my trip has been the best by far. I get family redemption time; they get to deeply explore the Seattle beer scene.

Chris has moved to the kitchen to grab something from the oven. He returns and places a plate of food in front of me: grilled salmon, roasted brussels sprouts, and wild rice.

While he's here, everyone assumes he'll cook—because Chris is a better cook than all of us combined. Each night I come home to find that he's saved me a plate, knowing that I'm never hungry when my dad eats at four thirty. I might have to reward him with a rooster-themed golf club set at the end of this trip. "You. Are. *Awesome*."

He tilts his chin to me in acknowledgment. "I know."

"I thought it smelled like farts when I walked in." I poke at a brussels sprout. "I assumed it was Ed."

Ed starts to argue with this, but seems to decide it isn't worth it.

I recognize the warmth spreading in my chest, and am not such an emotional idiot that I don't know it's gratitude, but I'm also working on being more vocal about these things. Expectant silence spreads through the room.

"Thanks for dinner," I tell Chris. "As usual, it's super yummy."

He nods, but the silence remains. We all know the quiet wasn't about my dinner gratitude, anyway.

"So, I brought it up with Dad today," I begin, "about feeling like I wanted to be closer to him."

"And?" Reid asks. He knows how nervous I've been about broaching these heavier conversations with my dad.

"He knew what I was going to say, immediately." I lean back into Reid, taking comfort in the broad weight of him behind me, the way his arms are banded firmly around my middle. "He talked—super openly—about what it was like for him when Mom died. It was hard, sort of, because I realized what a burden we were? Not that he ever said that. But, I mean, he was just broken, and on top of that, he knew he was failing us." I press my hand to my cheek. "I don't think I ever really thought about it like that before.

But I told him, 'Look at Elly. Look at me. We are fine. We're successful, and happy, and not murderers.'"

"See?" Ed interjects. "Murder kink."

"Anyway, he seemed to get it," I say. "I think he is relieved to see that I really am okay, and not a nutcase."

Alex clears his throat.

"Okay, not a *complete* nutcase."

Reid speaks quietly against the side of my head. "The craziest thing about parenting must be that it's this huge experiment and you have no idea whether it's successful until, like, decades later."

I turn around and kiss him. "You are so sublimely dorky."

After this, everyone is quiet for a few seconds. I realize how weird it must be for them to see me going through this, and I think I should probably say something about how much I love that they're here or what it means to have a family like this for the first time in my life. But then Alex rips an enormous, stinky burp, and Chris groans and stands up to open a window, and Ed starts pretending to beat Alex with the tiny lead pipe, and I think, *These idiots*.

Reid spreads his hands across my rib cage, with a quiet meaning. I love when he does that, when he spreads his hands wide like he wants to cover as much of me as he can. Heat pools low in my belly even though the rest of the room seems to be breaking into twelve-year-old-boy chaos of belching full sentences and jokes about lead pipes.

"I'm proud of you," he says quietly.

"I'm proud of me, too," I say. "And I really like that you're here."

"Do you think we can sneak out of here unnoticed?" he asks, lips pressed gently to my ear. "I'd like to go have sex now."

I nod. "On the count of three."

"One," he says.

"Two," I say.

"Three."

We stand, slowly backing away from the table. Alex has Ed in a headlock. Chris is leaning out the window, trying to reach the shoe that Alex just launched outside.

Reid and I manage to tiptoe all the way down the hall to the master bedroom before our absence is noticed.

"Don't think we didn't see that!" Alex yells.

"We're turning the music up tonight!" Ed says. "Don't be weird!"

"We'll do our best!" I call back.

Last night, I barked like a dog just to freak them out.

Tonight, we might make a lot of fake spanking noises.

But then we'll climb between the covers, pull them over our heads, turn on a flashlight, and make each other laugh with stupid stories that we never seem to run out of. I'll tell him I love him too many times, and he'll kiss me to shut me up. And from there, it will all go quiet, and sweeter than I could have ever imagined.

We'll get an entire night—every night, for the rest of our lives if we want it—and for those perfect eight hours, we can forget there's anyone else in the house, the city, the world.

acknowledgments

When we finished edits on this book, it felt a little like we were packing up abruptly and moving to a new town. It had been a couple books since we'd written an ensemble like we have in *My Favorite Half-Night Stand*, and although the ending sees everyone (mostly) settled and happy, it was still hard to walk away from the gang, their dynamic, their obvious love for each other. We hope you've enjoyed spending time with them as much as we did.

Both of us are long married, having met our husbands in the dark days when cell phones either flipped open or were the size of bricks, and so the idea of online dating, let alone a dating app, was foreign to us. Left to our own devices to write a dating-app story, we would no doubt sound like two octogenarians writing the user instructions for a 3-D printer. We are so indebted to our CLo & Friends group for helping us with an online dating questionnaire we designed for research purposes. Thank you to all of these sweeties: Dana H., Summer W., Kristensparkles, Stacey L.,

Chandelle C., Jenn C., Melissa H., Caroline K., Saam N., Crystal J., Jessica N., Tina A., Nena, Erica B., Jennifer N. B., Melissa B., Jacqueline, Angela I., Jessica T., Ashley H., Elle O., Cassandra L., Vera Charlotte, Floriane M., Britney B., Renata P., Sydney R., Kristen T., Amor C., Amy B., Angelica N. B., Brie S., Tabitha C., Kawtar T., Jennifer B., and Stacy Alice. They took the time to share stories that made us laugh and cringe, and any authenticity that rings from these pages is due to their help. Anything that feels wrong or ridiculous is, of course, our fault.

As always, our books come to our editor as words stuffed in garbage bags tied together with twine (only sort of joking), and we are forever enamored with Adam Wilson for making these pages into books. Thank you, Kate, for agreeing to join Team CLo—it feels like the most natural fit in the world. How lucky are we?! You two are *truly* amazing. Holly Root, our agent, has been unanimously voted The Person CLo Would Like to Be When They Grow Up. She keeps this train on the tracks, and some days that takes efforts that hint she may be a cyborg. Kristin Dwyer is our precious and our PR rep and if she weren't with us, we'd be lost somewhere in the Mediterranean with no wallets, no itinerary, and no Honest Trailers to watch. Thank you to our fantabulous team at Simon & Schuster: Carolyn Reidy, Jen Bergstrom, Jen Long, Aimée Bell, the entire sales department (you're our heroes), Rachel Brenner, Molly Gregory, Diana Velasquez, Mackenzie Hickey, Abby Zidle, Paul O'Halloran, John Vairo, Lisa Litwack, Sarah Lieberman, Louisa Solomon, Lauren Pires, and Ellen Gutoskey. Ed Schlesinger, you're not technically on Team CLo but we claim you anyway. Too late, no backsies.

Forever and ever and ever we love you, Erin Service, for reading our words in their most naked form and not laughing. Thank you, Marion Archer, for your happy flails and your critical feedback. Thank you to every blogger, Bookstagrammer, Booktuber, reviewer on Goodreads, Twitter/Instagram/Facebook follower—truly, your support of our books is what makes it possible for us to write them, and at the risk of sounding trite, you make our day when you tell us that you loved something we did.

Our families make us want to stay home and travel less, so thank you to our international readers for understanding why we've slowed down a bit. And thank you to our husbands for understanding why *I DON'T CARE WHAT WE HAVE FOR DINNER, JUST MAKE A DECISION* is not meant to sound rude, we're just on deadline. All the time. You're the best.

PQ, you make me laugh. I heart you.

Lo, you're perfect in every way and everyone should be more like you. It's so helpful when you decide what I would write in the acknowledgments about you and then just send it to our editor. You're the best.

Praise for the Novels of Christina Lauren

"With exuberant humor and unforgettable characters, this romantic comedy is a standout."

—*Kirkus Reviews* on *Josh and Hazel's Guide to Not Dating* (starred review)

"From Lauren's wit to her love of wordplay and literature to swoony love scenes to heroines who learn to set aside their own self-doubts . . . Lauren writes of the bittersweet pangs of love and loss with piercing clarity."

—*Entertainment Weekly* on *Love and Other Words*

"A triumph . . . a true joy from start to finish."

—Kristin Harmel, internationally bestselling author of *The Room on Rue Amélie* on *Love and Other Words*

"Lauren brings her characteristic charm to the story. Holland's tale is more than an unrequited crush; it's about self-expectations, problematic friendships, unconventional family, and the strange power of love."

—*Booklist* on *Roomies*

"Delightful."

—*People* on *Roomies*

"At turns hilarious and gut-wrenching, this is a tremendously fun slow burn."

—*The Washington Post* on *Dating You / Hating You* (a Best Romance of 2017 selection)

"Truly a romance for the twenty-first century. . . . A smart, sexy romance for readers who thrive on girl power."

—*Kirkus Reviews* on *Dating You / Hating You* (starred review)

"Christina Lauren hilariously depicts modern dating."

—*Us Weekly* on *Dating You / Hating You*

"A passionate and bittersweet tale of love in all of its wonderfully terrifying reality. . . . Lauren successfully tackles a weighty subject with both ferocity and compassion."

—*Booklist* on *Autoboyography*

"Perfectly captures the hunger, thrill, and doubt of young, modern love."

—*Kirkus Reviews* on *Wicked Sexy Liar*

"Christina Lauren's books have a place of honor on my bookshelf."

—Sarah J. Maas, bestselling author of *Throne of Glass*

"In our eyes, Christina Lauren can do no wrong."

—*Bookish*

"The perfect summer read."

—*Self* on *Sweet Filthy Boy*